Bent Red Moon

Bent Red Moon

A Western Story

RUSS HALL

Five Star • Waterville, Maine

First Edition
First Printing: July 2005

Published in 2005 in conjunction with
Golden West Literary Agency.

Set in 11 pt. Plantin by Elena Picard.

Printed in the United States on permanent paper.

Library of Congress Cataloging-in-Publication Data

Hall, Russ, 1949–
    Bent red moon : a western story / by Russ Hall.—1st ed.
        p. cm.
    ISBN 1-59414-135-5 (hc : alk. paper)
    1. Texas Hill Country (Tex.)—Fiction. 2. Indians of
    North America—Wars—Fiction. I. Title.
    PS3558.A37395B46 2005
    813′.54—dc22   2005005997

"It ain't what a man don't know
that makes him a fool,
but what he does know that ain't so."

—Josh Billings

Prologue

They rose from the water. As their long dark hair caught the first orange rays of the rising sun, it looked to be long flowing strings of fire. The horses bore no saddles and the soft thud of their hoofs on the bank said the stout paint steeds were unshod.

Some of the wagons and tents were on fire and the screams began. Mick stood and stared until an arm circled his waist and he was pulled up across the back of one of the horses where he could smell untanned leather and sense the wildness of these men. He watched a boy his own age, yelling, before he fell with arrows thick on his back.

Mick, for all the years that followed, didn't know why he hadn't screamed a warning, or if it would have mattered.

Chapter One

A scream ripped the harsh Texas air like the rending of a dry sheet. It snapped Mick Dixon awake and had him peering, hard, at the sky, seeing nothing but a blank pale gray slate of clouds. He was not sure, on waking, if it had been a scream or the shriek of an eagle, although at this hour of dawn that didn't seem likely. A dream or real? The way he'd grown up, a dream could matter just as much. He pushed up on one elbow from the hard ground, checking to see that Biscuit was where he'd staked her. She was. The light was a dim, faintly pink line at the bottom of the gray sky. He sat up and let the blanket fall off him. His look around turned up no snakes that had felt lonely or cold in the night and had wanted to huddle close. He'd slept with his boots on, so he didn't have to shake them to check for scorpions.

Biscuit tossed her head, letting him know that all was well, except the grass and bark he'd gathered for her were gone. Back on the ranch he'd have just hobbled her and let her graze. Out here, he didn't dare. He pushed himself up, stepped over the handful of arrows and bow he'd made. At first he had to use feathers he found; later he used ones he earned. It felt better having something like a weapon, if only this, and knapping the points had given him something to do while trying not to think about food. He'd been a damned fool to traipse out into these parts without a gun and only his belt knife.

He pulled more fodder and stripped bark from cotton-woods along the bank and carried the food to Biscuit, who barely glanced at him as she shoved her nose down to her breakfast.

"You're doing better than I am," Mick said into one ear while stroking her neck. She was long enough in the tooth not to snap her head at every whiff of a stallion, but her quirk was that she rarely missed a chance to snatch a graze, and he had to keep a firm hand on her when they passed through tall grass.

He watched her eat, then got his canteens as well as the small coffee pot, and went down to the bank. It was a good-size little river for Texas, and for this time of year. In places it narrowed down to a small rush between the pinch of tall rocks, while in other places, like the one beside him, it opened into moving pools. He looked around, had an idea this was the San Saba somewhere below Scalp Creek, which made staying by the water all that more dangerous. But he'd looked around for sign and, yesterday, a half mile back, had seen a bent-over tree that had been tied to the ground, pointing a different direction, which meant the Indian camp it pointed toward was not in the direction he was headed. That and finding no sign had encouraged him enough to stay, although this was no place to make a permanent camp. That was for sure. He'd seen plenty enough signs, the previous few days, before coming this far.

He filled the canteens and the coffee pot, getting fresh water in the morning from the stream the way he'd been told it should be done by Owl Snake Woman, who claimed that water left standing over night was dead water. It was the women in those days, though, who went to fetch live water each morning.

It had taken him longer to start a fire the first few times he tried because it had been a while. But now he got one going quickly enough and fed it sticks of dry mesquite. He stretched a small piece of skin on sticks to help the fire build against the breeze. Then he put the last of the coffee into the pot and put that on a rock, almost in the fire. He stood back, could see only a small trickle of smoke. It was risky, but worth it for a taste. Aunt Ruth, bless her departed soul, had been the one who had hooked him on coffee in the morning. Lord knows he'd been close enough to chewing some of the last during the past few days. It made him sorry to have just used up the very final bit of it on this small pot.

While the coffee was heating, he went back to the river. He slipped off his shirt, and, in a spot or two, it pulled slowly from his skin due to too many days of wearing it and sleeping in it. He dropped it beside a rounded pinkish stone, half in and half out of the water, with enough of a flat surface to serve. Then he pulled off his boots and pants. He waded into the cool water wearing only his socks. The moving water was cool, almost cold, but the warriors of his youth had made a ritual of plunging into the cold water every morning, believing it toughened them, and it probably did.

Mick dove down into the brownish flow that would have been clear had it not rained a day ago. He came up a few feet away, sputtering. He stood. The water was chest high here, but the current was strong enough and the rocks beneath his feet slippery enough that he had to take careful steps back to the rounded rock where he'd left his shirt. He tugged the shirt into the water and held it under until it was soaked. Twisting it and wringing it underwater, he got out all the dirt he could, then he rubbed it on the rock a few times, the way he'd seen done, although not so hard he tore it or wore it through. Then he rinsed and wrung it out before spreading it on the rock again. That would have to do. The sun wasn't out all the way yet, but, when it was, it would dry the shirt enough for him to wear it.

The next chore was harder. He slowly pulled off one sock and went through the same process. When he pulled it from the water, it was more holes than not. The other sock fared even worse, coming apart in his fingers while he washed it. He wadded the bits into a small lump and tossed it onto the shore. That meant he'd probably be barefoot in his boots for a while.

He was rubbing his chest and under his arms with handfuls of sand and gravel in place of soap when he heard a small *click* and looked over in time to see Biscuit lift her head. Mick measured the distance to where his bow and few arrows lay. Then he ducked low in the water behind the rock with only his head out of the water.

A horse pushed through a tangled chaparral of live oak and mesquite scrub that came only to the horse's withers. The figure on horseback wore a broad slouch hat and heavy chaps. The face was in shadow, and a blue bandanna encircled the neck above a gray flannel shirt.

"You'd best come out of the water. Your lips are going to turn blue." The voice was a forced bass, the kind Mick had used himself once when he was trying to seem older.

He stood up, and the morning air seemed as cool for a moment as the water had been. He waded out to the shore and let the water drip off him while he reached for his pants, looking over the rider the whole time. His naked skin glistened in a pale sheen over taut flesh with no fat and the ribs clearly showing.

The rider wore a pistol at the hip, hard to tell what kind from here, no rifle. The face was as clean shaved as Mick's own, although his came from being but seventeen, at least according to Aunt Ruth's family Bible that had been among the things lost in the train wreck. He was not prone to whiskers yet.

"That's the San Saba River you're camped on, and you're into the edge of the Comancheria, for sure," the rider said. "You're either brave or the height of foolish to be out in these parts on your own. My bet is on foolish."

"How many in your party?" Mick said.

"Just me."

"Seems like the pot's as black as the kettle."

The rider's hand slipped down to rest on the butt of the belt pistol.

Mick pulled on his pants. "If you had breakfast in mind, there's some dried turkey in my left saddlebag."

Normally he wasn't so open with strangers. But there was something to think about here. For one, the accent was of a person maybe from the West, but who'd been off to the East Coast, too. You come out here, you find all kinds of pockets of ways people speak. The fur trappers had their own lingo and style, the buffalo hunters another, the miner types a still different manner of speaking. The cowboys, with whom he'd most recently spent time, had still another way of talking, whether spinning fireside yarns or cussing at a roped calf that had tangled itself up in the brush of an arroyo. Coming out here from the East himself, as he had, Mick had an ear for it.

"Appreciate the offer," the rider said, "but it was the

smell of coffee that caught my fancy. It also told me you weren't Indian."

Mick glanced at the pot that held barely a cup, and the last of his coffee at that. "Help yourself," he said. Basic hospitality, the way he'd been taught it, demanded that.

The rider climbed down from the horse, a gray stallion with black mane and tail. The saddle looked Mexican to Mick. "Name's Syd." The rider took a tin cup out of a saddlebag and reached for the pot.

"Mick. Mick Dixon." He sat on his crumpled blanket to pull on his boots.

"You sure you've had yours? There's only a cup here."

"Go ahead." Mick stood and shook out his blanket, rolled it into shape, and put it down beside his saddle. He stood, realized nature called, and walked over to a thick clump of prickly pear, peeked in first, and then did his business. Not quite a week ago, tired, he'd climbed off the saddle to relieve himself and found he was peeing on a rattlesnake. It had so stymied the snake that it had barely rattled before wriggling off. Still, it was always worth taking a peek first.

Mick closed up his pants and turned back. Syd stood looking up the river, away from him. Mick grinned. "You hear something?" he said.

"Naw. Just checking." Syd took a sip of the coffee.

Mick could smell it, almost taste it. Over the rim of the cup, Syd's eyes glittered black and with a sparkle that could be anything from raw evil to humor. You meet a stranger out in the wilds like this, you take your chances, but Mick wasn't as worried as he might be. He figured Syd for maybe the same age as himself, or perhaps a year younger, sixteen, with some Mexican, even Indian blood somewhere. The smooth skin over those cheek bones showed more than just a few days in the sun.

With the coffee gone, there was no need for a fire, so Mick kicked dirt over the flames. He picked up the coffee pot and started for the river.

"You lost, or were you headed somewhere?" Syd said, following along, carrying the tin cup and taking an occasional sip.

"Headed where?" Mick said.

"The fort's manned again, I hear, as of 'Sixty-Eight. That's what had the Comanches so full of oats, don't you know. The Federals pulled all their troops out for the Civil War, and the Indians figured they'd won, drove the white men back where they came from. It's played hell with the settlers who came out here thinking the forts would hold them back."

"Which way's the fort?" Mick asked, bending over to rinse out the pot.

"McKavett's that way several days' ride," Syd said, pointing. "Fort Mason's the other way. The nearest big spreads, the Allen and Campbell and the Rolling R, are as far north the other way, maybe a bit farther. They've got as many hands riding gun as they do cow-poking, if you've a notion to get work. The rest of this area is up for grabs for any rancher with enough men to come out and pick up wild strays, if you're after that kind of work."

Mick dismissed that with a short shake of his head. He'd had his turn at being a cowhand on the McLaren spread, trying to put together a stake until the boss' daughter made off with Pretty Boy, the number one horse in his string. He and Hodges Laney, McLaren's *segundo*, had buried the girl, after Two Claws, their Tonk tracker, had found what was left of her. Pretty Boy's bones were probably white in the sun by now. The Comanche still had his rifle, for all Mick knew.

Going past his saddle and blanket, Syd looked down and stopped walking, then looked up at Mick. "Where'd you learn to make Cheyenne arrows?"

"What makes you think they're Cheyenne arrows?"

"I know arrows and have seen the like before. Did you find them?"

Mick shrugged.

"OK, you made them. Where'd you learn how?"

Mick finished rinsing the coffee pot, rubbing the inside out with his fingers. He straightened. "When I was a boy, I was taken by the Sioux, stolen by the Cheyennes, lived with them a few years before a Major Frank North and a bunch of Pawnees got me away from them." He didn't mention how he hadn't called out and warned anyone when the Indians that had carried him away had massacred his whole family, how that was one of the things he had never understood or been able to live with, a thing that drove him and gnawed at him to this day. He had not even told his Aunt Ruth when he'd been shipped back East to live with her.

"That still doesn't explain why you're all the way out here in the worst of Comanche country by yourself with only a bow and no gun," Syd said, eyes glittering over the rim of the cup again.

"My gun was stolen."

"How long you been out here, I mean right in the middle of where we are?"

"A few weeks."

"Well, you sure could have gone a different direction."

Mick shrugged.

"I hope you're not out to prove anything."

"The last letter my aunt got from my Uncle Bill was

from out this way. I came to Texas, this part of it, hoping to find him. It turned out to be a bigger place than I thought, and rougher." He left out how he had had to take work to eat.

"You're not going to tell me that your uncle's name has the Kid, or Buffalo, or Wild attached to it."

"I don't know any of those Bills first hand, but I suspect my Uncle Bill's not famous enough to have a nickname."

"What is his name?"

"Bill Hinton."

Syd's head gave the tiniest of jerks when Mick said the name, like a repressed snap.

"You heard of him?" Mick asked.

"No. Why would I have? He hasn't robbed any banks or trains, has he?"

Syd looked away when he spoke, a trait Mick associated with indirectness or a slight bending of the truth. Mick didn't pursue it. There seemed no point. This was the most Mick had talked in weeks, and it tired him, made his jaw almost hurt. He stood up slowly and stretched his back. His shirt lay stretched across the top of the pink rock beside the one sock that was too full of holes to use. The shirt was still too wet to put on, but he put the coffee pot on the rock and was reaching for the shirt when he saw Syd freeze.

"What?" he whispered.

Syd tossed out the last bit of coffee from the cup and put it down on the rock beside the pot. Each movement was slow, exaggerated, and made not the slightest sound.

Mick's head turned slowly in the direction Syd's was frozen. At first he saw nothing. Then a headband around long black hair hanging down to bare dark shoulders showed through the parting limbs along the shore upstream. Leather cords from a powder horn and a pouch crossed the chest. The Indian's leggings were pale yellow with fringes down the sides. He was no more than twenty yards away, all by himself. Mick's first thought was Comanche, although it was rare ever to see one off a horse, that is, unless others were close with horses.

He weighed his few advantages. The brave was on foot, and, for all Mick could tell, he seemed to be alone, for the moment. Then he saw the Indian's eyes narrow, widen, and a smile spread across his face, the kind he might get when looking at a couple of rabbits or a young antelope. The Comanche began to lift the rifle he held in his right hand.

Mick reached and grabbed Syd's arm, yanked hard, pulling them both down behind the shore side of the pink rock. The shot ricocheted off the top of the rock, with a metal *clang* as it swept away the coffee pot, cup, and shirt.

Mick stuck his head up, saw the Indian pouring powder down the barrel. Only the sock full of holes lay next to the fresh groove on the stone. *You missed the only thing worth hitting, you damned heathen,* the white-raised side of Mick thought.

Syd's head lifted and Mick reached to push it back down behind the rock while the Indian calmly used a rod to tamp a bullet into place down the barrel.

"Stay down," Mick said. "It's hard telling what they'll do to a woman."

"What makes you think . . . ?" Dark eyes glared at him from under the hat. But she stayed crouched low.

"You going to draw that gun, or talk?" Mick asked.

Syd still stared at him.

Mick touched the side of his nose. "I can tell when a deer's in season when it's on the other side of a hill," he said.

"Well, I'm not in season."

"Look, we can argue that later," he said, popping up to look toward the Indian just as the rifle's hammer clicked back. He ducked behind the rock again, pulling Syd with him.

Chapter Two

Bits of shattered pink rock sprayed over them. Syd looked over at Mick. He looked more irritated that his coffee pot had been shot than that they might be killed. He stood up straight and looked directly at the Comanche. Syd pulled out her five-shot cap-and-ball with the three-inch barrel the gunsmith had told her would be easier to carry and shoot. She aimed and fired three times as fast as she could cock the hammer with both thumbs and pull the trigger again. The brave had been moving closer, halving the distance between them. He squared his chest and looked right at the girl. The shots went left and right of him. His eyes widened a bit. It was hard to tell if the look of amazement was from someone shooting so fast, or from missing him three times. The look of surprise showed as each bullet whizzed past. He leveled his rifle again. Mick reached and shoved Syd's head down behind the rock.

"Don't do that," she snapped.

But Mick was too busy to hear. He hopped to one side, and the Comanche's shot kicked gravel along the shore behind where he'd been standing. Mick took off in a sprint back to where his saddle and blanket lay.

The girl stood up again, saw the Indian calmly pouring powder, then dropping a ball down the barrel of the rifle. He began to tamp the shot into place, grinning at her, as if aware now that she was female. She raised the Colt and fired again, her hand shaking as the last two shots whipped past him, clipping leaves and kicking up stones. His grin spread to a broad smile. He was now convinced he was invincible. He lifted his rifle toward her.

"Hey!" It was Mick, standing upright beside his saddle. He'd strung the bow and had an arrow notched.

The Comanche spun the barrel of his rifle Mick's way and fired. Mick leaned in a snapping jerk to one side in a rapid shift, straightened, pulled, and let the arrow loose. His movements were as if he was on horseback.

Syd's head shifted toward the Comanche where the arrow was buried to the feathers in his chest. The grin slipped off the warrior's face and he fell backward onto the gravel, the gun falling at his side.

Mick stood still for a second, with the same mix of surprise and relief on his face that she felt. Then he rushed over to the Comanche with another arrow drawn in the bow. But the Comanche was down, was never going to be up again. Mick dropped the bow and arrow to one side and lowered to his knees by the body.

"You going to scalp him?" she called over. She had the pouch on her belt open and was pulling out new caps, paper twists of powder, and pre-greased bullets, reloading as she spoke.

He stood, holding the powder horn and leather pouch of musket balls. In the other hand he held the rifle, then picked up his bow and arrow. He looked back down at the brave again, as if sorry he'd killed him.

"At least now you're not out here without a gun, are you?" she said.

One eye lowered and he squinted at her as he swept past her to his saddle. He reached in and got out a shirt. "It's my last one. He blew away my only other, *and* my coffee pot."

"You were out of coffee anyway, weren't you? That's why you only made one cup, isn't it?"

"Thanks for finding the bright side of that. Just what kind of shooting were you doing anyway? Were you trying to miss?"

"I do just fine shooting at blocks of wood for practice."

"Well, if a block of wood pulls a gun on us and tries to kill us, you'll be the first person I call on for help."

She felt the warm flush run up her face. "And what was that daring bit of facing him and letting him shoot at you? Were you after coup?"

"I was trying to keep him from shooting you," he said. He lifted his saddle and carried it over and put it on his tethered horse. After he tightened the cinch, he carried the big rifle over and slipped it into the empty scabbard. It wasn't a perfect fit, but it would probably ride OK that way.

"Where are you going?" Syd asked.

"Almost any place but here. I don't know what he was doing alone . . . hunting maybe . . . or even if he was alone. A dozen others might be heading this way right now. We were just lucky he was on foot. A Comanche on foot's always a better bet than one on horseback." He gathered up his blanket, tied it in place, and added the bow and remaining arrows to his rig.

"You coming?" Mick asked.

Every instinct and thought told her to ride off by herself in another direction. She'd made it this far. But he was seeking Bill Hinton—that name burned each time she thought it, the man she'd sworn to kill. She looked for her tin cup. It was as mangled as the coffee pot, but at least she was able to straighten the cup with her fingers so it would serve. Still, it was not a thing of beauty. She sighed. "Yeah, hold your horse."

When they rode past the warrior, she said: "You're probably going to raise some holy hell when one of his friends finds him killed with a Northern Cheyenne arrow. They'll think the savages have descended from the north."

Mick gave a cluck and nudged his horse on. "Well, they won't be that far from wrong," he muttered.

They wove through the edges of hills, Mick leading them away from the rivers and the trails where the Indian sign was thick. The leaves on the live oaks were a dark, sometimes dusty green at this time of year. Most of the mesquite leaves had yellowed and fallen. The grass, where it was thick, was long, bent, and yellow to brown.

She'd lived long enough in the Northeast herself—sent there by the sisters for schooling and manners—to forget how the leaves stayed on the live oak trees keeping them green when trees back East would have long ago lost their leaves. Coming to this notion at first had made her think the area was impervious to weather. But there was weather here, all kinds. Her first ice storm convinced her of that.

At a low crest of a ridge of hills Mick slowed, then stopped. He pointed below, as he edged his horse into the dark shadow of an old and large live oak tree. Syd followed, stopped when he did again, then looked where he was pointing. Down below, in the wide valley, were dark dots, the humped backs, short horns. Buffalo. There had to be a hundred in this group, nothing like they had been once, but still a sight to see. A number had gone north by now, along with the remaining buffalo hunters following them. While she watched, she saw a string of horses ride out from the woods in an organized semicircle, herding and driving the buffalo at the same time. The bison broke into a run, the calves big enough to keep up. The warriors closed on the back of the herd. Even from here she could hear the solid *thump* of arrows hitting their marks. Then there was an occasional shot. But most of the work with these Indians was still with the short bows favored by horseback tribes. They were far enough away, and occupied, so there was little risk. Syd glanced at Mick. His mouth was slightly parted, and his hands twisted at the reins, as if wanting more than anything to ride down and join the hunt.

He turned to her, saw her staring at him. She watched him wrestle with a smile, aware she had seen his itching desire to ride down and be one of them. He shrugged it off, turned his horse, and quietly led them away from the hunt.

"Old Biscuit here's not horse enough to ride down a buffalo, anyway," was all he had to say about it.

By evening, when the dark was settling over the land like a dog-hair blanket used to douse a fire, Mick found a spot to camp, not near water but in a semicircle of cactus. The other side was a tangle of sumac, scrub oak, and black locust. The grass was matted down. This was where deer had come to sleep during the day, ones out browsing now that the sun was slipping over the horizon.

She started to gather sticks, but Mick shook his head.

"No fire." His voice was low, careful. He went off and came back a few minutes later with his arms full of grass for the horses. She followed him on his next trip out and brought back fodder, too, this time.

By the time the sun was long gone and dark was setting in earnest, she was settled on her blanket and Mick was spreading his as far to the other side of the small clearing as he could. She'd have grinned if her insides weren't still fluttering nerves. He was a man, after all, just another damned one of them, and she would have slipped away and gone off on her own long ago if he hadn't said those two magic words: Bill Hinton.

The tilted wooden cross on her mother's grave had faded and grown worn since she'd been back to it. The flowers—late brown-eyed Susans mixed with the blue of chicory blooms, what she had been able to gather herself—did little to brighten the spot. She stood in a quiver of quiet rage, then went to get out of the clothes she had worn on the long trip back from the East to Virginia City.

Mick rummaged in his saddlebags and brought her a few stringy strips of dried turkey. She noticed he only took half as much for himself, so he must be getting low. He turned to go back to his blanket.

"Wait," she said. She reached into her near saddlebag and brought out a long rectangular paper-wrapped package of hardtack.

Mick's smile slipped a bit, but he stood waiting, probably expecting to have to gnaw at one of the brick-hard pieces of dried bread dough.

"Bring your cup over here," she said. He did, and she put her wrinkled cup down beside his, put a piece of hardtack in each, and then poured water from her canteen into each cup. While the bread was softening, she dug out a small dark brown cone from her bag, took her knife, and shaved off some of the cone into each cup. "Give it a little time," she said, and set her cup aside.

He carried his cup back to his blanket where he sat cross-legged, Indian style, and chewed at his turkey in a surprisingly genteel way for such a rough setting while being particularly careful not to stare her way. That made her almost grin again. It was a long time since she'd met anyone she would call shy, or who had anything like Mick's labored manners.

"Hey, this is good," he said.

She looked up from her cup, spoon poised, and saw him looking up from his tin cup, surprised. You'd think, from his expression, that he'd stumbled across a stack of flapjacks with syrup instead of the stony biscuits she'd improved on a bit.

"What'd you think, I was going to poison you?"

"No. I mean it's a dessert. I've always hated hardtack."

"You see?"

"See what?"

"You shouldn't always be quick with your opinions. There's something good in everything if you just know how to serve it up."

"How did you do it? I mean, make it sweet."

"Brown sugar."

"If I ever get supplies again, I'm going to have to round up some."

"I have to confess"—her grin was mischievous and well worth seeing—"I have a sweet tooth myself, so I knew to pack some. My mother and I used to have a cup of hot chocolate every morning. I tried bringing some chocolate, but in this heat that was a mistake."

"Your mother?"

"I'm. . . ." Syd looked away. "We're done talking about that."

A seven-year-old girl and her mother sharing a moment with cups raised to their lips. She could smell the chocolate, taste it, even now. But she could not recall the details of her mother's face, and for that she hated Bill Hinton all the more.

The tension of the moment hung over the tiny camp as the full dark of night settled in. She put away her things and stretched out, staring at the stars that seemed to hang down almost to her eyes. She lay there on her blanket, tired, but as alert as she'd ever been. This was the part she'd been dreading as much or more than encounters with Indians. A bath and a change of clothes might be nice, and not to have a medium-size rock poking in the small of her back. But that was only part of the discomfort. The worst was knowing he was right there, a man, this close to her, at night.

The way she pictured it was that she would start to doze and he would come creeping over, pulling back the blanket, wanting her. She played it over and over in her mind until she could feel his hot breath on her neck. Her shoulders stiffened, and it was hard to get comfortable. She waited, and finally all she could hear was his steady breathing.

The stars moved in and out of clouds that whisked past as briskly as those buffalo had run across the plain. The smell of dusty sage, and something musky and vaguely reptilian hung in the breeze that lightly swept across her face. Something small slithered through the dark from under the cactus just a few feet from her head.

"Mick?"

"Yeah? What?" Sounded like he had barely begun to sleep, only to be startled awake, yet he was trying to sound like he'd been awake the whole time.

"Oh, nothing."

He didn't reply, although she imagined she heard him sigh. He lowered his hat back down over his face. A few minutes went by.

"The roads," Syd said. "Why aren't you using them? I know why I'm not."

He sputtered awake again. He'd been deeper asleep this time, but he never complained. She heard him take a few deep breaths before he answered.

"I tried the roads earlier," he finally said. "I half thought of riding into Llano, even though I didn't have money for any supplies. I came around a bend through those hills on the eastside of the town and three riders were going by the other way. They gave a friendly wave, and kept going. But I caught them looking over my gear, checking my horse, noticing that I didn't have a rifle or belt gun."

"They look like robbers?"

"They looked like everyone does out here. Tired, hungry, and a little uncertain what to think about anyone they meet on the road."

"And?"

"They went on around the bend I'd just passed. I stopped and couldn't hear their hoofs."

"What'd you do?"

"I got off Biscuit, led her off trail, and backtracked on them. I got up higher than they were, on a stretch covered from the road by a thick chaparral. I tied Biscuit and slipped down closer to the road. The three men had stopped. They were checking their guns and looking back toward where they'd seen me. Then they kicked their horses back that way and rode around the bend, but they rode past where I'd slipped off the road and couldn't find my trail when they came back through. I could hear them cussing up a fair bit, though."

"You think everyone on the road is a robber and cutthroat?"

"It doesn't have to be everyone. Just one or two . . . or those three . . . would do it."

"Did you try mixing in with a group?"

"No. Did you, or were you afraid they'd see through that get-up?"

"I slipped in with one or two groups, and they didn't think a thing about me being out here alone, figured I was a runaway indentured boy from all I could tell. There are plenty of those."

"What's that?"

"A family can't make expenses and the sheriff shows up, tells the oldest boy he has to work off the debt. I'm surprised you haven't heard of it. So the boy is taken away from his family, made to do chores from before light until after dark. All for the money the family owes. That's all there is to that. A lot of the boys run away, and I don't blame them."

"It sounds like slavery."

"It's just another form of it, one that benefits those already a bit better off."

"The way some ranchers get hands to gather strays from the wild? The rancher gets richer, and the hands get beans and just enough money to drink up on a Saturday night trip into town."

"It's not a very fair world, is it?"

"No. No, it isn't," he said.

"You think that's worse than what happens to some girls?"

"No. What happens to girls is far worse." There was a long pause in the darkening night when she didn't respond, so he said: "You're not worried about me that way, are you?"

"No," she lied.

"Good." He pulled his hat down farther over his eyes.

She stared straight up at the sky, saw whole constellations of the stars lit up in strings of images she could only imagine. The black was so black, and the light from the stars and sliver of moon so bright. She waited and waited, but could only hear Mick's quiet breathing above a far-off owl. The scurrying in the sand was louder by her ear. She turned her head. It was a lizard. She could see it now, waddling briskly on its nocturnal hunt.

She was tired, but didn't think she could ever sleep. Then she felt herself dozing off and forced her eyes open with a snap, clenching the pistol grip tighter in her fist. She'd sworn to herself, several times, that no man would ever touch her again. And *live*.

The open stretches made her the most tense. The terrain around them rose to rounded or spiked hills, sometimes mesas, in the distance, light brown and gray rock showing through the clutter of cedar, cactus, and yucca that covered the steeper hills. They had to ride across these open places. There was no getting around that. She caught herself looking at every peak and cliff, expecting to see someone watching them, even though she knew the Comanches had lives just like other people and the men had to hunt and the women gather. Still, these people had the warrior instincts of all tribes, and a heightened sense of it because of all the people pouring into the land and using up the game.

There had been game enough in the last few hours, although Mick seemed reluctant to shoot, perhaps thinking of the noise. He'd made excuses. He passed on shooting a *zorillo,* a skunk, because he didn't want to clean it. He let a 'possum go because, he said, when you take the skin off, the body looks like that of a small human baby. The line between being brave and being careful is thin, and she watched him bob slowly on that sorrel mare, watching the ground, looking constantly about. If she hadn't seen him respond without hesitation and kill that lone hunter Comanche, she'd have worried about his bravery. For now, she rode and stayed alert as they crossed the tall grass heading toward a spine of hills that climbed to sharper points.

Back in Llano County there'd been big live oak trees that linked across the open places. Here, as they passed in their wandering way through Mason County headed toward Menard County, the ground was too open. Just staying away from water wasn't enough. That and staying away from anything like a road, too, had her shoulders tightening into knots. At any moment they could come across a band of Indians, and that would be all it would take.

For stretches the soil would be yellowish tan, then they'd climb a low ridge of hills and see red dirt and stone. On the slightly higher plateau the soil would be pale again, with occasional pink mounds of the very hard rock leading down to creeks and streams. They only visited the water when they had to, letting the horses get their fill. Then they moved with skittish haste away from the water, where they were most likely to run into Indians.

The sun came out from behind a cloud and she reached up to tug her hat down lower over her eyes. All day the cloud cover had come and gone, acting like it might rain, or it might not. Two days and nights of this so far, but at least Mick had kept to his own bedroll, a comfort of sorts. Other than a brace of long-eared rabbits he'd shot by bow and some roots he'd known to dig, they hadn't eaten anything other than the last of his dried turkey meat. At least the turkeys had been eating the tiny wild *pequin* peppers, so there was a spicy pepper flavor to the meat.

Mick slowed his horse as they neared a string of trees that marked a ravine heading up toward the hills they approached. He looked back at her, caught her scouring the tops of the hills around them. His lips twitched into as close to a smile as he'd given in a while, which told her he was just as antsy as she was about crossing the open stretches.

At the edge of the trees the dropping pitch of the ground

led down to thicker brush as the ravine sloped down to the stream. He slid off his horse and began to lead it. She did the same. He moved slowly, and she led her black-maned stallion up until they were pushing through the low scrub side-by-side. The sounds of the horse's flanks scraping the sides of bushes and the sporadic chatter of birds high in some of the bigger trees were all she could hear. Then a brisk rustle marked a squirrel rushing away. Even though she recognized all the sounds, she felt her heart beat faster. Thorns of a dried berry bush grabbed at her flannel shirt, and she paused to untangle herself. When she looked up, Mick was tying the reins of his horse to a low limb. She looked a question his way, but he was turned and staring ahead. He left the rifle in the sling and took his bow, strung it, and held three of his arrows in the bow hand as he eased forward without making a sound.

The air was damp here. She could smell the stream. But the rustle of drying leaves high in the trees that crowded above them now kept her from hearing the trickle of water. He moved quickly and without a sound. When she slowed to look to see where she stepped, he reached back toward her with one hand. She clasped it, felt the rough cowhand texture of it, didn't know how she felt about holding hands. He tugged her on through the thicker bushes until they stood on a rise looking down into the green hills that sloped down on either side to the water.

Below, thirty to forty feet, and a good bowshot away, four does and a buck had their heads bent to the low ripple of water that trickled across the rocks where the stream widened. The shallow water, barely over the deers' hoofs, caught the declining rays of the sun, turning the surface to a flickering sheet of gold. Now she could hear the water, a low murmur as it slid over the rounded rocks of the riverbed, the whisper of the leaves rustling, and here and there a bird chattering. It was as serene a thing as she'd ever seen, and she didn't think about their needing meat, or that Mick hadn't brought his gun. She watched the deer drinking their fill, the buck only lifting his head once, then dipping to the water again.

Syd felt rather than saw Mick slip closer, then his hand came around and clamped over her mouth, his other hand gripping her shoulder so she wouldn't squirm. The second she felt his hand clamp tight, she struggled, throwing an elbow back at his ribs, which he ducked, and she kicked back at him, which he side-stepped. He bent close to her ear.

"*Shhhh.*"

She bit down hard. But his hand didn't pull away. She felt her lips pressed hard against his calloused palm and her teeth sinking in until she tasted the first bit of blood.

Bam!

The shot made her stop. Her mouth relaxed. The does scrambled up the bank, bouncing away, their white tails lifting with each leap. The buck staggered to the shore, fell to his right, tried to get up, pulling with his forelegs, then flopped onto his side again, quivering and blowing hard.

One Indian rushed out of the brush on the near bank with a knife held high and ready. He dropped to the deer and cut its throat. Another Indian came out of the opposite thicket of brush. He carried a black powder muzzleloading rifle much like the one hanging on the side of Mick's saddle. An older Comanche followed shortly; he had an arrow notched, but lowered the bow as soon as he could see the deer was down. They looked around, and, just as their heads began to turn in Syd's direction, she felt Mick lowering her head behind the bushes. She let him.

His hand eased away from her face, and she saw blood on his palm. He held a finger up to his lips, although it was unnecessary. She stayed as still as she could manage. Below, the Comanches were talking, not loud, but back and forth as they dressed out the deer. The sounds carried up the hill. Mick turned and, as quietly as they'd come, was slipping back to the horses.

He spoke into the ear of the sorrel as he untied it and led it away. She untied the stallion and followed. The Comanches would be busy back there for a while.

Once they were far enough away, Mick slipped up onto his horse and waited for her to mount. She wanted to say something. They were far enough away for that now. But he sat his horse and looked ahead. Maybe she wouldn't have shouted when the gun went off. But he couldn't know that. He had just been careful. She could say she was sorry she bit him.

He turned and gave a nod to the right, with no expression on his face. They would go downstream and cross there. He held his reins as if one hand didn't have drying blood on the palm, blood she could still taste. There was nothing to say. They crossed the stream, then turned and rode off toward where the sun was nearing the horizon.

"Did someone, or something, steal your spirit?"

"What?" He looked up at her. Until now he'd been staring down at the sticks she had stuck in the ground by the low fire.

It was dark around them, and the flames from the fire caught and flickered in his surprised and blank eyes. They made Syd want to reach over and poke his arm with a sharp stick, see if there was any emotion, even pain she could detect.

She'd watched him earlier while she made the dough using fatback from the bacon for shortening. His eyes had stayed wide while she had brought salt, soda, the bacon, flour, and all manner of foodstuffs from her saddlebags. The three weeks he'd spent out here with nothing but what he could grab with his hands made him appreciate the least bit of real food.

Tonight's camp was located halfway up the lip of a half hill, half mesa, as far off any trail as they could get, where Mick thought they could risk a small fire. She'd made dough, rolled it into two strips, and had twined the strips around two sticks she'd stuck in the ground.

The bread was beginning to brown and smell like home by the fireside. The two horses were tethered close to the fire, and one of them, Syd's, made a low whinnying sound, not enough to carry far, but enough to cause Mick to glance that way.

Every minute out here was an on-edge reminder of danger. Indians everywhere and hostile, rattlesnakes, scorpions, every bush with stickers. Even the hot sun that had beat down on them all day had seemed to hammer that message home: Don't rest, don't let up. But there was no moon showing, just the black, and the far flicker of stars, and the smell of the bread. She reached and turned each stick, letting another side brown.

He looked impatiently at the bread, then at her. "My spirit. What about it?"

"It seems gone, like you're hollow inside, or confused, uncertain about something."

He shrugged, looked back at the bread.

She reached and turned the sticks again. There was hunger there. She could see that. But it was the simple gnawing kind, for food not tasted in far too long.

"Don't you feel anything?"

"When?" he said.

"Anytime."

"I don't know. What do you want me to feel?"

"I don't know. What do you think about?"

"When?"

"Right now, for instance. Or anytime . . . when you're in the saddle just plodding along through these woods."

"Oh. Well, I guess I think about apple pie a lot. I remember that Sunday was fried chicken day back at Aunt Ruth's. I can almost smell it, until I reach for another piece of dried turkey."

"All that's because of the bread cooking. What about when that Comanche was shooting at you. Weren't you afraid?"

"Of course."

"You didn't show it."

"I was using it. What do you think gave me what it took to shoot him first?"

"It's just that . . . you don't . . . show everything . . . anything."

"What do you want to know?"

"Why are you out here?"

"I told you. My uncle."

"You really think you'll come across your uncle out here?"

"The last letter Aunt Ruth got was from Austin, and he was outfitting and heading toward the upper ends of the river I was camped on this morning. So, it's possible."

"Didn't you say he left her? Were they still close?"

"Aunt Ruth and Uncle Bill? Are you kidding?"

"It seems unusual is all."

"I guess it does sound odd, him taking off like he did. I

know I've never heard of two people who split up who keep in such close touch with each other, but they did. He wrote letters full of his high expectations, and sometimes a glimmer that he'd had more than a bit of luck. But it never seemed to last long for him . . . long enough for him to send for her. For her part, she looked forward to the letters, though he was hardly still long enough for her to write back much. She told me that he was a snake oil salesman as much as anything, but his silver-tongued ways must've charmed her. She talked about their times together a lot, even though he was gone for good as far as she knew. Whatever bond had been there was still there, and, even though they'd split up, they needed each other, to the extent mail could get through from every spot in the country where gold or silver had been struck."

"I saw newspaper articles talking about silver mines out here in Comanche country," Syd said. "You don't think they're just trying to lure men out here to fix the Indian problem?"

"I don't know who 'they' are, or what they're up to. But this area's as likely for him to be in as anywhere in the country right now. He's the only family I have left, except a preacher uncle back in Philadelphia, and I said no to living with him when I went to stay with Aunt Ruth."

"Where is your Aunt Ruth?"

"She was heading out to Saint Louis to move her business there. But . . . well, she didn't make it."

"What happened?"

"Someone put some stuff . . . timber and tree trunks, that sort of thing . . . across the tracks. The train wrecked, went off its rails. The men who did it were busy robbing the mail car while the survivors of the derailment were picking through those who didn't make it. Aunt Ruth was one of those." His eyes slipped away from hers toward the fire. "Hey, the bread."

She pulled a stick from the ground and handed it to him before the bread got too brown.

Mick picked at it, and had a hard time holding back, but it was still too hot to eat.

"He's all there is? Don't you have any school chums or other friends?"

"I went to public school for three days, until a group of boys cornered me and said things about my aunt."

"They beat you up?"

"Tried. I was smaller, but they weren't used to scrapping as if it mattered. I was banged up, sure. But I sent two of them to hospital. After that I was educated at home. So, there weren't any school chums. No neighborhood pals, either."

"Oh." She was sorry she'd taken the conversation this direction. She picked up her stick with the bread wrapped around it.

He tore off an end of his bread, blew on it slowly to help it cool. "What about you?" he said.

When he looked at her this time, she could tell his eyes were brown. They showed a bit of genuine warmth for the first time. "There's nothing about me."

"Oh, right. A young woman, sixteen, seventeen . . . about in there . . . riding around alone in Indian Territory, disguised as a man. Armed, but with no real shooting experience. Sure, nothing off or a little odd there. Have you any idea what these men would do to you, if they caught you?"

"Yes. Yes, I do." She felt her own voice tremble just a tiny bit, more than she would have liked. But Mick didn't seem bothered. He was matter-of-fact about so much of his life. If hungry, eat, if sleepy, rest. It seemed alarmingly simple, although he was not. Something was under his skin the way it was under hers. But he didn't labor it. He popped the first piece of bread in his mouth, and his eyes smiled, even though his mouth was busy. She picked a warm end off her bread, popped it in her mouth, and chewed it slowly.

So far she'd gone through cities, small towns, and camps of men, and no one had seen through her wearing men's clothes. She'd been just another young man drifting through, and there were enough of those around. Mick had seen through in an instant, and yet he didn't seem to be disposed to do anything about it. She felt herself just beginning to relax in his presence. In so many ways he seemed like a version of herself, keeping much to himself, something pressing on his mind, but not anything he could share, or share well and easily.

Around them the sky seemed abnormally black, huddled closely by the fire as they were. An owl had given her a start earlier, and then a small group of deer had rustled through the brush, their hoofs clicking softly on stones. A pair of coyotes traded calls too far away for it to matter, even if it was Indians, instead.

"What makes you so worried about my spirit?" he said, already half done with his bread and pausing so as not to wolf it too fast, but to savor and stretch the rare taste out as long as possible.

She shrugged, glanced out into the dark past the horses. Now that she'd picked at this scab she realized she'd really been asking herself. It was amazing she'd been able to think that way, knowing him such a short time.

"You were out here three weeks, with no gun, nothing to eat at first, and yet you seem like you just rolled out of your blanket each morning like it was another day. How did you do that?"

"What you mean is why, don't you?"

"Yeah, I guess I do. I'd hate to think you're just wandering around out here with no purpose."

He said nothing.

"Alone and unarmed." She'd known men to do dumber things, but had not run into many that had survived. "You don't think any of this is being contrary, do you, that you're a savage in the city, and a gentleman in the wilds?"

"I don't think anything's as simple as all that."

"This Bill Hinton. He was your blood uncle, right?"

"Yeah, my mother's brother."

"Does any part of that worry you?"

"Right now, it's just about the furthest thing from my mind." He glanced over at the rifle that leaned against the cliff beside them, within easy reach. "That old muzzleloader's not the best, but it's sure a comfort after having nothing." He looked back at her. "Where'd you get that short-barreled gun of yours?"

"It's a Colt, the Wells Fargo Thirty-One-caliber model. A gunsmith said I'd find it easier to carry. He even suggested the holster, said it's a single-flap, whatever that means. I guess it was catching on in California. It doesn't have a flap over the top, so I'm supposed to get it out quickly."

"You got it out fine enough, but it's a stubby thing, a belly gun, OK for standing right up against someone and letting him have one below the ribs."

"A belly gun. Thanks."

"It's better than any pistol I have with me. Don't let me talk against it to you. I shouldn't poke fun. I had only the bow."

"Which you strung quickly and used well enough when you had to."

"I used to play a lot with a friend, Bear Cub. We were siblings, really, only he was blood Indian. I wasn't, though most days I didn't know that."

"Did you get along?"

"Most of the time. We wrestled our way out of any of the usual disagreements. He sometimes thought I got treated better than him. But that was in his head."

Mick went back to eating, giving her only an occasional glance. Here was someone who knew more about her than she liked, and it was still not a problem. Then what was gnawing at her?

"It's that you're so polite," she said.

"What?"

"You sound educated, East Coast, and your manners are almost too good for out here. If you're rich, why aren't you home?"

"I'm not rich. Haven't you figured that out?"

"You sound like you are."

He sighed. "My family had money, but lost most of it. Dad speculated, like I said. We were in a wagon heading West to start over when the Sioux ended that. When I got taken away from my life with the Cheyennes, I had a choice of going to live with a stuffy preacher uncle or my Aunt Ruth."

"Hard choice, eh?"

"It wasn't so bad, until a few of those public school kids decided to make my life rough."

"There was just that one incident?"

"Yeah, but a couple of those boys were hurt pretty good. So, my aunt decided I'd learn at home."

"She was good at it apparently."

"She had help. There were other ladies."

While he spoke she watched the slow movement behind him, coming closer to where the two horses were tied. It was so cautious and at one with the dark that she could barely detect each stealthy step. Her hand slid down to her holster, slipped the thong off the hammer. Her fingers tightened around the grip.

"Servants?"

"Not really."

She saw Mick stop eating and look past her. There was another one back there. Mick lowered what was left of the bread on its stick to the blanket beside him. His hand started to slide across the blanket to the rifle in its scabbard on the saddle beside him.

"That was almost the last of the coffee," she said, keeping words flowing now, her eyes locked on the slow shadow of movement coming along the rock wall. "Maybe we should try a town and get some more."

"Yeah, maybe we should." He knew, too, to keep the talk going. His eyes were still over her shoulder. He gave up all pretense of cautious movement and grabbed for the rifle.

She spun. The Comanche was almost on her, a knife coming down toward her. She had the gun out, hammer back, and fired. The warrior dropped back and rolled. There was no time. She spun the other way as another brave stood up. He put the knife he was going to use to cut the horses' tethers between his teeth and pulled a bow off his shoulder. It was such a practiced and skilled move that he had an arrow notched and was lifting it by the time Mick pulled the rifle out and Syd got the hammer back on the pistol and fired.

The Indian doubled over, dropped the bow, and fell to one knee. Mick rushed toward him, swinging the rifle like a club. Syd looked away, although she could hear the *thud* of the blow. She shuffled with bent knees until her back was to the rock wall where she pulled the hammer back again on the pistol while Mick rushed to where the other Comanche had fallen.

She winced at the sound of another blow. Mick came scrambling back to her.

"Are you OK?" he asked.

"Why wouldn't I be?"

"I don't know." He looked over to the horses that were just now acting skittish and pulling at their tethers. Syd's horse was usually the more hair-triggered of the two. But the two Comanches had been quiet. He looked away from the fire and around into the dark surrounding them.

"You think there are more?" Syd asked.

"I don't know," he said again. "But after those shots we'd better move."

She was tired, didn't want to go again, but she went over and started to roll up her bedroll.

"Thanks," Mick said. He was packing up his own gear, didn't look right at her.

"Did that hurt to say?"

"They were gut-shot. Both of them."

She tugged the rawhide string around her blankets tightly with a harder jerk than usual. "Well, you're the one said it was a belly gun."

Chapter Three

Mick woke and it was still too dark to rise, but he was done sleeping. He lay there thinking, as he often did at times like this—those stretches during his life when he'd been all by himself. By now he was used to it. Except this time there was someone else stretched out on a bedroll just a few feet away. That wasn't a bad feeling. He liked waking up and knowing she was there, that they would talk, and ride together. He'd expected to feel a bit crowded by her being along, but he didn't. Taking care of each other wasn't so bad, and it made everything—the bread, surviving—better.

The sky grew gradually lighter in slow gradual degrees of gray, until he could begin to see the sage in a row on one side, although the light was still too dim for him to make out the light purple blooms on some limbs. He could make out the horses where they were tethered, patient and quiet. When he turned his head, he could see Syd's face, and for the longest time he watched her breathe, fascinated, as if it was the first time he'd ever been aware that other people were alive.

Well over two years ago, he'd regained consciousness and felt something like this, but what he'd seen then was the twisted wreck of the train, the engine on its side as well as the first few cars after it above the bent rails and jutting black ties. The air had been thick with the black smoke from where the baggage cars had been set afire. He had heard the screams and moans of other injured passengers, but it had taken a while to soak in that Aunt Ruth was dead.

A woman he'd never seen before, or since, had been helping the injured. She'd told him about Aunt Ruth, and about the luggage being lost as she bathed his head with a scrap of cloth and water from a bucket. She was a Baptist, she told him. A much smaller boy laying on the ground beside Mick, who got the same treatment, had been young and confused enough to ask her if the water made him a Baptist now. She'd been too tired or full of something painful to laugh.

Now, as he lay beneath his blanket, as much in the middle of nowhere as he'd ever been, the sky had grown a pale white. It would be a clear cloudless blue soon. The first growing brightness off to the east hinted that the day was going to be another hot one. His eyes swept the area for critters, furry or scaly, found none, checked on the horses—OK—and then fell on Syd again.

Her eyes were barely open, yet, still half closed, they sent bolts of hot lightning through him. He lay in the warm glow, wondering why none of the girls at Aunt Ruth's had ever been able to look at him like that.

"What are you thinking about?" he said.

"That we're about out of coffee."

"Oh." Mick rolled onto his back, looked up at the flat white sheet of sky that hadn't turned into anything. "We'd probably better skip a fire this morning. Too out in the open."

"Not even to make bread?"

"You know how to make it sting."

She kicked off her blanket, let the cool air help her wake up. Mick was careful not to look that way. Even fully clothed, there was a rumpled "just up" look to her.

"Why are you out here?" he asked. "You've picked at me. But you never said." His words were slow, treading their way carefully as if through loose, slippery rocks.

"No, I didn't," she said.

"Not going to?"

"No. Not right now."

He wanted to ask why she was bothering to tag along with him, but there was the fear of breaking the spell. He stood up, rolled his blanket, and tied it in place behind his saddle. He didn't know what to make of the warm feeling inside him. He was a little light-headed, like he'd been when he'd gone three or four days without food. He hoped it wouldn't cloud his reason. If she would have asked him to light a fire, even out here where the thin trail of it could easily be seen for miles, he might have done it for her.

She packed up her gear and carried her saddle over to her horse, swung it into place, and ducked to grab the other end of the cinch.

"Something bad happened to you once, didn't it?" he said.

She stopped, and turned to look at him. The warmth wasn't there now.

"Yeah, something like that."

"A man?"

She nodded, turned back, and pulled the cinch tight, waited on the horse to take a breath, and then pulled it tighter.

"It's about my mother . . . and me, as well," she said. Reluctant.

"Oh."

"I was young, real young. The man was passing through. My father was dead. We lived in a town where there was an attraction that drew a lot of men for a while."

"And?"

"Now my mother's dead, too. I was sent off to be raised and educated in the East by the sisters. I guess that makes us a pair of orphans out here."

"I suppose it does."

She climbed up into her saddle.

Mick took a last glance around at the campsite, then slipped up onto Biscuit.

"You spend a lot of mornings without breakfast out here?" she said.

He scanned the area in all directions. The sun was still just a sliver of yellow on the horizon. "The young Cheyenne warriors used to have to go out every once in a while and fast. It made them think clearly, understand life better, hardened them for the warrior life. This *wu wun,* a starving, was also supposed to make the young man fortunate in battle."

"I wondered, being raised an Indian, how you felt out here now killing Indians the same as all the whites who just want to run them off the land."

"They're a different tribe. They've attacked us first every time."

"That's what this is to you, isn't it. Some damned kind of warrior test?"

He turned to her, surprised at the language, more surprised at the look she was giving him. He turned back to the trail, gave Biscuit a cluck, and started leading them out of there.

As Biscuit picked her way through a thick stand of chaparral, Mick was thinking that the terrain, from horseback, was a lot different, and better than being on foot. They'd come to the road and were running parallel to it, but staying off it, even though a stagecoach had rolled by, kicking up a huge cloud of dust. They could have ridden hard and kept up with it, but that wasn't what they wanted, even though it did feel good to be near a road and the hint of civilization that went with it.

They'd seen less game near the road, but there'd been less threat of a Comanche attack, too, although Mick had paused at one spot to get off Biscuit and look at sign where half a dozen Indians had sat their unshod horses and watched the road. He wondered how the people traveling by would have felt if they'd known that.

He would've been hard pressed to say why his heart beat a bit faster as they saw more houses as they neared the edge of town. With the homes came fences, too, and a barking dog. He veered left just as the houses began to get more frequent, and they rode toward the open stretches and thicker stands of trees.

Occasionally they came to strings of fence, even houses, out in the wild. Few houses, though, that were not banded together still stood. Twice they came upon open scorched ground and just a stone chimney sticking up from the black mound that had once been a cabin.

"I'm sorry about earlier," he said.

"What?"

"Asking you about your family. It upset you."

"Well, I'm sorry I snapped at you . . . about the Indian thing."

"It's the food really, isn't it? You're just hungry."

"I could eat." She hesitated, then said: "Well, OK. I'm very hungry. I don't know how you keep going."

"Down there. See where the stream widens?"

"Yes. It shouldn't widen there, should it? There's no natural reason."

"There's a reason, a natural enough one, and it's what's built a dam. You wait right here, and keep this for me." He slid the rifle out of its scabbard, checked the load, and handed it to her.

"Isn't it dangerous near the water? Indians."

"I'll be quiet." He slid off Biscuit, tied the reins to a cedar bush near a clump of grass she would want to nibble, and took his bow and a couple of the arrows.

The sun wasn't that much farther across the sky when he silently parted the stand of cedars and slipped back to the clearing where Syd sat waiting. The two horses were tied and she was looking off in the direction he'd followed down. She spun when she heard the rustle of limbs, and she saw the beaver he was carrying by the tail.

"Good eating?" she asked.

"And we get a skin we can sell."

"I've heard trappers had picked the rivers nearly clean."

"They didn't get them all." Mick took out his knife and began to clean their lunch. Syd started gathering twigs.

"If you'd believed in me as a hunter, you'd have already gotten firewood," he said.

"Look, I'm sorry about earlier. OK?"

"You said that. I wasn't meaning to pry about your life so much." He peeled the skin away from the muscled dark meat of the beaver, feathering the knife along to help as he pulled. He would stretch and dry the skin as soon as he got the meat cooking. He might not have money, but a beaver pelt is as good as green if he ever got to a town. Beaver meat wasn't so bad, either, if you got a young one. This one wasn't old enough for gray whiskers, but it wasn't so far from that. It was a good hide, though.

She came back with a big load of wood, dropped it on

the ground. "How big of a fire do we dare build?"

"We'll dig a hole, lay a bed of stones in it, start the fire down in there, then this old beav' will have a chance to stew. Wish I had some salt." He lay the cleaned beaver onto a bed of yarrow plants he'd gathered. The bruised leaves smelled as good as fennel, and were adequate for wrapping beaver, but were really good when wrapped around fish.

"I've got salt," Syd reminded him.

He got the small part of a broken-handled shovel from his bag. It was turning into one of his handiest tools out in these parts. You could bury anything, even dinner.

She watched him at the base of the only large live oak tree near them. He dug a hole almost at the trunk, and then started the fire in the hole. He worked it slowly and used only the most dead and dry twigs, so there was almost no smoke. What little smoke there was followed the line of the trunk upwards, and was filtered through the canopy of leaves at the top until there was no trace of a fire.

"I was too young to remember much of it, but the sisters told me all about it," Syd said.

Mick glanced up. She was staring off at sky, where, in the distance, a hawk was climbing, a small bird fluttering at its tail, harassing it.

"You don't have to tell me anything." He could tell something was gnawing at her, though.

"No. I want you to know. I think you *should* know."

That was a bit more ominous than he'd expected.

"My mother was Mexican, a widow. Some think my father was white . . . as white as you. Does that shock or upset you?"

"Why would it?"

"It would bother some people. Anyway, I don't actually remember all that happened, just what I learned."

She paused and Mick waited on his knees, looking up at her, knowing she needed time to ease up to it. When she didn't immediately pick up the story's thread, he bent again to the task of cutting the beaver into portions that would cook quicker. He sprinkled on some of the salt Syd had gotten out of her saddlebag. The fire had burned down until it was a flat bed of glowing embers at the bottom of the hole. He wrapped the beaver parts in the stalks of ferny-leafed yarrow, the only greenish ones that hadn't turned yellow or brown yet. He put that on the embers, lay on another layer of yarrow fronds, then, using his shovel blade, began to cover over the hole with loose dirt and gravel.

"There was a man," Syd began. "He was drifting along, like so many do, all out to make their fortunes and keep going. My mother . . . she didn't . . . she wasn't an easy woman to know. But this man seemed kind, I'm told, and could laugh."

"Did he hurt you?"

Syd had to think about that. "He didn't beat me, if that's what you mean."

Mick looked up at her, didn't know what to ask or say.

"I was young, only seven, and I didn't know . . . what was right . . . or normal . . . or expected. He started touching me"—without knowing it, she shivered as she spoke—"in certain ways . . . then, later, more. My mother caught him. There was a fight. I don't know that the man meant to kill my mother, but she was a passionate woman, and she fought hard, with everything she had. At some point she fell. When others came, they found her dead. The man was gone. That's when I was sent away. Later I learned all I know now."

Mick hadn't thought Syd's cheeks dusty, but he could see the trail the single slow tear made as it struggled slowly down the length of one cheek.

"The man never came back?"

"No. He was spotted in one or two places, ones similar to the town where we lived and where my mother's buried." Syd's chin quivered, and she bit at her lip, trying not to let Mick see her cry. He held out an arm, but she spun around, started to walk away. "If I ever find that man," she muttered, "if I ever do." She stood by the horses, her shoulders shaking.

Mick knew not to go to her right now. He looked up at the sky, checking again to confirm he couldn't see any trace of the smoke from his fire, and knew why he didn't tell her about the man by the stream where he had gotten the beaver. A trapper, probably. Although, with no clothes, Mick could only guess. Tied to a tree like that, his eyes had been plucked out by birds at least a week or more ago. His wrists and ankles had been bound with untanned leather strips. His genitals, penis as well as testicles, had been cut off in one slash and crammed into the man's mouth. One of the Indians, Comanche from the sign, had taken a knife and slashed open the man's stomach. They'd hooked an end of that to the man's burro, had it pull his intestines out in a string. Then they'd killed the burro and eaten parts of it, cooking it while the man died, slowly.

One thing about it. They wouldn't be back to that spot for a while—would give nature a chance to take its course. Indians, even Comanches, didn't much like to trespass on a burial ground, or hang around where there were dead. They'd probably not hunt around here for a bit. It's one reason Mick was so calm about cooking up his beaver so close to the spot.

He watched Syd, still softly twitching, reliving her own sorrow. *Yeah, probably best not to mention that guy down there at all.*

★ ★ ★ ★ ★

That night they lay with bellies full for a change and watched the stars grow closer as they lay back on their blankets, still with no fire, but Syd had put her bedroll closer to Mick's this time.

The wind rustled the tops of the bushes near them. A cricket made its noise near them, but it was otherwise quiet.

"It's so calm," she whispered.

"Do you want a story?"

"Oh, yes. Do tell me a story." The mocking edge to her tone was cheerful enough for him to continue.

"I'll tell you how the Cheyennes came to have guns. Is that OK?"

"I guess."

"It was a favorite of mine."

"Get on with it then."

"Long ago the Cheyennes were not as strong warriors as they became because they had no guns to fight the Ho Hee, the Assiniboines, only clubs and sharpened sticks. This was before the horses, and they moved from place to place by packing the dogs. One tribe had moved from their earth lodges to hunt buffalo, and after four days they had a great deal of meat."

"Is this story supposed to make me hungry?"

"Not after all *you* ate. Anyway, the tribe moved on along the stream and left one old woman behind. She stayed at the old camp because she wanted to pound up bones, boil them, and skim off the grease."

"Mmm. Mmm."

"The story doesn't need you to help it along," Mick said. "She was busy boiling the bones and skimming grease from the pot, and she'd made a torch and tied it to a stick and thrust the stick down her back, between her dress and her body so the torch was over her head and could throw light on the pot. She was blowing the grease off the water when a person came into the lodge and sat down at the head of her bed. She didn't look up, and soon, one after another, twenty Assiniboines had come into the lodge. She heard them say to each other that there was a lot of food in the lodge, dried meat hanging on all the walls, so they would eat first, then kill her."

"Does this . . . ?"

"*Shhh.* Just listen. The woman was scared. She knew what they intended. But she stayed as calm as she could manage. There was a big sheet of back fat . . . tallow . . . on the wall, and she took it down and roasted it, so the men would have it to eat with their dried meat. She put it on a stick and hung it over the fire. Soon it began to spatter and drop grease into the fire. When it was at its hottest, she grabbed the stick and whirled it around, throwing hot grease into the faces of the men as she spun. Then she dropped the stick and ran for the door.

"Near the lodge there was a high bank that ran along the river, high above it, with rocks below. She ran that way through the dark, but her torch told the enraged Ho Hee where to follow. They were furious, and raced after her. She came to the steep bank ahead of them and pulled the torch from her back and threw it over the cliff. The warriors came racing through the dark after her and ran, one by one and sometimes in groups, over the cliff to fall fifty or sixty feet to the rocks.

"The old woman ran to the new Cheyenne camp and told the men what had happened. In the morning they came and found all the Ho Hees with broken backs or legs. They killed them all and took their guns, and that's how the

Cheyennes first came to have guns. What do you think of that?"

"I like it. She's my new hero."

Two days later, the last of the beaver bones long picked clean, Syd turned in her saddle and said: "I'm hungry."

"What? Do you have a tapeworm?"

"We've been riding a long while. The horses have eaten more than we have."

Back with the Cheyennes, it had always been the job of the braves to gather meat. The women took care of water, wood, roots. But the meat had been men's work. It seemed natural enough to him.

"OK," he said. "But tell the truth. Is it that chocolate-loving sweet tooth of yours? Or are you really hungry?"

"Why? Do you know where there's chocolate?"

"No. But I just saw a bee go by."

"Which means?"

"Honey."

"Honey? You know where we can get honey?"

"It also means we're within a day's ride of a ranch or a town." Mick lifted high in his stirrups, looked around. "Honey bees are never too far from people in my experience."

"Where's the honey?"

"Down that way, closer to the stream."

"How do you know?"

"I've found I'm a good bee follower. Do you really want some?"

"Yes. Why are we still sitting here?"

He grinned, liking the idea of getting things for her she enjoyed. Oh, it might seem like the old story of the boy bringing a box of candy to the girl he was sweet on, but he still knew he was going to find that honey for her.

The closer they came to the stream, the more careful he was about watching for any sign or movement. The brown green of vegetation seemed to stretch all around them, the bare black bones that were mesquite trees, the low hillocks of the live oak trees, the sage tangled into the edge of cactus. Fires had swept through much of the area, set by the Indians to ensure the return of the buffalo each year. The thickets thinned the farther they got from the direction of the town he sensed to their north. Near the stream, the cottonwoods and other trees grew thicker. It was shady and cooler.

"I wish we could ride down here more," Syd whispered, riding closer.

Mick held a finger to his lips. He stopped, sat his horse, and watched. After a couple of minutes he nudged Biscuit back into motion, bearing to his right. A trail opened, and Mick didn't care much for that, but it was an animal trail. Any moccasin prints or hoof prints of unshod horses were old and buried beneath a clutter of raccoon, opossum, and other critter markings.

Biscuit wove through the thicker brush, past a stand of tall cane, then veering right as Mick followed after the occasional bee he saw buzz past. The bank to the right of the stream climbed into a steep cliff. Behind it, the other side of the hard rock came down the sharp pitch of hills in layers, leaving gaps, openings like stressed smiles in the rock, places snakes would love to hide.

Yucca plants and cactus managed to live, clinging to the rock face of this side of the hill. Where the cliff climbed to the top, a flurry of thicker trees and old berry bushes grew in profusion. He rode around and swung out wide around a patch of thicket that grew close to the base of the hill. Biscuit stopped, and Mick turned back to Syd.

"What?" Her horse danced a step sideways. Whatever had stopped Biscuit was affecting the stallion, too.

Mick slid off Biscuit, unfastened his riata, put it over a shoulder, then pulled the rifle from its scabbard and held out his reins to Syd. "You'd better take the horses to the top of the ridge over there." He nodded his head toward a rise at least 1,000 feet from where they stood.

"Why?"

"Just do it." He didn't care much for the way the brush was matted down near the front of the cave, nor did he like the way the horses had cut up at what they could smell. There could be snakes, anything. The ground was too hard for footprints or tracks of any kind. It was nearly solid rock here.

"You know, you could explain things more, sometimes," Syd complained, but she led the horses up the hill and out of sight.

He turned, took a deep breath, ducked low, and headed into the cave.

The smell was dank, musty. You'd expect that in a cave. He expected it to be dimmer, too, but, at least, near the entrance there was dim light. He could see the moist walls with moss growing along the dampest, brightest side. The wall wasn't sunlit, or anything, just less dim than the rest of the cave. When he eased close to that wall, he could look up, where a fissure ran to a thinner rift. Near the end was a small hole, too small for someone his size to crawl through, but enough to let in some sunlight on bright days, and perhaps a bit of rain on wet ones.

He was sliding his feet along, looking up, and his left foot went out over open air. His hands went out to the mossy wall, and his weight shifted toward his right hand, where he held the rifle, its counterbalance tipping him away from the opening in the floor. When he'd eased his left foot back, gotten it planted on the solid rock floor of the cave, he looked to where he had almost stepped. It was a hole, going straight down, barely wider than his shoulders. But he couldn't see the bottom from above. From the back of the cave he could hear a low *buzz* that he took to be the bees. There was another regular sound he couldn't make out. Crickets from the front of the cave chirped, as did something high along the top of the cave, probably a bat or two.

He eased around the hole into which he'd nearly tumbled, shuffling his feet, making sure of the floor as he edged back into the darker part of the cave. The top of the cave, its ceiling, dipped lower and lower, not in stalagmites, but jagged-edged rock that made him crouch low as he went deeper into the darkness. Maybe he should have brought a torch. He paused, thinking he could go back and make one. He would probably need to smoke the bees out of their hive, anyway. Well, no. He was making excuses. He slid back farther into the dark. Above him, the ceiling opened until he could stand now, although he was in near black, just the dim light coming in from the bottom of the entrance.

He could hear the bigger noise now, the one above the *hum* of bees and rasping harsh chirp of bats. Something was breathing. Mick froze where he stood, bent to listen closer.

"Mick?" The shout came from the front of the cave. He'd told her to stay on the hill with the horses.

"Are you all right in there? You don't need to do it."

Damn, he wished she'd quit shouting. Her voice boomed in echoes through the dark insides of the cave. In the silence that followed the last echo of her yell, he listened hard, but could no longer hear the deep breathing sound he'd heard before. He did hear a snuffle, then what sounded like an irritated snort.

"I don't need the honey that bad," came her voice again. "What's the matter with you? Why do you have to do these things?"

Maybe she'd seen everything he had outside the cave and was coming to the same conclusions, or apprehensions. He just wished she'd quit yelling.

The sound deep in the cave was no snort this time. It was the beginning of a snarl turning into a growl. He spun and, gripping the rifle as hard as he could, ran toward the cave entrance, ducking low where the cave dipped down at the top, then straightening and giving his legs everything he had as he ran out of the dark into the light of day that nearly staggered him it was so bright.

Syd stood there, head tilted and a hand on one hip. Her eyes opened wide.

"Run!" Mick shouted. "I mean it!"

She spun, but stayed where she was, staring.

From behind them a galloping black shape charged out of the cave's mouth. Then the bear stood, all six to seven hundred pounds of it. It roared, a loud hearty roar, then dropped to all fours and took after them in earnest.

Chapter Four

Syd saw the bear, and she heard Mick yelling, but she seemed frozen where she stood. Mick stopped, grabbed her, turned her in the same direction, and pulled to get Syd moving. "Run!" he repeated, tugging at her hand.

The bear's lumbering pace should have been something they could outrun, but Syd's first steps were stumbling ones. Then she shook her hand loose from Mick's, picked up her feet, and started moving, slowly at first, as if walking. In a few steps, though, with the bear gaining ground, she was moving briskly enough to pass Mick.

There must be a cub. Or was this just the crankiest bear that'd ever been woken from a nap? It wasn't stopping.

The ground around the front of the cave had been hard and flat. As Syd and Mick scrambled up the hill, it grew steeper and more uneven. Their running had taken them gradually farther apart. Splitting would cause the bear to make a decision to go after one or the other of them. Mick saw Syd stumble, go to one knee, and get up again. A quick glance back was enough to see the bear veer toward her.

"A tree!" Mick yelled. "Get up a tree!" He stopped, lifted the rifle, and tried to get a bead on the bear. A moving target was bad enough, but a bobbing one, with tongue hanging out, jaws open, and on their heels, was another thing altogether.

"Yo, bear, over here!" He shouted, waved his arms, whistled, but the bear stayed with its choice, rolling after Syd, whose legs were going as fast as she could make them.

Syd's hat flew off when she looked back. Her eyes got wider as she saw the bear was gaining. But the bear slowed, paused to smell at the hat that was still tumbling to a stop, then it started running after Syd again. She watched over her shoulder, then struggled to unknot the handkerchief around her neck while she ran. She let that flutter behind her, and again the bear slowed.

She keeps that up she's going to be naked soon, Mick thought for just the glimmer of a second, then kicked himself away from thinking like that. He raised the rifle and fired, only the gun didn't fire. He pulled the hammer back—no percussion cap. It must've fallen off somewhere. He pulled up the leather pouch that held the caps and balls. By the time he found one, Syd was flying, her hair rippling back in a short dark brown wave.

The bear was ten yards back, but gaining.

Ahead of Syd, halfway up the increasing pitch of the hill, was a live oak tree with a fork low enough for her to reach. The trunk was as big around as her waist. Still in stride, she sprang and pulled herself upward. The bear grew closer. Syd slipped, fell back a bit, and screamed, then she gave a surge and pulled herself all the way up and got one foot in the fork of the tree.

Mick was running toward them now, as fast as he could.

The bear started to climb the tree. Any screaming Syd had done earlier had just been for practice apparently. The bear's growls were louder now, too—confident, aggressive growls, expecting to be gnawing on something, or someone, soon.

Mick glanced around as he ran. All he needed now were for Indians to hear all this racket. He ran on, stumbling over a root that stuck out of the ground, but catching himself and staying upright after a staggering step or two. He'd never seen a bear this big, a full adult from the look of it, climb a tree before. Maybe they could. But he doubted it'd be easy for this one to haul its own bulk very high into a tree. The bear wasn't really trying to climb. Mick could see that as he got nearer. It was pulling itself up, then swiping with one long-clawed paw at Syd's feet. Then it got one. Syd screamed, a scream like a mountain lion turning inside out. It was a scream to make every Indian within two dozen miles shoot upward out of any war paint. The tips of the bear's curved claws raked along the side of Syd's leg, scraping down until they hooked in her boot top. The bear was pulling her foot toward its mouth.

"You! Stop it!" It was stupid, but Mick couldn't think what else to yell at a bear to make it turn his way.

Syd yanked her leg up just as the bear's mouth snapped on the boot's heel. Her foot pulled out and the bear tumbled back a step, it's mouth crunching down on the boot at the same moment Mick ran up to it, shoved the barrel tip under the bear's cheek, and pulled the trigger. The recoil almost tore the long gun from Mick's hands. He looked down at it, where his fingers barely held their grip, and then back up at the bear.

The bear was turning toward Mick, aware of his coming up close for the first time. Its mouth was full of boot, but it swung a heavy paw toward Mick, then fell directly onto him. All he could feel after the initial impact was the bristly black fur smashed against him and the hard muscle. The body was like a dirty rug full of anvils on him, and he couldn't move. The thick smell was overwhelming from this close, and the weight was enormous. But Mick realized the animal was not moving.

"Mick! Mick! Are you OK? Are you alive?" Syd cried.

He wished she'd quit shouting like that. Two things—it might call in Indians, or it might rile the bear, which was either dead or napping. It sure wasn't stirring. It smelled dead, but, for all he knew, it had smelled that way back in the cave. There was the added coppery smell of blood, though, lots of it.

"Mick, come on. Talk to me."

"I'm under here." His voice came in a gasp. He didn't want to say he was fine, because he wasn't sure about that yet, never having had a bear land on him before.

"Help me," she said, and that stirred him more than worrying about himself had. He wriggled and pushed with his feet, shoved with the heels of his hands. He left the gun lay where it was, under the bear.

"Oh, oh, oh."

"What?" he asked.

"Mick."

"What?"

"You're hurt, hurt bad." She rushed toward him, limping. He looked up at her, could see her with one eye only. He reached up and wiped at the other eye. His hand came away covered with blood.

"I'm all right," he insisted. "What about you? Your leg?"

"You're all right? Really?"

"Yes. What about . . . ?"

She bent and gave him a hug around his shoulders that surprised him as much as anything that had happened in the last few minutes. When she pulled back, she seemed as embarrassed with herself and as startled as he felt, but he also felt good, warm, and not just because his feet were still pinned under the thick coat of a dead bear.

"Let me clean some of that blood off you." Syd went to reach for her bandanna, and was surprised to find it not around her neck.

"You threw it at the bear," Mick said. "You're hurt. The bear got you on the leg."

"Oh, just scratches."

"You don't understand. Help me out of here."

With Syd tugging and Mick pushing, he got out from under the bear. It was going to be a chore cleaning it. But they'd eat well. Then he thought of Indians and all of Syd's yelling. He scanned the woods around them. Nothing.

Syd came back with her handkerchief, limping with one boot off and her leg scratched, and squatted down to swipe at Mick's face until there wasn't a clean spot left on it. She tossed it down beside the bear.

"Don't throw it away," Mick said. "I'll rinse it out at the stream. We've got to get more water. Now, let me look at those scratches."

Syd stood and took a step back, looked at the bear's head, where her boot was still in its mouth.

"There is nothing dirtier than a bear's claws. It's like they're poison. We've got to clean those scratches."

"OK, if you can get my boot back. I'll go to the stream with you."

Outside the cave, Syd's horse whinnied, and Mick went out to make sure it didn't mean company. But it was just the stallion settling in closer to the cave. The bear's skin hung stretched between a pair of saplings that bowed toward each other with the weight. It had taken him a while to get the horses used to that. Mick went back in the cave. Syd sat with her back to her saddle that rested against the stone wall where a little light came in, but not too close to the hole Mick had found earlier in the cave floor. Syd's face was coated with a light sheen of sweat.

"I was afraid of this," Mick said.

Syd looked up at him, tried to grin, but it was feeble and a little scared.

Mick had used an indented round dip in the cave floor for a mortar and a blunt stick for the pestle. He pushed and ground at the goo he'd made.

"What is that stuff?" Syd asked. "It smells awful."

"It's a mix of powdered skunk cabbage, the root pulp of wild parsnip, and some wild onions, all mixed with bear grease. We're lucky we had a bear handy." He looked up at her, his forced smile not masking his concern very well.

"What's it supposed to do?" she asked.

"Draw out the poison," Mick answered.

"What poison?"

"I don't know. It's something happens where a bear scratches. Our dad, well Bear Cub's, not mine, Iron Eyes, got scratched by a bear and his leg swelled up until I thought they'd have to cut it off. But Snake Owl Woman, who was medicine woman for our tribe, used something like this."

"Something's wrong with that story."

"What?"

"A woman as the medicine man?"

"You know more about the Cheyenne I lived with than me?"

"No," she responded, then: "What are you doing now?"

"These are leaves from a lizard tail plant. I was lucky to find them and the skunk cabbage near the water. None of it's too fresh. I'll tie the lizard tail leaves on top, then wrap this in place." He used slender strings of vine from which he'd stripped the leaves to tie the poultice in place. "That's all I can do for now," he said when he was done.

"And pray?" Syd said.

"If you like."

"I don't feel that bad, just tired, and too warm."

Mick went over to where his saddle lay close to the mouth of the cave. He got his canteen and took her bandanna from where it hung. He wet the bandanna, folded it, and put it on her forehead. She leaned back against her saddle. Her brown cheek bones were flushed darker. Her eyes, open only part of the way, watched him for a tired moment, then fluttered shut.

Mick felt a lurch in his stomach when he looked down at her. He didn't have all Snake Owl Woman's knowledge or skill. It made him feel helpless, and it made him aware, too, that he cared.

He finished dressing out the bear, making wooden racks from branches to hang the meat he wanted to save, inside the cave, and burying the bones and the rest to discourage any attention from scavengers. It had been a male, probably just cranky, so there'd been no cub to worry about, after all. He filled the water canteens, took down the hides, and rolled them, fed the horses, took a reconnoiter for half a mile around the cave's mouth, still watchful for Indians, and, when he came back, he still found little to do while Syd slept.

He gathered up the bear claws and the flattened bullet he'd taken out of the bear's skull, made a drill from a slender bit of flint on half an arrow shaft, and sat down to drill holes. By the time Syd's eyes fluttered open later, Mick had strung the bear claws into a necklace with the bullet in the middle. He held it up so Syd could see it as she woke. The metal, with its hole through its center, glittered brightly between the long claws, each drilled from side to side at the base.

"What's that for?" Her words were weak, like wounded butterflies staggering from her lips.

"Snake Owl Woman said it's big medicine if you keep something of what hurt you close. It helps you heal."

"You believe that?"

"I'm willing to try. You want it?"

"Sure." The word barely made it from her mouth before her eyes closed again. Her forehead and neck were soaked. Mick took the now warm handkerchief off her forehead, poured cool water on it, wrung it out, and wiped her face and neck before he rolled it and put it back on her forehead. He lay the necklace in her open hand, and her fingers closed over the bullet on its leather cord. *Argento,"* she whispered, and fell asleep again.

He swallowed, got up, and went to see to the horses.

From outside the cave he could hear her moan from time to time, so he took another scout of their perimeter, going out a mile each way this time. The area was clear, with not even a hint of recent traffic—no direction or trail markers, or moccasin or unshod hoof prints. Near the cave mouth he found a place on an old live oak where the head of a pickaxe had long ago been driven into the tree, but the handle had rotted off, and the rusty blade was gradually being swallowed as the tree grew. There was no other recent sign of any men having been around. He had a clear shot at half a dozen turkeys in a roost up on a limb, but knew there was all the bear meat they'd need hanging in the cave. There were some herbs close to the water he picked, thinking he might make Syd tea, if he could recall all that Owl Snake Woman used for a fever. There was much to pick, from the inner bark of a dogwood tree to the inner root bark of a red willow. He gathered some of each. It might not taste good, but that was not its purpose.

Syd was tossing and mumbling when he tiptoed into the cave. Outside, the sky was dimming. She'd knocked the cloth from her forehead, which sparkled with beads of sweat. The collar of her flannel shirt was soaked. Her eyes twitched, although they stayed closed, and her arms jerked about. She held tight to the necklace. She could not have clenched it tighter if it had been a lifeline.

He could make out a word or two and leaned closer, realized she was muttering in Spanish. She'd said her mother was Mexican, but the speech she used with him, so far, had reflected the education she'd gotten back East. He could make out *madre,* but little else. He straightened and looked for more chores to keep him busy.

It was dark outside, and he'd been comforted by seeing no one near. He brought in enough wood for a small fire. Behind the hole in the floor and beneath the spot where he'd seen sun coming in through a small hole high above, the cave floor formed a depression rising to a short stalagmite on the hole in the floor's side. The shallow bowl in the stone that he'd noticed earlier was blackened. He suspected this was not the first fire ever built in the cave.

When the pot with its fever barks was setting beside the low fire, Mick picked up a stick that was long enough to be a torch and went toward the back of the cave. He should have checked earlier to make sure nothing could bother Syd from this direction. The cave didn't go back too far, just a bit beyond on each side after it formed a fork. At the scratched walls of one dead-end he found the beehive, broken open where the bear had gotten into it. Bees were making repairs. Down the other fork the cave ran out, also, with signs where someone, long ago, had clawed at the rock, and more recent sign where the bear had slept.

He eased back to the front of the cave, put the stick back into the fire, touched the side of the pot to find it warming, and then turned back to Syd, who with wet face still mumbled to herself and tossed about. Mick picked up the handkerchief, and took it outside to wet it with the water he'd most recently brought from the stream. It was coolest, and was, according to Cheyenne custom, live water.

He went back in and, as quietly as he could, stepped to Syd. Her leg outside the wrap was a bit swollen. They'd removed the torn chaps long ago, and he'd cut her pants to her knee for the dressing. Her face was tinted darker by the flush of fever. Most of all, Mick didn't like the relentless fever and her tossing in what seemed bad dreams.

As he lowered the cool, rolled handkerchief to her forehead, he could feel the heat coming from her skin. The minute the damp cloth touched her skin, her eyes snapped open, unfocused and hysterical. She screamed: "Don't touch me! Get away!" Her face was a snarl, threatening, even with its unfocused eyes. Her arms thrashed and her right hand slashed at him, as if she held a knife, or wished she did, and she threw the necklace at him. He ducked as it sailed over his head as he backed away.

Mick's heel was on empty air, and he tottered back, looked behind, and saw the hole behind him. He'd almost stepped right into it. He caught himself, took a step away from the hole, and looked back at Syd. Her head had dropped back onto her saddle, her damp face rolling from side to side. Her hands clenched and unclenched, alternately making fists or claws. Mick gave her a few minutes until she seemed to sleep again. Then he eased up to her, put the cool cloth on her forehead, expecting anything. But she slept.

The tea was hot, so he moved the pot away from the fire. When she was awake, and not in a mood better suited to cutting out his liver, he'd see if he could get her to swallow some. Even cool it might help, and the coolness might be better for fever.

Outside, it was dark. He checked on the horses, then stood looking at the stars a while. Nothing much in that. To the north, once he'd taken a few steps away from the cave, he could see a dim yellow glow in the sky. There was a town in that direction, probably Mason. Knowing that didn't help much at the moment. He went inside, decided to look for the necklace.

It wasn't anywhere on the cave floor that he searched with a torch taken from the smoldering fire. He whipped the flame into a brighter state and held it down the mouth of the hole. There it was. The necklace had hooked itself on the top of a leaning wood pole near the bottom. It was too far away to reach.

He got his riata from his saddle and looped one end over the stalagmite beside the hole, then he dropped the other end down into the dark. The torch he carried in his teeth, and it made him think of the Cheyenne woman who'd led the Ho Hees off the cliff.

Climbing down the riata, using his arms and one leg looped around it, wasn't hard. He was agile, quick, and the weight he'd lost during the past few weeks made it easier for him to maneuver.

Mick could see the hewed walls of the chute enough to know it was man-made. Streaks of different rock ran in veins, and these had been gouged in places. With the torch in his mouth, he had to turn carefully to look down. The log pole had once had smaller pieces of wood tied to it, but the leather straps, holding these, had rotted or been eaten away. The smaller pieces of wood lay on the floor of the hole. Against one edge of the bottom of the chute wall sat a bullet mold. It hadn't fallen there from above, but had been carefully placed there, out of the way.

The necklace hung, its top end against the rock wall, across the tip of the wooden pole that had once been a ladder. Mick eased down the riata, hand over hand. Perhaps it was silly to try to rescue it, but he'd spent a lot of time making it. More than that, there was Owl Snake Woman's saying this sort of thing was big medicine. He should know better, after his own years back in the heart of so-called civilization. But here he was.

He was close now. With the torch in his teeth, he leaned back, holding with his left hand, stretching all the way back with his right. Maybe it was premonition, or his extraordinary good reflexes—he snapped back his hand just as a scale-covered arrowhead, with mouth wide and fangs poised to sink in, shot out from a crevice in the wall, the thick diamondback body following the lunge. Its weight far out of its hiding spot, the snake tumbled below to the floor of the shaft, where it coiled, ready to strike again, although Mick was now beyond its reach. The sound of many rattles filled the shaft, letting Mick know it wasn't the only one down here. He reached and got the necklace, let it slide onto his wrist, then he used both arms to pull himself quickly to the rim and out of the hole.

He looked back down, but could barely make out the bottom, and he couldn't see the snake. It had been at least eight feet long. He'd heard of some ten, even twelve feet long, but only in spots like this, where they'd had a chance to grow old and mean enough to have long rows of rattles.

His heart was still hammering fast. He took the necklace over to Syd, lowered it into her open hand, and the fingers closed over the shiny bullet again. She seemed to breathe a little easier. Maybe there was something to what Snake Owl Woman had said.

The fire had grown low, so he put on more wood until he could clearly see her face. Then he sat by her side into the night, watching. She seemed weaker, but was sleeping better. There were no more dreams and she didn't leap at him when he refreshed the bandanna on her brow a few times through the early part of the night.

Lying in deep sleep at last, her face was serene. With all her efforts to wear a hat low and her face shadowed, he hadn't really noticed before that she was beautiful. The clean lines of her face, even beaded in sweat, were something to see. He got up from beside her and went to lay on his own bedroll, between Syd and the cave entrance.

The fire slowly died down and sputtered out, leaving the cave in blackness. A breeze swept through the front and up through the hole that had drafted the smoke out.

He lay for a long time, unable to put his finger at first on what it was that felt so different. Then, after a while, he realized what it was. He felt lonely.

Chapter Five

Mick woke. He couldn't remember falling asleep. Nor could he recall how he came to be within a couple of feet of where Syd lay. He was sitting cross-legged, and his legs tingled; he wondered if he'd be able to stand. He looked at her and saw that her brown eyes were open, that she was watching him. But her eyes were only half open, like she was willing them to stay propped there until he was awake. A smile worried its way onto her face.

Before she had seemed driven, as if she wanted something as much as he did. Her languid look now scared him more than anything. He'd been drawn to the side of her personality that was fire, and here her embers seemed to barely flicker.

"I'm kind of a bother, aren't I?" she asked.

He tried to smile back, but his face just felt stretched and worried. His legs were all a-tingle as he struggled to his feet. He rubbed them, and then hobbled over to where the pot sat with the tea that had cooled through the night. He filled her cup half full and carried it over to her.

"What's that? More of that snake lady's stuff?"

"It's a cold tea," he explained, "that's supposed to help ease the fever some. I was going to get you to drink it last night, but . . . well, it'll be just as good for you now."

There was no need to tell her how she'd almost knocked

him into that snake hole. He doubted if she remembered much of last night. He helped her lift the cup to her mouth. The skin of her cheek felt smooth and warm against his rough hand. "How's that?" he asked.

"Awful." She tried again for that smile that slid off her lips in a tired wave.

"That's fine. We were always told that any medicine that tasted good couldn't be good for you."

"It. . . ."

"What?"

"It does relax me, though. I feel it."

"That's good. I'm going to try to ride to town."

"There's a town?"

"A bit north of here."

"Why?"

"You need medicine."

"You don't trust the Indian medicine you've been using?"

"I don't know what to trust. I just . . . I don't want to take chances with you."

"Don't go getting goopy on me."

"I'm . . . I'm not. What do you think I should do?"

"I think you should go boil your fat head."

He stood up and was sorry he did. His legs felt the rush of blood burning all the way up and down. Some of it was in his cheeks, too. He went outside, looked around, then moved the horses and got them feed. Biscuit seemed pleased to feel the saddle put into place, and Syd's horse pranced nervously—or jealously. When Mick tied on the rolled bear and beaver skin behind his saddle, the prance of Syd's horse was downright skittish.

The rifle he slid out of the scabbard and took in to lay beside Syd. He put the powder and bag of bullets and caps beside it. He left his unstrung bow and the arrows there, too, not that she could use them. He just couldn't very well carry those into a town.

"What am I supposed to do with all this?" Syd said.

"Hopefully you won't need to do anything. You've got your belly gun, too, don't you?"

"Just going to leave me out here, huh?"

Mick didn't get it. How could she practically smile at him one moment, and the next chew him out like he was the hand and she was the foreman?

"Listen to me," he said. "Behind where you're lying, there's a hole, a shaft of some kind, old mine or something."

"What's that to me?"

"Just don't go near it, unless you want a bad fall . . ."

"I'm not going to. . . ."

"or like snakes," he finished.

Her mouth clamped shut, as if she'd determined not to speak to him again. But that was just the fever, he told himself. The beads of sweat stood out on her forehead, and her shirt was soaked through. The tea, although cool, must have had an effect. He made her drink another cup of it, even though she fussed. Before he left, he filled all the water containers, decided to take only one of his own canteens with him. He carried her canteen along with his other and put them by her side.

She sat up now and looked at him with those half-lowered fevered eyes. He noticed she wore the necklace around her neck, the bullet hanging down in the front, the claws making a nice spray across her upper chest. It was a necklace any brave would be glad to have, but Mick wasn't so sure it was right for her, now that she wore it. Perhaps it would seem more appropriate when she was back to dressing and looking like a male.

"Here." She held out one arm, the small brown fingers facing down in a fist.

"What?"

"Hold out your hand. Don't be so difficult."

"I'm not. . . ." He forced himself not to say any more. He opened his hand under hers and something fell into his palm. He pulled his hand back, saw a coin, a $20 gold piece, the first he'd seen since, as a cowhand, he and Hodges Laney had brought back a small sack of them for 300 head of cattle sold after gathering them from the brush while McLaren had been all cozy back at his ranch. All that seemed a lifetime ago now.

"You may need that," she said.

It was hot in his hand, almost burned, although he didn't know if that was because it came from her, that she had a fever, or if it just embarrassed him to take money from a woman, someone younger than himself. Yet his pockets were empty, and he was going for medicine. Maybe the fur would be enough, but he'd better take the coin.

"Thanks," he managed to choke out. He spun and started for the cave opening. He was angry, for reasons he didn't understand.

"Mick," she said.

He stopped, turned back to her.

"Hurry back. OK?" She was barely able to keep her eyes open. Her head eased back on the saddle and she closed her eyes.

There was no road to Mason from this direction, at least none he'd found so far. But it bothered him little to ride the same way he had been, staying away from the likely Indian spots and neither showing himself on high ground nor riding out in the open, even though that meant skirting some open areas across which he could have made better time.

He could tell he was getting closer to a town when he came to a fence. Old Hodges Laney had told Mick he remembered when there wasn't a barbed-wire fence in the state, but that folks were starting to put them up from one end of the state to the other, which seemed more than a bit of a stretch of the truth to Mick.

The morning was still early when he came up along a road that led in to Mason. He heard the rumble of a stagecoach first. In a few minutes he was close enough to see the brown line of the road weave past a stand of tall trees on its side. In the distance he could hear a rider coming.

The rider passed in a moderate gallop. Just someone getting from here to there, unaware of anyone who might be looking on from the copse of woods where Mick sat his horse and watched.

Once the rider was past and the trailing cloud of reddish dust had settled, Mick clucked to Biscuit and moved out onto the road himself. He turned toward town, taking a more sedate gait. It would be early yet. The stores might not be open.

As he neared the town and could see the cluster of buildings ahead, he noticed a small steep-roofed building to his left. The stone used to build it was of reddish squares, some darkened to a near black. At the top of the front of the pitched roof was a wooden cross, not a carved one, but one tied together in the manner of some small ones he'd seen in cemeteries. He slowed Biscuit, then veered left and jumped down, tied the reins to the hitching rail in a loose looping knot.

Inside the church the light was dim. The trees that

crowded the eastern side were live oaks, so they still had leaves, unlike the tall winged elms scattered through the rest of the churchyard that had lost their leaves. A row of candles glittered up along the altar. A woman with a shawl over her head knelt at the front altar. Mick took off his hat, slid into one of the back hand-hewn pews. It was quiet in here, restful. Wind swept over the steep roof of the church, and a draft through the cracked-open window bottoms made the candle flames leap in unison for a moment.

Mick had no idea why he was here, what had lured him into this place. But he used the time to think of Syd, to hope she pulled through—well, more than to hope. He had never been one to need much in the way of other people. Aunt Ruth had been always busy, and had encouraged him to occupy himself. He'd been fine alone in the woods, too, until now.

The woman at the altar stood slowly, as if her bones and muscle resisted. When she came past, Mick could see she was very old. But there was something in her face. Hope? She paused at the door, dipped her fingers in the holy water contained there, made the sign of the cross, and went out.

Alone in the church, he tried to pray. But he didn't know any of the words he thought might be expected of him. So he sat and thought of Syd, and finally said out loud: "Just do what you can to make her better, if anyone can hear this." Mick sat for a few more minutes. Then he finally rose. At the door, he paused, looked around. There was a white stone image of Mary, with a tiny basin of water at her feet. Mick dipped his fingertips in the water, imitated the sign he'd seen the woman make, then went out of the church, almost running into a man in a brown cassock.

"Pardon me," the priest said.

Mick didn't know what to say. The man had a silver

chain with big links around his waist with a large silver crucifix hanging from it. The cross caught the sun in flashes of light, and Mick realized he was bowing his head in a prolonged nod. "I'm sorry."

"No need to be sorry, son. Is there something you're looking for?"

"No. I was just . . . getting out of the heat."

The priest looked up at the sun, which was bright, but which hadn't really heated up the day yet.

Oh, great, Mick thought as he untied the reins and swung himself up onto Biscuit. *Now I've lied to a priest, too. Add that to my day.*

His first glimpse of the town did little to impress Mick with the advantages of civilization. The few people on the streets moved with an awkward precision when contrasted with the smoother, more natural movement of the Indians or game that lived in the surrounding wilderness. The haste of the people he saw, their urgency as they went about their tasks, seemed false, artificial. He tried to recall if the people of Philadelphia had seemed like this to him. Not at the time, he guessed, but he'd probably have the same reaction now. Who was he to come out of the woods and be judging people?

A picket house he passed had a fading sign on its porch—**Bridge's Hotel**. He wouldn't be staying overnight, so that wasn't for him.

The downtown had a few buildings of stone or brick, but more of wood, some weathered considerably by the winds that blew through, like the breeze trying to knock off Mick's hat today. In a few places, new, stone buildings were in the process of being erected. The place seemed to be growing at a steady pace for not being near a railroad. He rode down the street, looking at the signs, trying to figure which would be most likely to have medical supplies.

A man wearing a homespun butternut shirt was loading a wagon out in front of Ranck's General Store. His shirt, his pants tied with a length of braided rope, and the broad slouchy straw hat marked him as a farmer, that and the kind of supplies he was putting in the wagon. The yoke on top of feed sacks confirmed that bit of insight.

Mick rode Biscuit up to the man's wagon. The man put a cloth bag of Arbuckles coffee beans into the back of the wagon, which Mick would have very much liked to have had. He caught the man's eye, but the farmer turned away to the stack of goods he was loading.

"Do they have medicines inside?" Mick called to him.

The man turned with a small barrel he could barely lift. He settled it onto the back of the wagon with a *thud* and started to turn away again.

"Hey!" Mick yelled. Manners were one thing, but this wasn't the time.

The farmer turned, frowned, and nodded toward the store's door. It was as if Mick had been speaking in another language.

Mick headed toward the door of the store, passing a large pile of cowhides stacked nearly to the top of the portion of the store that amounted to a porch. Down the street, a man in red flannel shirt, suspenders, and jeans was approaching. But none of Mick's answers was out here on the street. He went inside.

The store's interior was like a wonderland to him after being out in the wild so long. It seemed everything desirable he could imagine crowded the shelves. Behind the counter at the store's rear stood a tall man with sandy tousled hair, graying at the temples. He wore wire-rim spectacles and waited on a lady looking at bolts of gingham cloth. It gave Mick a moment or two to look at the stacked leaded tins of food, jars of molasses, piles of new, never-used blankets, stacks of buffalo-hair pillows, tools, traps, mining gear, tall jars of bright-colored twists of candy, a sweating block of yellow cheese, plugs of Lorillard tobacco, factory-made shirts and pants. A wonderland! Although he'd been in stores back East, he couldn't imagine how all this stuff had gotten out here and into this little town's store. Still, this was a fair-size town with its own courthouse and jail, which he'd passed, and somewhere on the other side of town would be the rounded stone walls of Fort Mason.

Near the back of the store a rack of guns lined the wall, one or two of them even new. There was a long-barreled Hawkins rifle, an Army Enfield, a couple of Springfields, an old brass-band American musket, a Gallagher, Spencer, a Sharps carbine. He hoped to see one of those newer Winchesters, but supposed they'd been snapped up, which accounted for some of these trade-ins. Beside these stood twenty-five-pound and six-pound cans of Dupont powder, and there were primers and St. Louis shot tower lead in bars done up in twenty-five-pound sacks. There were even various caliber bullet molds on the order of the one he'd seen down the shaft in the cave. With this kind of gear he could stay out in the woods for years.

"Can I be helping you, son?"

Mick looked up. The tall man was done with the woman and had moved close, keeping an eye on the weapons. All the pistols were in a locked case, so he didn't have to worry.

The front door opened and the man in the red shirt, from the street, came inside.

"Be along in a minute!" the tall man called. "Now, what is it you'll be having, son?"

"I need medicine. Something for fever."

"Nothing new in weapons?"

"No, sir."

"Oh." The man moved over to an apothecary cabinet along the wall. "Fever, you say? You look OK."

"It's not for me, and I don't have money."

The man had opened a drawer and was looking through it. He stopped.

"But I have a couple pelts. Can I trade for the medicine?"

"Cowhides? I'm only offering a dollar per."

"No. A beaver pelt and a bear skin."

The man in the red shirt browsed his way closer, glancing up with a soft grin when Mick looked awkwardly his way, amused by the conversation between Mick and the clerk.

"I'd have to see the hides," the man said.

Outside, he gave the hides a quick check, seemed glad the bear had been taken with a head shot, saved having a hole in the hide. "Still need a bit of tanning, but I'll stand for the medicine," he said, leading the way back inside. "Who's sick? Be it one of your folks?"

"My . . . my brother."

"Aconite. That's what you need. You give him one drop per teaspoon every two hours. Should take his fever down."

Mick knew he didn't have a teaspoon, but he'd figure something out. Then he remembered Syd had one. "Does that make us even?" he asked of the man. "Or does that leave room for anything else?"

Red Shirt seemed amused by that. He stood by the rifles, looking closely at a crack in the stock of one of the guns.

"What is it you've a mind about?"

Mick would have loved to get a bag of coffee. But he

didn't know how much medicine ran, and didn't want to push his luck.

"Chocolate or cocoa."

The clerk's lips narrowed, then he smiled over at another customer, but he went and added a small tin of cocoa powder beside the small bag in front of Mick. "This for your . . . brother, too, now is it?"

Mick nodded, knowing he had Syd's gold piece in his pocket, but having vowed not to spend it if he could help it. That was none of his money. He had felt badly enough taking it, and looked forward to being able to hand it back.

"What is it, son?"

Mick hesitated. "Have you ever heard of someone named Bill Hinton? He's my uncle."

"No. But lots of fellas come through here and don't give a name, or their own, at any rate."

Mick took his things and went outside and was slipping them into one saddlebag when the man in the red shirt came outside, saw him, and stepped closer.

"James got you on that exchange, boy. You could have gotten more for those skins."

Mick couldn't figure what business it was of this fellow's. "This was all I really need," he said.

"Where are you off to?"

"Out there." Mick nodded vaguely.

"My name's Bob. Bob Pattie. What's yours?"

Mick told him. He waited politely for the man to finish and move on. If he rode hard, Mick could get this medicine back to Syd before night. He didn't much care if someone got the better of him with a couple of skins. The woods were full of fur—hides or skins of one kind or another—if that was his game. All he wanted to do now was to get back to Syd.

"You look like you haven't eaten right in a spell. I'd be honored to stand you to lunch, if you've a mind."

"No . . . thanks. Sorry."

"Oh, your sick brother. Right?"

"That's it, sir."

"He must be real sick for you to pass up home-baked biscuits, steak, potatoes, and pie I smelled baking this morning."

Mick's stomach gave an unforgiving lurch. "He's sick enough, sir."

Mick waited, but the man stood there, looking at him. This Bob Pattie was a bit taller than Mick, but not that much more. He was slender and losing some hair on the front of his head, graying a little at the back and sides. He looked over Mick's horse and Mick in a way that made the youngster uncomfortable.

"If you two are looking for work, there's a bit of tension building up around here," Pattie said. "You could work for one of the ranchers . . . could make even more if you're handy with a gun."

"What kind of tension?"

Bob looked up the street toward the jail. One deputy was walking this way down the street, and another leaned against the front stone wall with a rifle.

"Some of the cattle ranching kind. You're not unfamiliar with that, are you?"

"No, sir."

"If some folks won't talk back to you out this way, try using German. *Verstehen?*"

Mick shook his head.

"Folks moved up here from Fredricksburg. Area's mostly German. When the state voted whether to secede or not, this county voted Union. What'd they care about seceding? They were making good lives for themselves. Now there's a Reb or two back from the big disturbance that think they ought to have a lively time of it. Understand?"

Mick frowned, looked up at the sun, then politely back to the man who seemed driven to chat. After a minute of this awkwardness Mick untied Biscuit and hoisted himself up into the saddle. "Gotta go," he said.

The man reached up to touch his hat brim, realized he wasn't wearing one, so just gave a short wave as Mick turned the horse and started off down the street.

Mick rode faster going back than he had coming in. He wanted to get this medicine to Syd as soon as he could. If something had happened to her . . . well, he didn't want to think about that.

When he eased up to the cave, after giving the surrounding area a thorough but quick scout first, Mick reined Biscuit to a stop. Syd's horse was gone. His heart leaped up high in his chest and hammered away. He tied Biscuit to a scrub sage and rushed inside the cave. Everything was gone. There was no sign of her, or any sign of a struggle for all that, either. The cave floor had been swept clean.

Mick went out and stood in front of the cave. There was no movement in any direction he looked. He pulled himself back up into the saddle and slowly started tracking in circles wider and wider around the cave.

At last, almost half a mile away, he picked up the first hoof print. Twice he lost the trail, had to stop, trace it past where the prints had been wiped out on purpose and then she'd backtracked. Each time he'd find the trail again and surge forward, wondering if he'd be welcomed or if she'd shoot at him.

It was late afternoon and the sun was turning orange in

the distance when he started down the slope of the far side of a hill. He looked up, and there sat Syd on her horse, watching him.

He rode closer. Her eyes were rimmed with red, and she could barely hold herself upright. The long ride all day had taken what little she had out of her. The shirt she wore was different than the one he'd seen her in that morning, although she couldn't have much packed in her saddlebags. This one was soaked through with sweat now, too. But she wore the necklace. Her mouth twitched, and he realized she was trying to smile, but was too tired and worn to manage it. There was a good deal he would have liked to have asked her—Why she'd taken off like that?—although he had a hunch it had to do with men in her past. But before he could say a word, she waved a tired hand in a short sweep beside them. "This look like a good place to camp to you?" she asked.

Mick had to hop from his horse and rush forward to catch her as she fell sideways into his arms.

Chapter Six

Syd woke and looked up into the wide nostrils of two horses. She blinked. One was her own horse, the other Mick's. Her horse gave a low nicker, sensing her awakening.

"Your horse was so skittish I had to tie them close," Mick explained. "Out here we don't want to make any more noise than we have to until I can determine how alone we are." His words were soft and careful, the way a person gets when cautious about disturbing the calm of early morning.

She forced her head up, found Mick. He stood looking out over a hedge of piled bramble and stacked loose brush that surrounded them—dead dusty brown mesquite limbs woven in a tangle with living sage and thorny locust—a small fortress in the wild that either the wind had blown that way or Mick had helped along a bit. She had no idea how long she'd been sleeping, although she felt clammy in her clothes, and groggy and foggy of mind, like cobwebs needed to be swept from the corners of her brain.

He turned and came to her, helped her sit up against her saddle. Then he went over and poured her a cup of the Indian red willow root tea from the pot. He handed her a cup. It was cool. He dug out some of the medicine he'd gotten in town from his saddlebag, had her take a dose of that with the cool tea.

"Still aren't sure whether to lean on white man's medicine or red, are you?" she said, striving for a kidding lilt to her voice, and almost making it.

His shrug was tired and labored. "Can't hurt to keep trying both. Hasn't killed you yet. In fact, I think your fever broke in the night."

She could remember him making her cocoa a couple of the times when she was awake, how that had been a welcome treat and had made her think of her mother more than ever. Much of the past couple of days she'd lost while in the grip of the fever. She did feel better, even though tired, but, for a change, refreshed from the sleep. A bath and a change into clean clothes would be just too precious right now. Best try not to think too much about that. She looked down, saw his blanket on top of hers where they'd both tumbled to her waist when she had sat up. Then the significance of his blanket being tangled with hers sank in.

She felt heat shoot up in flames to either cheek. "Where did you sleep?"

"I didn't. I've been up all night, tending you through all this."

"Oh. I'm . . . I'm sorry I snapped," she said, adding: "It seems I'm always sorry."

His slow smile was tired, and his eyes were edged in the red that comes from sitting up and listening to the coyotes beyond the point where that is fun.

"Don't be," Mick said. "I shouldn't have gone in that cave once I had any notion there was a bear inside."

"But you were being brave, weren't you, because that's what you expect and require of yourself?"

He turned away, then froze, held up the flat of his hand.

She sighed, realizing how she sounded. "I guess I owe you another. . . ."

Mick looked back at her, held a finger to his lips. *"Shhh."*

She listened, could hear nothing. She tried to stand, but her legs felt like bags of sand. She looked to see if anything lay across them, but there were just the blankets. It was the fever that had made her weak. The one leg still felt slightly swollen and a little numb, but she had more feeling in it now. After a full minute she began to hear the slow *clop* of hoofs, shod ones. The careful steps said that whoever was coming didn't mind their knowing, but didn't want the whole valley to hear.

Mick eased over, nevertheless, and picked up his rifle, had it ready to raise.

The first thing Syd saw was a man in a bright red flannel shirt, suspenders, and a flat straw hat with a red and black ribbon around it and a brim that seemed narrow compared to cowboy hats. The only time she'd ever seen sporty straw hats like that was back East. The man's horse pushed its way through the opening in the brambles Mick had used to get in and out. The horse was at least sixteen hands high, a dappled gray gelding with an almost regal bearing. She didn't know what kind it was, although it was one handsome horse. The only one she'd ever seen like it, with a thin neck, the high arching neck and tail, was a jumper.

"Why'd you follow me, Pattie?" Mick said.

"That's a heck of a trail you two laid down back there. There were backtracks, and switches across granite, and places you'd stopped to wipe out tracks. Why, I've seen people running from the law who were less careful than you two." He looked down at Syd. "Is this the brother?"

"I asked you a question," Mick said. Syd had never heard his voice have so much edge to it, and, to add emphasis, he pulled back the hammer of his rifle.

"There's an Indian trail not too far back from here," Pattie advised. "You sure you want to discharge that firearm so near them. Probably Comanches on the war-path."

He seemed as cool as the center seed of a cucumber on a shadowy vine after a morning rain. *Awfully cool,* Syd was thinking, *and with a gun pointed right at him.*

"That's a travois trail," Mick shot back, "made by Ki-owas, and it's two weeks old. Quit trying to scare her."

The man grinned down at Syd. "Sorry, ma'am. Bob Pattie here, since it doesn't seem likely he's going to intro-duce me." He touched the rim of his hat with two fingers and a thumb. "I was led to believe you were his brother, anyway." He saw her looking at his hat, grinned again, and slid off his horse, ignoring the barrel of Mick's gun that swung with the movement. Heading toward Syd, he walked right past the barrel of the gun, brushing it casually aside with his hand as he went by. He wasn't that much taller than Mick, maybe an inch or two, but his upright bearing made him seem a bit taller than that. He came close enough to look down on her. "It's a boater . . . the hat. Don't see many of these west of the Mississippi, do you? That's the point, you see? You add a low voice like mine, with a bit of a drawl, folks don't know whether I'm from the North or South, are, in general, confused. The rest of the rig is miner get-up. Folks see all the parts, can't decide on the whole. It's better to cast a mixed picture out here. Let people sort it out and think what they will, or what you want at that moment. You'll find that out, if you're in these parts long enough."

He talked fast, smooth, kept his eyes moving to both of them, and made slow clear gestures with his hands. He wore a gun on his belt, but wore it high, unlike gunslingers, who wore their guns low for faster drawing. She had seen someone who moved and even acted like him. She struggled to remember where. *Damned fever.* Made her thinking slow. *Oh, that was it. On a riverboat . . . a man with three cards, moving them fast, picking everyone for big money until a couple of the men rushed him and threw him overboard, somewhere just south of Memphis.* She wondered if the fellow ever had made it to shore, weighted down as he was with all the silver, gold, and bills he'd fast-talked from the other passengers before taking his abrupt departure. This man had the same smooth, oiled quickness and relaxed ease, over-confidence.

"How's the fever, by the way. Did that aconite do its job?"

For some reason, the whole situation struck Syd as funny. Mick looked mad and territorial with this blustering fellow just blabbing along.

"I believe it was the willow bark that did the trick," she said.

"Willow bark?"

"Although the skunk cabbage might've had a hand in it."

Now it was the newcomer's turn to look dumbfounded. He glanced back at Mick, who was trying to hold back the beginning of a smile himself just then. But the man didn't lose his confidence for long. He put two fingers up to his mouth and gave a short whistle. "Sancho!" he called out. "Where have you gotten to?"

There was a rustle from the cut in the brush where Pattie had entered, but nothing came into the small enclosure.

"Must be stuck," Pattie said, and walked past Mick's lowered gun barrel, back to the opening, reached through, and gave a tug. "There you go."

Past the extended red sleeves of his shirt, Syd saw a gray head with huge curious dark eyes in a rectangular box of a bushy gray face topped by an almost black mane and long furry ears. It looked a bit like a horse, but was a third the size, not even as big as a pony. Two loads, in thick canvas coverings, were packing on either side of the tiny mule. It's what had caused it to get stuck.

"Wondered why she wasn't coming in," Pattie mumbled. "She's usually curious as a baby raccoon. These little bronco mules can pack a load, though."

As if to live up to her description, Sancho, once through the opening and free at last, scampered over to the two horses tied by Syd's head. She pressed her nose up against theirs. They didn't seem to mind, even Syd's horse, who could be stand-offish. With the man and his two animals inside now, too, the enclosure seemed a lot smaller. All Syd could see above her were snuffling animal heads. It was getting downright crowded in here, not helped by the little mule being full of energy and banging around with whatever was packed on her sides. There had to be 150 to 200 pounds of gear. She lowered her dark muzzle to sniff Syd and to nudge at her face, as if eager for petting.

"Why Sancho?" Syd asked. "Why'd you name her that?"

"Didn't bother to look at first. Damn' thing thinks she's a puppy. Was owned by a family who made a pet of her, probably. Well, she's working for her meals, now."

Syd tried to push the furry gray head to one side. Mick still looked put out, but it was hard for Syd to think this man dangerous, with his near comic pack animal and his wind-bag blustery style. Then the man said something that changed the look on Mick's face.

"I've got quite a load of supplies. I'd be glad to share. I've even got coffee. Lots of it. I saw that look on your face, back there, when you got the cocoa while eyeing those bags of coffee beans."

Syd, who'd so enjoyed those cups of cocoa in the rare moments she wasn't sleeping through her bout with the fever, watched a flush of pink spread over Mick's face. She knew, then, that Mick had done without so she could enjoy the chocolate. He'd never said a thing about that when he'd given back the gold coin.

"You didn't answer me yet," Mick persisted. "Why'd you follow me out here?" There was less edge in Mick's voice this time, but his expression was still intent.

"You said you were looking for your uncle. Figured you weren't just wandering around blind out here, so you must be hitting the logical places. I have some business myself over Menardville way, and you probably need to look in at Fort McKavett. No sense two green young things like you being alone out here. For that matter, I don't fancy being alone. This is dangerous country. We're safer if we're together. Right?"

Mick's eyes narrowed at something Pattie had said. Maybe he just wasn't happy about being called a green sprout, so Bob Pattie turned to Syd with the question on his face, one for which he already seemed to know the answer.

Sancho pushed her nose against Syd and nuzzled her hard enough to stir her. Bracing herself, Syd used the little burro as support to pull herself up to a wobbly, but erect, position. Sancho didn't seem to mind, even began rubbing her neck against Syd's leg like she was a puppy.

"Well, the bronco mule's done what I haven't been able to do all day," Mick said, "which is get you out of your bedroll. This'll be good for you."

Bob Pattie glanced from Mick's to Syd's face while he went over to the mule and started digging through the packing on one side. After a minute he pulled out a cloth sack of coffee beans. Syd watched Mick try not to drool openly. Well, she'd missed coffee quite a bit herself. There was nearly a festive mood to the camp as Pattie and Mick hustled to get a pot of it going.

Syd hadn't thought for a while how very young Mick was. Beside the bigger and older man, it showed. Mick might be able to stand up to the toughest and bravest Indian, and even to a bear, but he wasn't a match for this fast-talking, partially bald man.

"What gave you the fever?" Pattie asked while cutting a hole in one corner of a bag and bringing out a small square coffee grinder.

"A bear scratched me."

"You're lucky someone was with you to nurse you through that."

"Yes. Yes, I am."

Pattie turned to Mick. "But you think that's hard to doctor, you ought to try patching a guy who's had his leg shot off just below the knee by a Fifty-Eight-caliber Minié ball, another one through his side, bits of dirty shirt going along through the wound with that one, him going into shock, quivering all over the place, and the doctor with no antiseptic."

"You were in the war?"

"No sensible man would be *in* it. But I heard plenty from the ones who were."

Syd and Mick exchanged looks. Mick was too young to have served, but, to Syd, he didn't seem the sort who would have side-stepped the chance to be in it if he had been the right age.

"You need a hand with anything?" Mick asked.

Bob was fishing a new-looking large blue coffee pot with black speckles out from one side of Sancho's load. "I'll need fresh water, and I suppose one of us ought to have a quick sign scout around if we're going to light a fire. I'll go, since it's too early for you to trust me alone here with the lady. Better tie Sancho to your horses, though, or the little scamp will follow me."

When he'd loaded three big empty canteens onto his saddle horn and rode back out through the cut in the bramble wall, Syd turned to Mick and asked: "Well, what do you think?"

Mick was leaning his rifle back beside his saddle. He straightened slowly and looked back at her. "I don't know what to think. I'm tired to the bone just having listened to him a short spell."

There are times out in the open, under a darkening sky, with the smell of freshly brewed coffee mingling with the dusty sage carried on the breeze when it's hard to imagine that a tribe of hostile Indians might be out beyond the barrier, or cattlemen feuding, or that there were bears, even mountain lions—Syd had only heard that shriek in the night once, and it had been enough to freeze her blood. Right now, though, in that special glow of coming out at the end of a sickness, she leaned back against her saddle and felt like this was the most peaceful place in the world.

Sometimes, it seemed, the constant, hanging sense that you could die at any moment from a dozen different causes never lets up. But now, for whatever reason, they were in a place that didn't appear to be on the crossroads of any of those threats. She didn't know how long it would last—they couldn't stay here forever—but the relief was so profound she wanted to lie back and enjoy this, savor it, for as long as she could. The peace was delicious.

Bam! A shot sounded just outside the enclosure. The little mule's head snapped up off her lap, and she scrambled upright in a flurry of clambering gray legs. Always curious, Sancho shot for what amounted to the doorway to see what was going on outside the barrier where the three horses had been tied up.

A few minutes later, Mick led the way in, with an antelope's haunch over his shoulder. Bob Pattie's bright shirt appeared next. He carried the Winchester .44 carbine, although it was clear to Syd that Pattie had let Mick do the shooting.

"That's a sweet gun, a real pleasure," Mick announced, "especially after lugging around the blunderbuss I've been using." He had a few sticks in his free hand, and he swung the haunch up onto a bush, off the ground, and started sharpening both ends of the stakes.

"That's another reason for going along this direction," Pattie began explaining. "There's a little place, just outside Fort McKavett, where you can swap for just about anything."

"It helps to have something worth swapping, doesn't it?" Mick asked.

"Oh, you might be surprised."

Syd didn't know what to make of the constant twinkle in Pattie's eyes. It seemed he was always in on a joke, one he hadn't gotten around to share yet with others.

"I take it there wasn't any Comanche sign near us," Syd said as she stood, no longer wobbling as she took a few steps. Sancho scampered over, and Syd leaned on the mule, who didn't seem to mind. She moved over to Mick who was piling up more wood beside the fire they had built to make coffee.

"Seems odd there's so little sign," Mick said. His eyes stayed fixed on his knife work.

Pattie tucked his Winchester away, and then noticed Syd's necklace for the first time, apparently. "Say, that's some bit of medicine there. You kill a bear?"

"Mick did."

"Come to think of it, I saw the bearskin in town. *Hmmm*. And he gave you that? In some tribes a necklace like that'd be as big an engagement sign as if he put his blanket over your shoulders and the two of you sat under it at the lodge." Before Syd could respond, Pattie turned to Mick. "You have some Cheyenne in your background? Or did you find that bow and the arrows on your saddle?"

Mick looked up at Pattie, squinted, but didn't respond. Once he had thin strips of meat hanging around the fire, he said to Syd: "Keep an eye on Sancho, so she doesn't knock over those sticks."

"That a polite way of getting me to tend to the cooking?" Syd asked.

Mick shrugged, but had to wrestle back the beginning of a grin. He went out the cut in their bramble wall.

While he was gone, Pattie asked Syd: "That the bullet that killed the bear? The one on your necklace?"

"Yeah. Mick may not care for that rifle he carries, but I might not be here if he didn't have it."

"He get it off a Comanche?"

She nodded, turning the meat, stick by stick. When she looked up, Pattie was over by Mick's saddle.

"I wouldn't mess with any of his gear," Syd said.

"Oh, I'm not. Got the powder horn and bag of bullets from the Comanche, too?"

Mick pushed his way through the opening with a rustle. He had all the meat he could carry.

Pattie moved out of the way while Mick rigged up a few racks to smoke and dry the meat by the fire.

"That's a lot of meat," Pattie commented, watching Mick salt down some of it and then hang it. It wouldn't be smoked all the way by morning, so salt was the only way of keeping the meat edible once they mounted and rode out. "You can talk of the cavalry out here," Pattie said, changing subjects, "now that the Union has its troops out this way again and these new bunches of Texas Rangers we're hearing about, but they're not what is going to drive the Indians out of here. It's the buffalo hunter who'll do that. You take away a man's food and where is he?"

"Leaving all that meat out there," Mick said, "and just taking the hides ought to be against the law. It's a waste. Someone, somewhere, is going hungry, and the buzzards are the only ones eating good."

"Just Indians going hungry," Pattie said.

"They're people, too," Mick said. "I don't think much of someone who'd starve another to death."

"Well, you sure don't waste, do you, boy?"

"I prefer not to be called boy," Mick said.

"Oh, you prefer Mister Dixon?"

Syd looked up, she couldn't recall Mick telling Bob his name.

"I just don't care for the term 'boy', if that's all right with you. Sir."

The conversation was becoming more interesting to Syd. She'd felt a bit of tension from Mick earlier, and now it was almost a part of the air. Pattie didn't seem to notice, but he'd not seen as much of Mick as she had.

"Mick is one of the most polite young men I've ever come across," Syd declared. She watched Pattie for a reaction and didn't have to wait long.

"Those are whorehouse manners, ma'am." Pattie looked at Mick and winked.

"What do you mean?" she said. "Mick, you don't have to take that."

Mick, though, was almost grinning. "Well, it's true enough," he said. "Aunt Ruth did run a cathouse in Philadelphia and was headed to Saint Louis to run one there. I don't have any problem admitting to that. How do you come to know so much about me?"

"I don't," Pattie replied. "But I know the tone and delivery. 'Leave the money on the dresser, sir.' No impoliteness meant to you, of course."

"I don't know how you can say that," Syd said.

"It won't bother Aunt Ruth where she's buried." Mick's eyes stayed fixed on the spot where a heart would be beneath Pattie's red shirt.

Pattie's head rocked back a half inch. "Your aunt's dead. I'm sorry . . . sorry to have pried at a tender spot. When?"

"Two years ago. Train wreck outside Saint Louis."

That sure seemed like a real enough bit of emotion from Pattie, Syd thought. But she said nothing.

All three were quiet through the meal, which, given the conditions, wasn't formal. Pattie cut at his meat with his belt knife. Mick had cut some of the strips into smaller pieces, so Syd could be a bit more dainty.

Hungry as Syd was, she watched Bob Pattie with newfound interest. After a while, in as casual a conversation tone as she could manage, she said: "You said those are mining clothes?"

"You see a lot like these in California, Colorado. . . ."

"Virginia City?" she said.

"Yeah. Damnedest place. They were throwing aside huge piles of funny-colored sludge they couldn't figure out for the longest time. All they knew was they were after gold, never knew they were sitting on one of the biggest silver lodes ever found."

"You stayed in the International Hotel?"

"Heavens, no. I had a little one-room place near Union Square, once. But mostly I lived out in the camps."

"Those togs aren't just to confuse other people, like the hat, then?" Mick said.

Pattie looked at Mick in what Syd would have taken as an unfriendly way, yet the next moment he smiled and shrugged it off. There was tension here, and she hadn't figured it all out yet. But it was fun being full, sitting around a fire with the sky growing dimmer, and guessing what would happen next.

"Tell me, young Mister Dixon," Pattie said. "What color is gold ore? Would you know it if you came by any?"

Mick glanced at Syd. It seemed a trick question to her, too.

Pattie dug in his pocket and came out with a small lump of rock that glittered as gold as anything Syd had ever seen. "What's that?" he asked.

After a hesitation, Mick said: "Gold?"

"No. It's iron pyrite. Fool's gold. Some nuggets and dust are actually gold-colored, but not like this. Like as not, any vein you found in the quartz of a hillside would be black with a dark green tinge to it. That's the color of dirt you look for along a stream, too, if you've a mind to do any panning."

"I guess I don't know that much about mining," Mick admitted.

"OK. Say you have a stack of buffalo hides you want to sell, so you stake them out and tie them down. You even have someone staying guard with the piles. Is that all you need to do?"

Mick didn't answer, which was an answer.

"No." Pattie winked in Syd's direction. "Before you stack them, you have to poison the hides or the hide bugs will ruin them before any wagon can haul them to market."

"Why are you doing this?" Syd asked.

"Doing what?"

"Trying to make Mick look bad."

Pattie held up a hand to her, but looked at Mick. "If you're going to make it out in these parts, and, by that I mean accumulating any wealth, you have to know things. It isn't enough just to be able to grab."

"I get along all right," Mick said as he sat in his only shirt with no money whatsoever in his pockets and a slow-working muzzleloader leaning against his saddle.

"Now, boy . . . Mister Dixon . . . you're riding along and you see a single cattleman by a downed calf. He stands up and waves at you. What do you do?"

"Keep riding, heading another direction."

"Why's that?" Pattie seemed a little taken aback this time by Mick's answer.

"Because, like as not, he's over there with a running iron."

"And what would he be doing with that?"

"Putting his own brand on cattle. The calf might be unbranded, or, more likely, the fellow is a hand on a spread near there and he did some hair branding during roundup."

"Hair branding?"

"If you're the one with the iron at branding time, you burn down just far enough so the calf looks branded, but isn't. The hide doesn't take the brand. The hair grows back, and later you put your own brand on the calf. Or, you change a brand into a new one with a running iron, which is why it's as good as hanging for a cowhand to be caught owning one."

That one goes to Mick, Syd thought.

"Why, I believe you've spent some time as a saddle

tramp," Pattie said. "How about this? Will a raccoon tree in a dead tree?"

"Never."

"You catch a carp in a stream, what do you have to do before you cook it?"

"Take out the mud vein, along the inside of the spine. But, if it's all the same with you, I'll eat a turkey that's been eating off a soapberry tree before I eat a carp."

"Well, you might get by after all, at that," Pattie announced. "You'd eat, but would you get rich?"

"You've been tossing everything at him," Syd said to Pattie. "Try this one, both of you. You're out here with nothing. What do you take for a headache?"

Pattie looked blank.

"Pennyroyal tea," Mick said.

"Swelling?"

"Witch hazel," Mick said. Pattie didn't try.

"Burns?"

"Boiled yellow-spined thistle."

"A cold?"

"Boneset tea."

"An insect repellent?"

"Goldenseal." Mick was grinning.

"Life's one god-damn' tea party for you, isn't it, boy?" Pattie wasn't hiding scorn from his face now.

"All I'm saying," Syd said, "is that Mick knows his bit of lore, and I'm convinced it saved my life more than his riding to town. Though the cocoa was worth that. But you should be careful. Wasn't it you said we all need each other out here, Mister Pattie?"

"Well, that's true enough." Still Pattie wasn't smiling when he went off to see to his horse. Sancho had been fed some of the grain carried in the bundles, and she was curled up, again, within petting distance of Syd.

It was getting dark in earnest by the time Pattie came back to the campfire.

"I'll take the first watch," Mick said. "All that coffee."

"Mick," Syd said, "you didn't sleep all last night. Why don't you let Mister Pattie have a turn?"

Pattie smiled. "I had plenty too much coffee, too. It's no problem for me. I'll be glad to pull my weight."

When he slipped through the cut with his Winchester, Syd whispered to Mick who was already stretched out on his blanket with his hat pulled down over his eyes. "Mick. Mick."

There was a pause, then a drowsy—"What?"—proving he wasn't as ready to be up longer as he'd indicated.

"This Pattie?"

"Yeah?"

"He sure seems to know a lot about you, don't he?"

"Uhn-huh."

"He seems eager to help you look for your uncle. Why's he being so nice to you, if you're a stranger to him?"

"I don't know."

"You think there's any chance he might *be* Bill Hinton?"

"That's what's been puzzling me most of the afternoon," Mick said.

Chapter Seven

First light was still an hour or so off when there was move-ment in the small camp. The coffee was going and Mick was packing the partially dried meat into one saddlebag. As soon as Bob Pattie had taken his saddle out through the cut, using Sancho to do the carrying, Syd rushed close to Mick and whispered: "If he's your uncle, why didn't he just say so?"

"I don't know," Mick replied.

"It would explain why he took to you in town the way you say he did, and why he rode all the way out here to team up with you."

"But, like you said," Mick said, "why didn't he just say who he was then? And what was that mining business you were asking him about . . . his being in Virginia City?"

"You said Bill Hinton fancied himself a miner, and this person who calls himself Bob Pattie, he's been there. I know that now."

Mick nodded, as if he understood, although Syd knew he didn't, and she couldn't tell him why she longed to cross paths with Bill Hinton.

"Still, we do need him. It'll make getting places a little easier," Mick admitted. But his expression wasn't eager.

"I guess we do." It would give her time to find out if the man were Bill Hinton, too.

"Are you fit to be in the saddle all day?" Mick asked Syd.

She nodded. "I'm not altogether well yet, but I'm better, and I owe you for that."

"You don't owe me for anything. You'd have done the same for me."

"Now, how do you know that, Mick? Maybe I wouldn't have, earlier, if I didn't know you as I do now."

When they were saddled, Pattie leaned close to Mick and said something low. Syd heard just enough to make out: ". . . sure enough looks like a Mex boy now. If the light's not too good. . . ."

Mick turned away, and Syd could see what looked like disgust on his face, or perhaps disappointment. If this man were really his uncle, it would be a blow.

It didn't seem to be in Mick to hate or even dislike anyone. He had treated her, a Mexican, with nothing but kindness. He even seemed more sympathetic with the Indians being driven out by white settlers than not, even though he had had to kill some in defense. For all the cleverness that this so-called Bob Pattie possessed, he didn't seem able to sense that clearly.

"*Cogito ergo sum!*" Pattie suddenly called out loudly, as if it were a battle cry. He raised one arm.

"*Pro quo esse videris!*" Syd shouted back almost as loudly.

"Catholic school, eh? It figures," Pattie said, waving his arm forward, then letting it drop and giving his horse a nudge with his spurs.

They were a sight as they headed southwest. Bob with his straw hat and red shirt. Mick with the muzzleloader stuck high out of his scabbard and the grim look of determination he usually wore when they moved about, and Syd in her slouch hat and with Sancho beside her. The little mule had become very attached to her, felt Syd needed the mule's help or something, and stayed close, even though the thick canvas-covered bundles on her sides sometimes banged into Syd's leg when their travels took them through narrow places.

Syd felt good, but knew she'd have to grit it out on this trek, as close as it was to the tail end of her fever. But she watched Bob Pattie and felt motivated. If Mick was out in these parts to find his courage, to see if he lived up to whatever warrior training he'd had living in an Indian village as a boy, she would have to draw on her endurance, and she knew it would stretch her. But that was all right, as long as that red shirt bobbed along ahead of her. Maybe someday she'd put a bullet through it.

All day they rode across valleys and up the sides of hills, through rocky passes, always staying clear of any sign or established trails. A strong breeze blew and tossed the tops of the long brown grass and the cedars and live oaks that still held some dusty green to them. The rest of the trees stood up like dark dried sticks, and the air was cooler, although hardly the October weather Syd had experienced back East.

Mick scouted each stream before they neared to cross. He said there was little except for some sign of squaws gathering water and a solitary hunter or two. But he didn't see the Comanche sign he had expected through here.

At first Syd worried that Sancho's not being on a lead rope might mean she'd scamper away. But she stayed close to Syd's side, except to shoot ahead if one of the horses shied at a snake in a prairie dog hole, or something equally interesting. Sancho seemed to have adopted the idea that she was the caretaker and protector of the bigger horses, even though she carried nearly as much weight as they did.

By noon the sun had warmed, and they were glad of the little shade Mick put them under so they could have a bite to eat. The meat he handed each of them was salty and a bit pink, but was edible with water from the canteen—they'd had no problem keeping the canteens filled. In late summer, half or more of the streams in this area were probably dried stone beds of washes and draws that you could ride on like roads. But the sporadic rains of fall had put enough water high in the hills to have them crossing water often enough to fill their canteens.

Mick and Pattie had gotten along fine while alert on the trail. There'd been no time or place for the jostling they'd done earlier. Now, with the wind rustling the leaves high in the live oak above them, Pattie asked Mick: "When you were getting all injunned up as a boy, were you in that tomahawk society of theirs or anything?"

"You're thinking of the Arapahoes. The Cheyennes have a dog soldier warrior society, but I was too young for that. My friend, Bear Cub, wanted in bad, but he probably had to wait a while, too." Mick seemed oblivious to Pattie's attempt to ruffle him, or he was a lot calmer under that kind of pressure than Syd would have been.

She asked Bob: "Pattie's a funny kind of name. How did you come by it?"

"Come by it? I was born with it. You think I'd make up a name like that?"

"I don't know. People do a lot of funny things that aren't clear to me."

"You'd better get used to that in life, young lady."

In the afternoon Mick stopped along the inside lip of a small stone cliff to stare ahead. He could see nothing of either Menardville or Fort McKavett. Pattie stood his horse on the near side, and Syd and Sancho pulled up closely on the other side. The horses seemed fine with the break, but Sancho broke away to nose at a couple of spots along the cliff.

"What caused that?" Syd pointed out the big gouges in the earth along the open stretch.

"Buffalo wallows," Mick said. They'd seen only small clumps of buffalo, sometimes eight or ten, at other times even fewer. His eyes were fixed in the distance.

Far away, almost as far as Syd could see, a spiral of black dots circled. "Buzzards?" she said.

"Yeah," Mick answered. "See the slight bend to the center of the wings."

"Sometimes they'll just ride the wind like that, if the wind's the way they want it," Pattie added.

"Those are fixed on something," Mick said. As he said it, one or two of the dots peeled off and lowered, didn't fly back up to join the others.

The sky had grown mottled, as if unclear about what to do next, more gray than blue. The puffy clouds that had been white were bruised and blacker.

In the dark shadows of thick trees and brush, most of the trees were bare. Syd and Pattie sat their horses while Mick went up and down the river, looking for a safe place to ford. He was also looking for sign, she could tell. Once or twice he got off his horse, looked more closely, then would remount. He went out of sight up ahead and, after a good stretch of time, rode back. He waved them forward.

Where they had crossed, there were plenty of signs that this side had been heavily traveled by Indians, but Mick said the sign was old. Across the stream they came up a bank steep enough to make them careful with the horses. At the top the ground leveled off into an open area that Syd knew had to be an abandoned Indian camp.

"There are the pits there, and scaffolds where they dried meat," Mick said, riding a bit ahead. "Over there you can see where they dressed hides. By that bent mesquite tree antelope hair is matted down by rain, but it's over a foot deep. There must be thirty-five, forty skulls in the pile behind it. They've been gone from here for over a month, but I can see everything as plainly as if they were camped here right now. The women coming in from gathering roots, the children playing."

Mick stopped his horse and stared at the blackened spots where there had been campfires. A few minutes later he still hadn't moved when Pattie said: "We've got places to get to, son. You're too young to worry about the past. You're part of the future."

Mick didn't say anything, although his glance at Syd carried a lot. He gave a cluck, nudged his horse, and they rode down and across the edge of the open dried plain.

The dim yellow light became brighter, and the noises became louder, less a blur, as slowly they made out a male whoop and an occasional female scream. After what felt like half a lifetime in the backwoods, it should have looked like a welcome metropolis to Syd, but it didn't. They pulled up outside the halo of light that came from Scabtown.

"Better put a lead on that mule before we go," said Pattie who had been particularly and unusually quiet for the last few miles. "Stupid little thing will walk right up to anything. She's stopped a streetcar before by standing in front of the mule pulling it, curious and not caring about some streetcar's schedule."

Syd bent and held one of Sancho's ears until she could loop a line over the little mule's head.

"This isn't any ordinary town," Pattie said, nodding toward the dim light and belaboring the obvious, Syd felt. "It's a barnacle on the side of Fort McKavett . . . you won't see the dark side of the place on the drill fields and bandstand by daylight. And you're liable to hear language that'd grow hair on a Mexican dog."

"What is it we need here?" Mick asked.

"Several things. You want to ask around about your uncle, don't you?"

"And you?" Syd asked, sensing what Mick had been after. "What do you need here?"

"I've got the unloading of the trade goods to do, and a bit of swapping about. Wonderful place for swapping about, this is. You'd better not go in with that bow and those arrows on your saddle, though, son."

Mick looked around for a place he could hide them, but saw nothing except the bare sticks of hackberry trees denuded of their leaves.

"Here, I can put them in one of Sancho's long packs," Pattie said, dismounting and taking the bow and arrows. He untied one side of the restless Sancho's packs, the longer side, and put in Mick's bow and arrows, tied them into place beside a bundle of long metal rods.

"You may have to act the part of a servant, Syd," Pattie said, looking up at her. "It would be hard to swallow that the likes of us are riding as equals with a Mex boy, you understand. No offense meant, of course."

"Of course not," Syd said. She looked over at Mick. "Just trade goods in there, right?"

"Yeah. Right," Pattie said, went back to his horse, and remounted.

Syd sat there wondering what a running iron looked like for sure, and why Bob Pattie seemed to have more than a dozen of them packed among the goods he planned to trade or sell.

They rode into a town made of rough sheets of tin and bad lumber. Very little paint had been wasted on decorating. But it was a busy town. Street lamps burned in a makeshift way here and there, mostly mounted by store owners to cast some light on their store front at night. People milled in doorways, and a few straggled across streets that were dirt now but would be mud in any kind of rain.

The looks on the faces of most the people worried Syd at first. These were survivors—some clinging to the small town that had formed with no plan except to exist off the scraps of one of the bigger military posts on the Indian frontier. A few of the men were dressed in garb made of homespun butternut, a cloth made by their wives on home looms. Most of the men wore old scraps of Army uniforms—sky blue pants, navy blue jackets that ordinarily would have the American eagle on its brass buttons. This late in the evening one or two wore a long overcoat, with short or long cape, depending on whether they'd been infantry or cavalry. As many or more of the men wore mixed-matched parts of clothing incorporating the Confederate gray. Which side they'd fought on didn't seem to matter as much at the moment, although the troops at the adjacent fort were Union troops. The faces in this town looked worn, some a bit scared, and then those who looked resigned to a fate that this was nothing like they'd expected when they'd headed West. A few would be writing letters back East, bragging how they were doing well—letters like Bill Hinton had been sending to Mick's Aunt Ruth, Syd figured. She wondered again if they'd find him out here, or if they already had.

She rode up beside Mick. Pattie was speaking in a low voice to him as they rode.

"We'll not stay in any of the inns. Dirty places most of

them, anyway . . . the ones that aren't running a more prof-
itable business altogether. The outlying campfire sites'll be
good enough for us. We're likely to learn more there. But
first, there's the matter of getting you a better gun."

Most of the stores, if you could go so far as to call them
that, seemed closed for the night and boarded tight. There
were plenty of saloons—loud and the open doors bright
spots on the dim street. A few men sat in the dirt at the corners of buildings or in entrances to alleys, their heads
thrown back or bowed forward in sleep—one with his
pockets turned out.

By a store front that looked as close to a general store as
anything they'd seen yet, Pattie turned into the alley that
ran alongside the building. Behind the high wooden false
front of the place, the building was a squat wooden struc-
ture of makeshift pieces. From what Syd could see, although the alley got dark, most of the other buildings in
town followed this model of promising more up front than
they delivered behind. Pattie seemed to know his way
around well enough, and led them to the store's back door.

Light came from behind faded calico fabric with moth
holes that had been hung as curtains behind two windows
with cracked panes of glass and covered with wooden bars.
Pattie dismounted and banged on the door.

"Go away."

Pattie banged again.

"If I have to turn ol' Trig loose on you, there'll be
nothing but bones to bury."

"Why don't you bark a bit, too? Trig's been dead three
years now, Ponce. Open the damn' door."

The bolt rattled, two locks clicked, and the door swung
open. A man with less hair than Pattie—only a couple of
very long strings of black locks on an otherwise dirty and

nearly pointed dome—stood holding an oil lamp and looking out at them. He wore a long-sleeved red woolen undershirt missing a couple of buttons and worn through at the elbows—this over trousers wrinkled enough to look like he slept in them.

"Who're these with you?"

"Well, you're no Diogenes with his lamp," Pattie joked. "Don't worry about these two. I'll speak for them. They're here to swap a bit, and I've brought what you wanted. We're just in from over Mason way." Pattie turned to Mick. "Bring that muzzleloader and its powder and balls, and we'll do better by you, here."

Syd tied up her horse and Sancho to one of the bars on a window. Pattie and Mick were doing the same with their reins at the other window.

Inside the door, the smell almost knocked Syd back a step. A pile of worn blankets against one wall served as a cot. The room had the odor of dried sweat and dust, a manly mixture of bedclothes never washed and a back door left open often enough to let some of nature's aroma inside, and not the better part of that. A piece of cheese, oily and dark on one side, stood in the center of the small table with its single chair. A handful of crackers and crumbs lay beside the cheese.

"Didn't mean to intrude while you're dining in style," Pattie said.

In the far corner of the small back room, there was a small circle of matted old cloth with a bowl beside it. That's where the late Trig had no doubt lived—still the same as it was, which made it even sadder than the rest of the room.

"Let's get on with it." The clerk, who Pattie had called Ponce, led the way through a curtain into the back of what proved to be the rear of the long store front. The lantern's glow lit an array of goods, although Syd couldn't see any soap amidst the mix; she had thought about buying Ponce a bar, maybe two. At the back of the store was a rack of the usual mix of used long guns behind a lower chipped-glass case containing small arms.

"None of these," Pattie said, giving a wave at the rack. "You know what I'm after."

"For that?" Ponce nodded toward Mick's rifle.

"Show him the powder horn, Mick. And the bag of bullets. Pay especial attention to the bullets, Ponce. The Comanches made them."

Syd was surprised at the change in Ponce. The man's eyes lit like a fox's with one paw in a hen house. He grabbed at the leather pouch Mick held, ignoring the powder horn and the rifle. He tugged open the thongs that held the bag shut and reached inside, drew out one of the bullets. He held it up to the light, where it glittered, not quite as bright as the flattened bullet in Syd's necklace, but brighter than lead. His head snapped toward Pattie. "Do you know where?"

The eagerness in his tone matched the sparkle in Pattie's eyes. "Let's talk of that in a bit. For now, will you trade?"

Ponce's nod was slow. He turned to Mick and took the rifle and powder horn.

"I believe a carbine'll do," Pattie said. "Right, Mick?"

"I don't have any money to make up any difference," Mick said.

"Don't you worry about that just now."

Ponce had gone to the front of the store, lifted the top off a display of cheaper goods, and from below he pulled out a rifle. He put everything back the way it had been and carried the rifle back to them.

"This is the Eighteen Seventy-Three model Forty-Four

Winchester carbine. I usually get forty dollars for one, fifty for the rifle. The Sharps carbine is only seventeen fifty, if you want to make a little back." He let the last bit hang as a question.

Pattie shook his head, nodded toward Mick. Ponce held out the carbine to him.

"Better round him up a couple of boxes of shells, too," Pattie said.

Ponce winced.

"Remember our deal," Pattie said.

Mick was running a hand up and down the sides of the gun. He worked the lever, looked in the chamber, ran his hand along the blued-octagonal barrel and the dark wood of the stock. His eyes were wide enough to be a kid's at Christmas.

Ponce put two boxes of ammo on the counter by Mick, who looked up and said: "We're square? Is that right?"

It didn't make sense, but Syd was thinking about the bullets, the Indian ones. She could see Comanche warriors visiting a spot where they could dig lead, only it wasn't all lead where they were digging. They had the same bullet-making kits, and it wouldn't matter to them if they were melting down and firing bullets of lead, or silver.

She watched the two men, Ponce and Pattie, send signals to each other right around Mick. Something was going on here, and poor Mick was too swept up in his new carbine to see what it was.

Ponce took Mick's old rifle, the muzzleloader, and set it in a corner, not putting it on the rack with the other guns. He tossed the powder horn aside, too, but he clung to the bag of bullets.

"What happens to that?" Mick said, pointing a thumb toward the gun he'd been carrying.

"Oh, I wouldn't worry about that," Ponce said.

"But no one's likely to buy it," Mick said, still a bit surprised, even puzzled, to have come out with a new gun.

"No white man," Pattie whispered to Ponce, low, but not so low Syd didn't catch it.

Outside, Mick slipped his new rifle into his scabbard while Ponce and Pattie carried in part of the load Sancho had been carrying. When Pattie finally came out and swung himself up into his saddle, he said: "Now what sounds good?"

"A bath, and a room," Syd said.

"Better hold onto that thought. . . ." Pattie stopped himself before he said "little lady".

So far, with her hat down and riding along at a slightly deferential space behind the other two, no one had paid her any attention. Part of that could be that everyone they'd met so far in town had been caught up in their own business. It was that kind of place, and that was probably why Pattie had brought them here. You could lose yourself in a smelly soup of people like this. Even though she'd spent far too many days without bathing, Syd felt her skin creep more by being near this sort of people than anything she'd encountered out in the wilds.

Shrieks came from an open window, and it was hard to tell if it was pain or joy. As they rode down the street, men, alone or in groups, some passing a bottle, would turn to hoot at a female, who as often as not would yell back in as coarse a way as Syd had ever heard.

"How about it, Mick?" Pattie asked. "You think you'd like something wet for your frog?"

"What?" Mick said.

"Want to get a little mud for the ol' turtle?"

"I think we'd better find some place we can camp for the night."

"It's what I had in mind, boy. But if you want something tamer, that's OK. I need to check up on what news I can find."

Mick glanced at Syd, and his face was far more embarrassed than it had been that time he had stood naked and dripping in front of her as he'd stepped out of the stream. Their eyes might have stayed locked a bit more, but a gunshot drew their heads forward. A man came reeling out of one of the saloon doors. Before they could speculate on whether he'd been shot, he spun and wildly fired another shot into the air. Then he holstered his gun and staggered off down an alley.

"Just letting off a bit of steam," Pattie explained. "I hear Johnny Ringo was fined for discharging a firearm in the downtown square of the little town of Burnet. Can you imagine that happening here? Not the shooting, but the being fined for it."

Syd could imagine a lot happening in this place. She was beginning to realize she'd felt far safer out in the wilds than here.

At the edge of Scabtown, Pattie moved into the lead and veered off into the dark. But it wasn't dark long before they came to a cluster of campfires. He knew his way well here, too, and wove close enough to be recognized by men who called out to him. This puzzled Syd who had nearly come to the conclusion that this *was* Bill Hinton. Yet these men called him by the name he'd given.

On the outer circle of the camps, Pattie found an abandoned site. There was even a small stack of firewood left. "We'll camp here," he said.

Already one or two of the men who'd seen Pattie ride past began to come this way and signal to him furtively while Mick got the fire going. Pattie had set his bundles off to one side, almost in the dark. Syd watched as he would go over, do a little business, and then return.

Any thoughts Syd had entertained of sitting down to a red-and-white checked cloth in a tiny home-style restaurant and having a real meal were gone. They'd flittered away like one of the bats that swooped in a sharp flutter of wings down through the edge of the light cast by their fire. But her hopes picked up when Pattie brought over a small slab of bacon, with just a bit of green on the edges that Mick had to shave off. Later, Pattie managed to trade for a jar of molasses.

With the smell of bacon going over the fire, and absolutely no threat of Indians for the moment, it was a delightful time—even though no bath, hotel, or restaurant was involved. A crusty old fellow with hands almost as black as the evening contributed a double handful of sourdough rolls, and with that they were in heaven. She kept telling herself that the cooking had probably taken care of any incidental dirt that had worked into the dough as she tore open another roll and poured molasses into the opening.

When you haven't eaten certain things in a long time, the taste was intoxicating. It was hard to tell how Mick felt about it, since he'd gone quite a while in the wilds with almost nothing. She had Pattie figured for someone who would trade for something to drink. His pile of goods seemed to be diminishing. But he appeared not be a drinker. He had traded off most of his tobacco, too, keeping none for himself. No one is immune to all vices. She began to wonder which one was his.

Mick's blanket and saddle were not far from hers, and he leaned back against his saddle, too full to take another bite. Syd forced down the last of her roll, then got up and went over to let Sancho lick her fingers clean. When she came back, she plopped onto her blanket and reached for her cup, took a sip of her coffee. It had cooled, but she felt too slow and stuffed to reach for the pot to add some to it. She leaned back on her elbows and looked up at the stars where Mick was staring. The flicker of warm fire was around them, and the evening was getting cooler, as if a weather change was coming.

Pattie was wrangling with some fellow in worn buckskin shirt and pants. Syd turned to Mick: "Did you know he had a whole bundle of running irons in that bit of trade goods he's dealing in?"

Mick didn't seem surprised. "He's a careful man, and one who knows a dollar as well as he would his own kin. I've been wondering why we got the kind of deal we did on that Winchester we traded for."

"Have you given thought to the notion that the lead bullets you got from that Indian might not be lead? What if they were silver?"

"Oh, I reckoned for that part. I've seen Pattie eyeing that silver on your necklace often enough. At least that was what I hope he was eyeing."

Syd rolled toward him, and, if he'd been close enough she'd have popped him one on the arm. But she was till too content and full to move.

"But even with that in mind," Mick said, "we still got too good of a deal for my new gun, though I'm glad enough to have it."

"I'd have bought you one, if it came to that," she said. "I owe you at least that for getting me through everything so far."

"I wouldn't let Pattie know anything about that money belt, if I were you."

"What? Oh, I won't."

When Pattie had tracked Mick back then, had he had time to put his nose inside the cave, or had he been in such a lather to catch up with Mick that he had skipped it and just followed hard on the trail? Probably the latter. But none of it made Mick feel better.

There was silence for a while, except for the rumble of talk from other camps and the faraway scream or whoop coming from Scabtown.

Mick took his new rifle out of its scabbard on the saddle, jacked out all the shells in the tube, worked the lever a couple times, then reloaded the gun, rubbed it a couple of reassuring times, making sure it was really there. Then he slid it back into its place, and he scooted back closer to the fire.

"Do you think he might really be your uncle, Bill Hinton?" Syd asked.

"These people don't seem to think so. They all call him Pattie."

"What will you do? I mean . . . if it is him. If you've found the one you were after. Does that end whatever's driving you?"

"I don't know," Mick said. "It just felt good to want something, and for the first time in my life to have half a notion of what it was. I don't know what to do if that's over."

"Might be a bit of a let-down if this Pattie's the one, though," Syd said. "What do you think?"

Before Mick could answer, Syd saw Pattie coming back toward them, and this time three strangers were moving along behind him. He had been snatching food each time he had come back to sit beside the fire. This time he didn't look hungry. Syd sat up, let her hat slip low until most of her face was in shadow, looking, she hoped, just like the boy she sought to be in this crowd.

"Got someone here says he knows you, Mick!" Pattie called out.

Mick sat up, not an easy job as full as he was. "Why, Hodges Laney," he said as soon as he recognized the man, "how have you been keeping?" He jumped to his feet, a whole lot more nimbly than Syd thought she could accomplish just then.

The man stepped around Pattie to shake Mick's hand. He was a tall man in a worn, dirty, and much mended buckskin shirt. His face was long, lean, and lightly stubbled—it was as weathered a face as the rocky and cactus-prickled terrain through which they'd passed. He was a stark contrast, Syd thought, to Mick and his round boyish face, and, although Mick had hopped up heartily enough to extend a hand, he seemed a boy among men. Yet, between them, there was the quick, genuine warmth of men who'd shared campfires, or sat a herd in the rain, and knew other hardships just to earn a plate of beans and a wage that would never make any of them rich.

Laney towered over Mick, and the man behind him was even taller, with a thick beard hanging down to the middle of his chest and long hair that didn't look like it had ever seen a comb. He wore all buckskins, a newer outfit with fringes, but stained with dark brown spots and smears in many places. The smaller third man seemed to drift along with the others. With the smashed-down silk hat he wore— a token of some former glory or belonging once to someone else—he should have stood out. But he was hard to notice at all. He seemed to cultivate that, staying to the shadow side of the big men, his eyes darting, catching everything. His face was narrow, the nose a bit like that of a predator bird, although shorter. A mark that could be dirt, a powder burn, or a dim birthmark spread from the bridge of his nose across his left cheek. He wore dark pants and the vest of a gambler's outfit—a wide pin stripe showing even in the dim light. The shirt had been white once, and new, but was neither now. His pistol was one of the new Colts, with a smooth dark grip, and it was worn much lower on his hip than Pattie wore his.

"This is Mythological Jim," Hodges introduced the near giant to Mick. The man just nodded, leaning on a big Sharps Fifty he carried. It was the long one, with telescopic sight. Both hands were high on the barrel, and his glance seemed to be on the constant hunt for something.

"And this is Weasel." He nodded toward the small man who, closer to Mick's size, was staring with unblinking eyes off into a clump of leafless trees to their left.

The group came over to the fire, and Pattie offered up what hadn't been already eaten. True to the ways of these camps, the three newcomers ate all that was handed to them as if they'd just come in off the trail themselves. The men glanced at Syd, but, as soon as they caught the tint of her and guessed it wasn't a tan, they said nothing.

"That sure all seems like a long time ago," Mick said after the men had finished off everything and traded a couple of belches. "You decide to leave McLaren?"

"Had to," Laney answered. "Place burned down, with McLaren in it."

"That man sure had some hard luck," Mick said.

Laney held back some sort of look and glanced at the stone face of Weasel, then at the man in buckskin, but it was hard to see any expression on his face behind all the beard fur. In the reflection of the campfire his eyes twinkled and glittered brightly, like those of a snake peering from a crevice. "You haven't said the half of it," he finally agreed, and he pulled a short twist of tobacco out of one pocket—the kind that Syd had heard was cheaper than cut plug—and bit off an inch. He held it out to the others, and only the man in buckskins reached for it and bit off a length.

"Which way did you come in?" Laney asked Pattie.

"Across from Mason, the back way."

Laney didn't ask why Pattie hadn't used any roads, instead said: "See much sign?"

"No, not really." He looked to Mick.

Mick shook his head.

"Tell them why, Mytho," Laney urged.

Mythological Jim was just getting his chew going well, but he tucked it off into his left cheek, bent, and spit into the dark. When he turned back, he wiped at the spot on his thick beard where the corner of his mouth must have been, and he said: "Up quite a ways ride from here I saw a big mess of 'em. Cheyenne, Comanche, and Kiowa all riding together."

His voice was a low rumble, each word coming out as if after a reluctant struggle—clearly a man not used to speaking much, or not caring to. Without realizing he'd done it, perhaps, he'd made the wavy hand sign for a snake, the symbol of the Comanches.

"That can't be right," Mick said. He looked from Jim back to Laney. "Cheyennes don't ride with Comanches."

"They do if it's Quanah and Isa-tai at the head of them," Laney pronounced. "There's gonna be big trouble up that way." Then he looked off to the north, where there was only black now.

"Raw hunger's what's done it," Mick said. "That's the only thing would make them ride together."

"Hell, starve the whole lot of 'em for all I care," Mytho

said, "though it's got 'em stirred up enough."

"That why you're not up there with the other buffalo runners?" Pattie asked Mytho.

"I ain't up there 'cause there's hardly enough buffs to make do. Used to be you could shoot a hundred and twenty, even a hundred and fifty from a stand once you took down the leader. Now you spend all your time movin' 'round, settin' up all over again. But all them Injuns heading that way don't add to the bargain, neither."

"Explains why there are fewer Indians down this way, maybe," Pattie said. "Better they have troubles up there than we have them down here." He reached with a long stick to poke at the fire, knocking a few of the embers closer together.

Weasel, who had said not a word so far, stood abruptly and stalked off into the dark.

Pattie glanced at Laney, who shrugged and said: "Off to shake hands with the devil, I reckon."

"Or wring the chicken's neck for Sunday dinner," Pattie said.

Laney leaned forward, working at the chew in his mouth, thinking in much the same way it seemed to Syd. The night seemed suddenly darker. She looked up, could see no stars or the sliver of moon that had been there on and off earlier.

"Maybe you could have better luck now yourself," Laney said to Pattie. "Hard to say how long things'll stay spread out like this."

"Heard you were by to see Ponce already," Mytho said. "Like I said, the days of runnin' buffs are pretty well over. Might could be you should cut us in." He was looking from the corner of his eye at Syd as each word rumbled out, not at her face, but at the necklace she wore, at the bright shining bead hanging lowest at the heart of it.

"Maybe we should step back over by the goods . . . ," Pattie suggested, and stood, trying to get the two men to move away from the fire for a quieter talk.

A voice came through the dark toward them. "You the fella with the trade goods jus' brought in?" There was no sound to the man's foot falls.

"I'm done for tonight. See me tomorrow." Pattie waved a hand to go away.

The man stepped into the light cast by the fire, and Syd nearly gasped out loud. In size he was somewhere between Mick and the tallest of the men who had just arrived. He wore a black hat, matching vest over a dark blue shirt with pearl buttons, and his gun was worn low, very low. He smiled, and his teeth shown bright white against the mahogany of his skin.

"You don't know about the buffalo soldiers, do you?" Laney said to Mick, who had to turn his head to see the latest arrival.

"No." Mick was still staring, in spite of what looked like an effort not to.

"Ninth and Tenth Cavalry are both all made up of darkies . . . like this mustered out one . . . troops with all white officers. Why, this county's more'n half darkies right now. The ones done with duty haven't all found their way home yet. But they will, given time, and encouragement." Laney's eyes were narrow. One hand moved up slowly to the handle of his big knife.

"You want to do any bid'ness, o' not?" the man said to Pattie. "Only wanted to buy that map o' yours. You know which one. I got the price you axed." His head tilted an inch to one side now, and he grinned, the fingers of his right hand open.

125

"Said he wasn't open," Mytho growled.

"Wasn't talkin' to you, stinkweed."

Mytho's mouth may have opened a bit. All Syd could make out was the gap increasing in the fur, and the glitter in the eye picking up.

Laney looked the man up and down, as if sizing him for a box. "To talk like that, you must be pretty. . . ."

The gun was in the man's hand, the hammer back, and it was leveled at Laney's throat.

". . . fast," Laney finished, and let his mouth snap shut. His hand eased away from the knife handle.

"Name's Harlan," the man said, his eyes sweeping all of them. "All I was axing fo' was a touch o' kindness. Now I'm takin' it." He turned to Pattie. "You . . . les go see what you have. I'll pay. Don' you worry that."

"Yes. . . ." Pattie bit off the "sir" he'd nearly tagged on. He stood up slowly, moved around the others, and went in the direction where the rest of his goods lay. Then Pattie stopped. "Behind you, nig. Seems someone has the drop on you."

"About time you shot you a buff, Weasel," Mytho said.

Syd saw Weasel ease into the light, his pistol out and pointed at Harlan's back.

"All I wanted was do a bit o' bid'ness," Harlan said, but didn't lower his gun.

"You'd better sing small and drop the pistol, Mister Harlan." Pattie's voice had as much a snarl to it as Syd had heard. *The true colors emerge,* she thought.

"I'd hang onto it, Harlan." Mick's voice came from behind Weasel. It was punctuated by the sound of the lever working on his Winchester.

Syd hadn't seen or heard him slip away from beside the fire. But there he was, coming into the light behind Weasel, giving the man a nudge until Weasel slowly put his gun back into its holster.

"Better take a walk, Harlan," Mick said, his voice as steady as the rifle. "Seems like Mister Pattie's store is closed, like he said."

"I heard that," Harlan said. "All I wanted was a bit o' bid'ness." He backed slowly away, then he was gone.

Weasel walked on toward the fire, gave Mytho a look that had a tugged-up corner to one side of his lips. It might have been a smile, but probably wasn't. After a minute, Mick came closer, too. But he held his rifle and didn't sit.

"Uppity," Laney said, and spat into the fire. "That's what they are."

"But can fight the Injuns like dammit," Mytho said, staring off in the dark to where Harlan had vanished. His hand had moved to the stock of his long rifle, but it slid off now, and he turned to look back into the fire.

Pattie glared at Mick as he lowered himself back down near the fire.

"And you, young Mick," Laney began, "I thought you a mite green, but not a fool. Come in here riding with a Mex, and now you take up sides with the like of that." He spat again.

"Get your things, Syd," Mick said, not looking at her. "We're pulling camp."

Full as she was, she managed to scramble to her feet. There was no nonsense in his voice. She lifted her saddle and carried it over to the horses, came back in a minute for the blanket. She was going to miss little Sancho.

Mick stood looking at the three men. "Get my stuff, too, if you don't mind."

"You can't go off like that, boy. I've an investment in you," Pattie said.

"I thought you were thinking like that. But, next time, ask first."

Syd lifted Mick's saddle and looked around at the faces beside the fire. No, they sure hadn't made any friends here.

Chapter Eight

Mick woke to the rustle of something stirring in the brush near him. He twisted on his blanket, saw a ground squirrel with its black head and shoulders—the rest of the variegated body and long bushy tail were pale—clamber in darting spurts across dead leaves and onto the rock cliff beside which they'd camped. Everything around him was otherwise still, too still, in the dim grays of early morning light. The high tops of the trees, whether bare sticks or dusty green live oak, were just beginning to take on any real color. No wind was moving the few leaves.

Too tired last night to make a fire after riding as long and hard as they could to remove themselves from the Scabtown area, they'd staked the horses and dropped onto their blankets. He looked over to Syd's blanket now, expecting to catch a glimpse of her sleeping. But she was gone. Her bedroll was empty.

He bent at the waist and lifted up, looking around. The horses were still there. He jumped to his feet, letting the blanket slide to the ground, and started studying the ground by her blanket. There were just her prints—no sign of moccasins or anything that might have snatched her away. Maybe it was just a call of nature. He spread his blanket, sat on it. But, after a few more minutes, he pulled on his boots and started along her trail.

Her steps led past the horses and down the sloping hill to weave past a spur of a short cliff down toward the river they'd paralleled in the long night ride. Mick hadn't seen any Indian sign, but it had been dark. They were still close enough to the fort, he'd figured, for there to be frequent bluecoat patrols through this area, letting him discount the idea of the area being thick with Comanches.

He heard her before he saw her—the splashing. Even this late in the year the berry brambles were pushing out new purple limbs among their fading, older, green ones. Mick eased around a big patch of the stickery plants, then past a small stand of cottonwood, keeping his head down, until he could peek over the tips of the yucca spikes of a tall plant that had long ago dropped its flowers and gone to seed.

Syd had her back to him in the river up to just below her shoulders. Her soft brown skin was wet, her hair matted and hanging flat in a black wave even though cut short so she could pass as a young man. He swallowed hard, but otherwise moved no more than a statue.

Mick had made no sound, but Syd suddenly spun and ducked lower in the water, staring at him, with just her head out, the big dark eyes alarmed. "Mick."

"I was . . . I was just checking on you."

"Well, you've checked. Get on back to the camp and let me finish my bath. You don't know how much I've craved being clean."

The way her hair hung down, dark and pressed against her head framed that smooth, brown face he'd found himself thinking about more than a little. He tried to speak, but there was nothing he could think of to say. He began tugging off each boot.

"Now, Mick."

He undid his trousers and dropped those.

"Mick."

"I want to be clean, too," he said. Well, there he'd said something. But it didn't seem to calm her.

She was looking to the shore where her clothes were piled. If she got out, he'd see her. If she didn't . . . well, he was coming in.

The water was cool as he waded in, bracingly cool. He dived under the water, rubbing his head to clean his hair and face as he went, then opened his eyes and bobbed to the surface, facing her. She was trying to back away.

In her splashing, more than her shoulders showed above the water. She did not have a big chest, but it was pert and proud. She crossed her arms over the hardened dark dots on breasts that were bigger than Mick could have guessed. His thoughts drifted for a second to wondering how she'd bound herself up to look like a boy in the saddle.

"Mick, I mean it. Keep away." She moved back, but stepped on a sharp rock, a crawfish, something that propelled her soft smooth self against him, until her body was flush against his. She stumbled back in the water, her eyes near tears. "Please."

"What?"

"It's . . . it's just that. I have bad memories. Bill Hinton."

Even in the cool water she had felt so soft and warm in that brief touch, Mick had been tempted to press closer. But Hinton's name stopped him.

"Uncle Bill? My Uncle Bill? What about him?"

"Don't you understand? He's the one who did things to me, awful things. My mother died defending me."

"That's why . . . ?" Mick began, but Syd cut him off.

"That's why I swore I'd kill him, if I ever found him."

"That's why you rode with me," Mick said, "knowing I was looking for him, too?"

"Well, yes."

For a few seconds Mick had felt his blood pumping in a warm rush, his emotion and passion as stirred as it had ever been. Now he felt how cool the water was. Above them a mockingbird was making chatter in the trees. The babble of the water slipping over rocks where the river narrowed upstream and emptied into this pool along the edge of the shore seemed louder. He felt a little mad, and a little used. That stirred and conflicted with the other emotions she'd lit in him, the ones that made him want to touch her again, feel her pressed against him. He said: "And you thought Bob Pattie might *be* my Uncle Bill. Were you thinking of killing him?"

"I . . . yes. I thought about that."

"If he'd have said . . . 'Yes, I'm Bill Hinton' . . . you'd have shot him?"

"I . . . don't know if I have it in me to do it. But I'd want to, if it was him."

"He said he wasn't Hinton. All the other men call him Pattie."

"But he's after the lost San Saba Mine. He's been in Virginia City. He knows about you . . . about your Aunt Ruth. It's an easy enough thing out here to change a name and grab a new identity. Come on, Mick."

"You'd have really killed him?"

"I don't know. It's like I said. When it comes down to it, I don't know if I have that in me. I stared at Pattie's back plenty of times and wondered if I could pull the trigger, but I still don't know."

Looking at that warm face only a foot or two away, Mick couldn't tell now if it was water dripping from her hair or the beginning of tears. He held open his arms.

This time she moved closer, let his arms close over her shoulders, and the side of her face press against his neck. He held her, gently, reassuring her, making no other move than just being close. He knew clearly then, for the first time, the level of his care for her, that it went far beyond anything about just two healthy young people of mating age. He would do anything for her, take care of her, even make sacrifices for her. That felt new to him, and fresh, and strong. All that he'd craved, the wanting to be connected, to belong, it was already here. Why hadn't he seen or sensed this before?

Mick reckoned he could have stood there, up to his chest in water, like that for the rest of his life, holding her that way. But the water was cool and running by with a vigor that swept an occasional leaf past them. They both began to shiver, although pressed warmly close otherwise.

"It was a silly thing to do," he said, knowing it wasn't a wise thing to say. He realized that as soon as he'd said it.

"What was?" Syd asked.

"Coming out into this mess on your own, all to hunt for a man and kill him?"

"Silly?"

"Dangerous . . . I should have said. Unnecessarily so."

"Oh, so it's OK for you to come out here and wander around with nothing but a slingshot. . . ."

"Bow," Mick corrected.

". . . while I'm too delicate. Is that it?"

Mick wanted to say he'd only said what he had because he cared. But he didn't know if he dared say that, either.

She pushed away from his chest with the flats of both hands, her face pinched in anger. She whirled and started to move out of the water. She'd have stomped if the water hadn't slowed her so.

"Wait." Mick started after her. "Let's not argue."

They both stopped at a rustling sound coming from the brush ahead of them. A gray head came bursting through the brushes, and whatever mood Syd was in shifted abruptly as she said: "Sancho! I've missed you, you little rascal."

Mick froze where he was, half out of the water, aware that his gun was with his saddle back at the camp. "Syd," he whispered. There was warning in his whisper, but she missed it.

She rushed toward the furry little bronco mule who was just as eager to clamber down the slope to her. As she stepped out of the water, with drops glistening on that smooth tan-looking skin, Mick was thinking: *Well, this was sure a short lifetime of paradise.*

His thoughts were confirmed and punctuated by the sound of a lever working. Above them, on the sloping bank, stood Hodges Laney, with what looked like Mick's gun pointing at them.

A rustle in the bushes to the right of him preceded Bob Pattie's red shirt and straw hat emerging from the woods. He grinned at them. "Well, now. If this isn't a cheerful sight."

Syd was trying to cover herself with her hands, and wasn't completely successful beneath Laney's slow, grinning leer. Mick waded up out of the water, trying to get between Syd and Laney.

"Well, well, boy," Pattie chuckled. "Is this the unicorn pursuing the young damsel from the waves?"

Mick almost lowered his hands to cover himself. Then thought: *To hell with it.*

Sancho nuzzled at Syd's side, but she didn't reach out to pet the mule, even though it wasn't the mule's fault she'd been used to help track the way to them for the others.

Pattie gathered up their clothes and Laney marched them, naked, back to their camp, where Mythological Jim and Weasel were digging through their things. Mytho paused to stare at the dripping, nude girl.

A bare mesquite tree stood gaunt and black beside their camp. Thorns stuck out long and sharp from its upper branches. "Untie the horses from that," Pattie said to Laney. "You know what to do."

Weasel led the horses away, looping a line around Sancho's neck and leading the mule away, too. The animal had done harm, without knowing it. Laney pulled Mick back against the rough bark and began to tie his hands together behind it. Syd screamed, and started to rush toward them. But, at a nod from Pattie, Mytho grabbed Syd and held her by the upper arms, pulling her tightly against him. She was dwarfed by the big man, and Mick saw the others leering at her struggling wet nakedness now.

His arms were yanked up high as Laney threw one end of Mick's own riata over a limb and pulled tight. He looped the other end around Mick's waist and pulled that tight, too, knotted it on the other side of the trunk until Mick was pressed tightly against the tree. His toes barely touched the ground.

"Why are you doing this, Hodges?" Mick said.

Laney didn't speak, just grunted with the effort of tying a tight knot.

"Because he's about the worst man around a deck of pasteboards this side of the Mississippi," Pattie said. "I just wish I'd been sitting in on some of those games while he went through McLaren's money."

Talk like this confirmed Mick's notion of what lay ahead. There wasn't any reason for Pattie to hide anything at this point. With Mick bound tightly, and Syd squirming in the big buffalo runner's grip, Pattie stepped forward until his face was less than a foot from Mick's. There was no reason to shout, or even talk loudly. No sense in stirring up any Indians, if there were some in the area.

"Are you Bill Hinton?" Mick said.

"You're in no position to be asking that." But there was a flicker of a smile. It didn't confirm anything, just that Pattie loved the power of his current position.

"Running into you in Mason was just chance?" Mick said.

Pattie's smile slipped to a near sneer. "Chance isn't a part of anything. Anyone worth salt makes their own fate."

"Let him go!" Syd shouted.

That was the last Mick heard from her, although he could hear her struggle with Mytho as he tied something across Syd's mouth. Mick couldn't see around Pattie at the moment, and not having to watch Syd's nude body squirm was a blessing of sorts.

As if knowing that, Pattie stepped to one side, let Mick have a look of the raw terror in Syd's eyes as she thrashed against the stained buckskin of Mytho's chest. Pattie's grin let Mick imagine all kinds of awful things happening to Syd next.

"I think you know what I want to know about, boy," Pattie stated. "The sooner you tell me, the sooner all this will be over, for both of you."

Mick could think of no way to save Syd from her worst fears. He hadn't begun to think about himself. He struggled against the riata that bound him. It didn't give at all.

"The mine, boy," Pattie said. "Fix your thoughts on that. Where is it?"

"I don't know about any mine," Mick answered.

"The lost San Saba Mine. You know it. You were

tromping around all over the area where it should be. I know. I've tromped that part of this stickery, stinking, sun-baked state enough myself."

"I still don't know."

Pattie stepped back, went over to the pile of their clothes, and picked up Syd's money belt, which he tossed over his shoulder. In his other hand he held the necklace. He pulled the knife at his belt, cut the leather thong just beside the bullet at the center of the necklace, the rest he knotted back together, and dropped onto Mick's head so the bear teeth hung down in a row around his forehead, like some tired crown.

"Where did you kill the Indian, then, the one you got the bag of silver bullets from?" Pattie said. He held the bullet up, and shoved it almost to Mick's nose. "Did you ever realize these bullets were silver you were using to shoot game with?"

"Yeah," Mick said. He was careful not to let his eyes go to Syd. He knew he was destined to die here, but all he could hope for was to buy some time for Syd, the slightest sliver, so she could survive, maybe escape.

"Where?" Pattie insisted.

Mick shook his head.

"Do you know?" Pattie glanced over at Syd.

Her eyes were wide, but she couldn't have talked if she'd wanted to with the gag in place.

Pattie turned to Mytho, whose grin now was as sinister as anything Mick had seen so far from anyone in this bunch. Mytho was a kid being turned loose in a candy store. He held out Syd, and Laney stepped over to hold her, copping a quick feel as he did.

"Leave her alone," Pattie ordered, "for now. We may need her."

Mythological Jim loomed bigger as he stepped toward Mick. The man was a giant, and a pretty foul-smelling one. From one of his back pockets he pulled a soiled and worn pair of gloves, the same kind of tough gloves cowpunchers buy, if they can afford them, knowing the kind of work they'll be doing all day with ropes and irons. He tugged them on, and the grin behind all the fur of his face stretched wider.

"You'll understand why I didn't ask Weasel to handle this," Pattie said. "He's not capable of going easy, the way Mytho can. You'd be dead by now if it was Weasel's turn. Just so you understand all I want's a bit of information. Weasel had so many notches on his gun we had to buy him new grips, didn't we?"

Mick followed Pattie's eyes to Weasel, who stood off to a side, watching, his arms folded, his already squinty eyes tightened down to narrow slits.

"From shooting people in the back?" Mick said. The expression on his face didn't change.

But the one on Mytho's face did, and he said: "You hear that, Wease?"

As Mytho turned back to Mick, his shoulder lowered and a fist pounded hard into Mick's abdomen. He could hear what sounded like a couple of snaps as the pain made him want to double over even though the ropes held him in place. His legs had snapped up, and he drooped against the tree trunk, trying to breathe.

"A mite easier there, Mytho. Make it last," was all Pattie said. He walked away, going over to stand in front of Syd who was tugging hard in Laney's grip and managing only a muffled scream through the gag.

The big buffalo runner switched to slaps, rocking Mick's face back and forth, occasionally throwing a punch that tried to go all the way through to the tree. Mick never uttered a sound—not a scream, not a moan. That somehow egged the giant on.

The beating seemed to last for hours. Mick lost track of what part of him hurt the worst. His insides felt like beaten jelly. Cracked ribs throbbed, and his neck felt ready to twist off. He could understand now the feeling of wanting death to come, for the hurting to stop. But all of the Cheyenne training of his youth wouldn't let him ask for that, to want it out loud.

"OK, give it a rest," Pattie finally said.

Mick's head hung and he could see Pattie's boots approaching, could see drops of his own blood form along his nose and chin, drip to the splattered ground.

"Understand this, boy," Pattie said. "I've been all through the area where the mine is supposed to be. Likely as not it's a spot where the Comanches can dig out the silver in gouges, just like they would a vein of lead. They may not know or care that they're using silver. But think of the nice touch it makes for a white man to die by a silver bullet. Touching, isn't it?" He grabbed Mick's hair and lifted his face until he could lean in closely, and Mick could see into hazel eyes that no longer carried the charm he needed to sucker people along.

"Tell me what I want to know, and all this goes easier," Pattie said.

Mick tried to shake his head, but Pattie just tightened his grip.

"You know, boy, when I go to a little chamber pot of a place like Scabtown to trade, it's not just for money, it's for information. One tidbit I got that amused me is that the white man's medicine, aconite, is really just monkshood. Would you have known it by its plant name? Is that the Indian way? Yet you doubted yourself and ended up going to town for something you could have gathered yourself, if you just knew how to trust what you know."

Mick felt ripples and spasms of pain shooting up and down his body wherever one of those hammer blows or slaps had landed. But he forced himself to think about Syd. *Don't listen to Pattie. What will keep Syd alive?*

"You see, you may know more than you think you do," persisted Pattie. "Think hard. Where is that mine?"

"Why don't you buy one of the maps that are circulating around?"

"Because, boy, I'm the one who made most of those maps." Pattie glanced over at Laney, who was staring at the nude girl, instead of paying attention to Mick. He turned back to Mick. "What do you think one of the things I was selling back at Scabtown was? I've got men, who bought that map, roaming all through Comanche and Kiowa terri-tory looking in every place I know the mine isn't. You see, all you need to do is include a detail or two of what was on a real map, age the parchment or old cloth by the fire a bit, fold and refold it, make sure there's a big X somewhere a fool can believe is the mine, and you have it. For my bit, I used the pick blade stuck in a live oak tree from the real maps."

Syd's head snapped up. She'd tired herself enough, trying to get free, to be hanging limply in Laney's rough hands—until now. Pattie caught the sudden movement of her head lifting, even though she lowered it as soon as she realized she'd shared more than she meant to, and Pattie let a sly grin show. He turned away from Mick, went over to Syd. He lifted her head up by putting a finger under her chin.

"Now, my spirited little Mex," he began, "I'm only

going to ask once, so remember that Mick's life hangs on your answer. Do you know where he killed the Comanche with the bullets?"

Her head turned to Mick, and he barely had strength to lift his head and look at her. She winced. Then she slowly nodded.

"And the pick in the tree. You've seen *that?*" Pattie's tone was more urgent. She didn't nod or shake her head, so Pattie reached and impatiently undid the gag. "Tell me."

She worked her mouth, as if it'd been full of dirty cotton, and looked at Mick. "Only if you give me your absolute word he lives."

Laney, who held her, started to say something, but Pattie held up a hand. "That's easy enough. Of course I'll let him live, if you promise to show me everything you can. You'd know the spot, if we find it?"

She hesitated.

"Mytho," Pattie said.

Mythological Jim's fist hit the side of Mick's head hard enough to knock it to one side. Mick's ear burned and he heard a steady buzz and roar from that side of his head. He tried to look up to Syd, to tell her something, anything.

She nodded, unable to look into Mick's face. "Yes," she muttered.

"OK," Pattie said.

Mytho stepped around in front of Mick and drew his Bowie knife.

"No!" Syd screamed. "You gave your word! I'll show you nothing!"

"Hold on there, Mytho," Pattie instructed, and went over and said something to the buffalo hunter. Mick couldn't hear clearly now, but it made Mytho chuckle.

Weasel stepped away from where he'd been watching

and started to gather up what gear Mick and Syd had. He started packing the animals, even saddled Syd's horse. Mytho still stood in front of Mick.

"Hurry up with that packing," Pattie snapped. He had Syd's money belt and was opening it while Weasel packed.

Laney kept close watch on Syd while she struggled into clothes, which is all Mick could hope for now.

"You like to seem kinda tough, eh?" Mytho said to Mick. He took the tip of his knife and very lightly let it run across Mick's chest, carving a message there. Mick watched each line turn red and begin to trickle. He couldn't make it out. But when Mytho finally stepped back, Mick's knees buckled and his head lowered. Before he struggled back up into a less painful upright position, he could read the message. It said: **INJUN, KOON, MEX LUVER.** The Ns were upside down, the letters big and bold, one word after the other down the middle of his chest.

Mytho stooped low, grabbed a handful of loose dusty soil, and rubbed it across Mick's chest, smearing the dripping blood and causing it to sting where the dirt was pushed into the open wounds of the letters. He grinned, stepped back, admired his work for a second, then headed for his horse.

Syd was already tied to her horse, and Weasel was leading Biscuit and the little mule on lead lines.

Mick looked up. The sky was darker and thunder had begun to sound in one slow rumbling roar after another. Syd's head hung, but she glanced back at Mick once before Laney gave the lead to her horse a tug. The initial drops of rain hit the dusty soil at Mick's feet, each one tossing up a small ring of dust before becoming a dark spot of mud. Slowly at first, then in a growing urgency.

"Now if that isn't just what we need," Laney commented. He swung his horse in a deliberate wide loop, with Syd's horse trailing along behind, until he could circle past Mick. As they went by, he spit down a stream of tobacco juice that hit Mick in the chest and trickled down, burning across the open cuts.

Mick listened to the *click* of hoofs fade, drowned out by the din of rain hammering down in sheets that looked like angled steel needles. The cool water washed across him as he slumped, straightened, finally slumped again as he hung against the tree in the growing, increasingly frenetic pounding rain.

Chapter Nine

Syd rode in a slow, rhythmic bounce with each step of the horse, head bowed and miserable, tied to Pattie's saddle. Rain poured off her hat and splashed down across her shirt that long ago had soaked all the way through and couldn't get any wetter or chillier. The downpour had not stopped once and her hat was plastered to her damp forehead. Her hands were tied together so tightly in front of her that her fingers were growing numb, and the loop of leather from those bindings was tied around the blanket behind his saddle. In the early going, they'd tried tying her to the saddle horn of her own horse, led by Weasel. But, twice, she'd tried to get the horse to break away and run. So they'd moved her behind Pattie, where now his musty man smell was closer to that of a wet sheep in this relentless torrent.

Lightning cracked. Pattie's horse slipped in the mud as it struggled up a hill. The rain continued to hammer down, nonstop, in steady sheets around them, twisting in the hard gusts of wind as it had all day since they'd left poor Mick back there to die.

Why had she argued with Mick? Why couldn't her last moments alone with him have been more tender, more caring, the way he'd wanted. Well, the way she'd wanted, too. Instead, they'd argued. *Damn. Now these men are going to take from me what I should have given freely to Mick. It's only a matter of time before it happens.* Only the urgency to ride had kept her from being handled more by them back there.

If her hands were free, she'd like to reach up and choke the neck above the wet red shirt in front of her. But even that was stupid. She wouldn't have the strength. Why hadn't she just shot him in the back when she had had the chance? She had to face that she hadn't been up to that, either. What had she been doing out here all this time, taking so many risks when she couldn't begin to do what she'd set out to do? She realized that now. Angry tears ran down her face. They hadn't even gotten to their first campsite yet, and God knew what would happen when they did. Laney and Mytho had both been giving her glances all day, still remembering her naked, no doubt. Weasel didn't speak or look at her, and somehow that was as bad or worse. He was the one who'd taken her little .31-caliber Wells Fargo gun, had tucked it down into one boot. The others had divided up the rest of her things, along with what little they had taken of Mick's. Pattie had handed out the gold coins from her money belt, one by one, to each of the men, keeping a share for himself. Everything she had owned when she arrived back in Virginia City had been sold for the money that was supposed to do one thing—get her close to Bill Hinton, just once. Now she was a failure, and Mick was dead or dying because of it.

Stupid. Stupid. Stupid. She alternated between being mad with herself, and being sorry and guilty about Mick—watching him being beaten by that hulk of a buffalo hunter, tied and helpless. Why couldn't it have been her left back there? She deserved it, not him.

Around them it was so dark she couldn't tell the time of

day. It seemed they'd been riding forever. She wished they would stop, but also dreaded the time when they would, had feared it since they set out. That's when anything could happen. Pattie wanted what she knew to get him to his stupid mine, but could he defend her against the likes of these men?

Pattie got to the top of the ridge and waited until the others were up and within hearing. "We need to camp soon . . . somewhere on high ground. Hodges, why don't you scout ahead and see what looks good."

Hodges Laney was as soaked as any of them. But to someone who'd been a cowhand as long as he'd been, this was nothing. He went by, gave Syd a promising leer, spit a stream of dark juice, and rode ahead into the rain. In minutes he was out of sight.

Pattie gave his horse a nudge, and they started ahead again. "Let's take it slow through here," he said. "Give him a chance to ride back."

They were sidling along a narrow path that jutted out from a ridge of rock that swept all the way down to the small river below, their horses single file, when, through the mud and rain, Laney came galloping up to Pattie, who was in the lead. Laney reined in his panting horse. His soaked clothes were torn in a couple of places. He was panting almost as much as his horse when he said: "Kiowa camp up ahead. Wiped out. Nothing but women and children killed. Whoever did it missed the warriors."

"How long ago?" Pattie said.

Laney gulped down some air. "Scavengers haven't given it much of a go yet. I'd say yesterday, maybe."

"Who?"

"Don't know. Whoever it was wiped out any traces . . . whatever the rain hasn't cleared. That tells me it's not In-

146

dians. Maybe the Rangers, but my guess is cavalry. Saw they'd missed the braves and didn't want to leave anything behind."

"What's your worry, then?" Pattie said.

"Hornet's nest," Laney said, still breathing hard. "Someone's kicked over the hornet's nest."

"What the hell are you talking about, man?" Pattie asked.

But before Laney could answer, an arrow appeared as it shoved all the way through his upper left arm.

Pattie dove off the side of his horse. "Down everyone!"

Laney fell or jumped off the side of his horse, and tugged the reins to pull the horse in front of him as a shield. The others all jumped from their horses, but Syd had to sit there, tied upright as she was, while arrows flew at them from several directions, one sticking into the cliff's side just a foot from her face, until Pattie realized she was an easy target. Not that he cared for her, she figured, but she would provide directions to the mine. He reached up, cut the bonds holding her to the back of the saddle, and yanked her down beside him, her wrists still tied.

"Kiowa arrows," Mytho said, easing his rifle out and turning it in the direction from which most of the arrows were coming. That big gun of his boomed, and a scream of anger or anguish erupted from the brush.

A rustle loud enough to carry over the rain came from in front of them. Laney fired twice, using his pistol. "Got two of them who were coming this way," he said, reaching up and yanking the Winchester, which had been Mick's briefly, from the scabbard along his saddle.

"Where the hell's that Weasel?" Pattie yelled.

As if in answer, a flurry of pistol shots came from the heart of the rain. Then, except for the rain, it was silent.

147

Next came a single shot, a pause, and another single shot. Syd couldn't see anything. But the arrows stopped, except one or two straggling ones. There was another single shot.

Pattie, Mytho, Laney, and Syd all crouched behind the horses, two of which were whinnying in pain. No more arrows came their way. The rain beat down on them. Then a rustle from the brush to their right made everyone swing guns that way. Weasel eased through, with a pistol in each hand. Syd realized she'd stopped breathing. She took a gulp of air that was part rain and it made her choke and gasp. Pattie clubbed her lightly on the back of her head with his pistol barrel.

"Shut up," he said, and looked toward Weasel, who was now over by his saddle. Weasel shook his head.

Pattie slowly stood. "It's OK for now," he announced. "They've cut out. Hodges, see to those horses." That apparently meant shoot the two wounded ones—an arrow was through the high arching neck of Pattie's gray, dappled Morgan horse, which made Pattie swear, and the horse Weasel had been riding was lamed.

Laney shot both in the head, and the animals dropped where they were. Then it was a struggle, in the rain, to get the saddles off and switch them over to Mick's horse and Syd's.

Pattie broke off one end of the arrow through Laney's arm and yanked the other side through. "Fix it now, or ride?" he asked.

"Let's get the hell out of here," Laney answered. "If the Indians come back, they'll be busy butchering these horses for a feed."

Pattie tied a handkerchief tightly around Laney's upper arm, directly across where blood was oozing, darkening the worn buckskin of Hodges's shirt. "Let's go, then," Pattie said. His eyes snapped nervously back and forth, trying to probe the dark and rain surrounding them as he boosted Syd back up into place and tied her bound hands again to the back of his saddle.

The others mounted, and they headed off along the trail they'd been following.

Mick watched the edges of the clearing as far as he could see through the thick rain. But not so much as a deer stirred. The grass and low bushes were being beaten down by the force of the rain. Tiny streams swept past the base of trees, joining to form a bigger rivulet running past the place where the fire had been and gathering in a rush toward the river.

He'd lost track of time. He hung from the mesquite tree in the rain, as alone and as hurt as he'd ever been in his life. If he relaxed the least bit, his arms stretched and hurt, and the leather around his wrists bit deeper. He was best when standing upright, which was fine as long as he didn't tire. At times he forced himself to tilt his head back and gather rain, swallowing as much of it as he could, knowing later he might crave water. He worked at the leather around his wrists, knowing that, although he couldn't wrestle himself free, he could stretch the leather that was prone to loosen when wet, because, if he didn't, it would dry tighter and cut off all circulation in his hands later. As it was, if he rested just a moment and found himself drooping, the leather bit into his wrists. When he stood again, the blood flowed back into his hands with a painfully tingling surge.

The worst, though, was imaging what would happen to Syd, what may have already happened. That's where his thoughts returned again and again, beyond any pain he felt. He wrestled to keep that out of mind, but the picture of her twisting in rough hands kept coming back to him.

He grew tired, slumped, snapped awake, and stood, feeling the stinging needles in his hands, and thinking again of Syd. The rain was cold now, and the sky dark. He tried to stare off into it, to think of anything else. He thought back to his earliest memories of the wagon train, of the Indians who'd swept him away.

Try as hard as he might, searching every bit of his memories, he was unable to remember the faces of either parent. He could no longer recall what his parents looked like. It was as if they had never been.

As they came out the other side of the river with Pattie holding the lead line to the tiny bronco mule as she swam across parts that were only to the pasterns on the horses, Syd caught her first glimpse of the Indian village Laney had found earlier, before the attack. Unlike Mick, she couldn't tell a Kiowa village from a Comanche one. They both used similar lodging. But she could see the scattered remains of the women and children when the wet black buzzards lifted to sit on low limbs of trees, watching them pass, waiting. One woman, about the same age as Syd, lay on her side. Her face had been picked open by scavengers. Three large holes, made by bullets, had blasted openings across the elk-tooth vest she'd been wearing. Mick had told Syd that an elk-tooth vest was supposed to make a woman irresistible to the young warriors, although that would have mattered little to her now. Syd wondered if one of the braves who had been firing arrows at them had been the one who cared for her.

The small forms, eyes gone from their picked at faces, were the children. Here and there lay a beaded moccasin or a small toy bow. Even the dogs had been shot and their limp, twisted forms lay among the bodies. No wonder the men who'd returned to the village were on the warpath.

The rain swept away their tracks almost as they made them. When they'd passed through the village, Syd turned back and saw the dark shadows of the birds lower to the ground again. She was glad the rain meant no smell to remember. But it would be a while before she forgot the village.

Pattie pushed on hard, seeking to put as much distance as possible from the village and the spot where they'd been attacked. One small river, a creek that was building rapidly in the rain, they could ford. The next one, a few miles later, the horses had to swim across. Pattie got off and hung onto the horse's tail, pulling at Sancho's rope as the little mule swam hard against the lighter but still hefty load of supplies she carried. Syd, he left tied upright in the saddle, where she felt the horse being pulled by the current, almost tugged away once. They all scrambled to the muddy shore on the other side, where, after three tries, Mytho had to come up and help Laney remount. Then they rode on through the rain.

It was hard for Syd to tell how long they'd been riding. It seemed like forever. They continued to push on hard. It was dark around them, and the rain had not let up.

Laney, who rode out front, began to bend more and more in his saddle, and Pattie called out: "Laney, find a campsite! We'll stop for the night."

Laney rode ahead, and, a mile later, the group found Laney swaying in his saddle and waiting. His face was pale behind the scruff of the dark stubble of his chin and cheeks. He must have lost quite a bit of blood. Still, he led the way up to the curl of a cliff side where the lip of the cliff protected a slim strip from the wind and rain. They would be able to have a fire here, if they could find wood and get it lit.

"Weasel, you and Mytho round up some wood," Pattie ordered. "I'll take a look at Hodges's arm and see what we can do."

The cowhand was still in his saddle. He swayed a bit as he got off, then walked his horse to the nearest tree, tied it without removing the saddle, and went over to slump in the lee with his back against the inwardly curved rock wall of the cliff.

Pattie got Syd off his horse and put her down a few feet from Laney. Then he staked his and Laney's horse close enough so they could be watched—there'd be no hobbling them, with the Indians this stirred up. He came back and took the packs from Sancho's back. Relieved of its burden, the little mule stood close by Syd, looking as exhausted as any of them. Pattie frowned at the mule, but didn't bother to tie her beside the horses. It didn't look like she was going anywhere. From Sancho's packs he got out a roll of tarp and, from nearby trees, cut poles to make a shelter, thus extending the dry spot where Laney sat. Syd and Sancho were at the other edge of the dry area. Syd couldn't believe how good it felt for just a few moments not to have rain beating down on her.

Weasel and Mytho made several trips to bring in wood. In this rain they wouldn't need to worry about a fire or the smoke showing, and there would be smoke with the wood as damp as it was. Pattie tore a few pages out of a book from his saddlebags and used those to help get the first frail start of the fire going. After the flames took, the men piled on more wood, and soon the warmth from the fire was as heavenly as anything Syd could remember. Her clothes were still soaked, and her hands tied, but she felt better, until she remembered Mick. Then she felt awful again, that is, until she looked up and saw Mytho leering at her, then she felt fear. She glanced to Pattie, who was digging around in one of the packs that had been on Sancho's back. Would he be able to stop the men, if they wanted her?

After Pattie found whatever it was he'd been hunting, he turned to Laney. "Let's have a look at it," he said as he handed the item he had pulled from his pack to Mythological Jim.

Before, Laney had looked big, burly, able to do anything. But now, Syd could see that his face was pale, and that Pattie had to help him peel off the buckskin shirt that was glued to his arm in places with dried blood.

Pattie gave Mytho a quick glance as he slipped one end of the long metal rod into the fire. "Weasel," Pattie said, "why don't you take a quick scout around, see if we're alone, in case there's any noise."

Although the wind hurled hard sheets of rain against the top of the tarp, Weasel didn't hesitate, knowing that whatever might be out in the storm couldn't be as bad as what was going to happen in the next few minutes.

Syd knew that Laney could hear the others talking and that he knew what they were up to. But he avoided their eyes, even hers. Earlier he'd been a threat to her, but not now. She had never seen an arrow wound before, but she'd seen infection. The arm, around the spots where the arrow had gone in and come out, was swollen and red. The holes themselves were raw. The arrow might have been poisoned, but, more likely, it had just been dirty or had pulled parts of Laney's soiled shirt into the wound. Redness had spread to his cheek bones and temples, an indication a fever was setting in.

"Sit here by the fire, Hodges," Pattie suggested.

"Mytho, why don't you gather 'round and hold him still."

Mytho grabbed Laney awkwardly by the chest and back, one arm curling around his side below the hurt arm. He seemed unsure of just how to grip the cowpoke, but he was so much bigger, it might not matter. Laney closed his eyes, waiting.

Pattie slipped on a pair of gloves and reached for the iron rod Mytho had put in the fire. Syd felt herself pressing back against the rock wall, with her tied hands on Sancho's tough, thick fur, for comfort. The end of the running iron that had been in the fire was glowing. There was nothing funny about the cowhand who'd clearly done some rustling in his day being burned by a running iron.

Syd wanted to look in another direction, but she was unable to tear her eyes away. Laney was breathing faster, panting. His hands were balled into fists. Mytho crouched closer, squeezing him. Outside the tarp, the rain swirled, lashed like a whip, and thunder rumbled. But Syd hardly noticed the storm. Sancho gave a jerk and sat up, and Syd realized she was twisting the little mule's fur.

As the tip of iron got closer, Pattie was watching Laney's face. Then the iron touched, and the sizzle and smell filled the area under the tarp. Laney never yelled, but his teeth clenched until his jawbones were defined against his rough cheeks. His eyes were clenched shut, and tears ran down across his cheeks.

Syd blinked, realized tears were running down her cheeks, and she didn't even like Laney, had, in fact, feared him earlier. But you can't smell another person's flesh being burned and be unmoved, even if you hate the person.

Pattie stepped back, held the end of the iron in the fire again. Mytho kept his tight grip and Laney trembled, his eyes still tightly shut and hands squeezed into fists. Sweat poured down the hair of his chest and back. He knew there was one more burning to endure.

This time Syd was able to twist her head away, stare off into the rain. But she heard the sear of the iron touching flesh again, smelled the flesh burning, heard a whimper from one of the men. When she looked back, Pattie was finishing wrapping torn strips of cloth around the arm, and then Mytho stepped in and helped pull on Laney's buckskin shirt. The patient looked dazed, and, as soon as they were done, he slid as close as he could lie to the rock wall and pulled a blanket over himself.

Pattie busied himself putting things away and had just finished when Weasel came back, dripping. He shook his head at Pattie.

"That's good," Pattie muttered.

Syd was watching Mytho, who was staring at her. The look was half leer and half promise.

Pattie saw it, too. "We need her to get to the mine," he said, as if that dismissed the subject. He could have easily said "until" we get to the mine. "I'll take first watch," he informed them. "Weasel, you take the second."

Mythological Jim shrugged and put his blanket across the fire from Syd. Pattie sat down beside Sancho. Without looking Syd's way, he said: "You'd better get some sleep. We want to be moving early."

Between the flickers of fire, at times, Syd could see Mytho's face. His head was turned toward her, and he was staring without blinking. She thought about Mick, wondered what it was like for him right now, tried to stay fixed on him, instead of worrying about her own plight. But those eyes that could see hundreds of feet into a buffalo herd to pick the exact place for the next shot stared at her until they burned.

Weasel was already snoring in his bedroll, and Pattie was tossing another log on the fire as Syd, thinking she would never be able to sleep, dozed off.

Chapter Ten

On the second day the wolves came.

Mick's drooping head lifted. The first of the two big lobos, with a gray face with black ears and black splotches on its fur like a shaggy paint horse version of a wolf, pushed through the brush and stood growling, its teeth bared. Then the second and bigger wolf came in view, almost white, with piercing blue eyes. The first wolf deferred to it, and moved forward only when the white one had. They were cautious, but determined-looking and hungry.

Mick hung still against the tree and tugged at the leather around his wrists. There was no give. Back when he'd been on his own, he'd had another pair of wolves come right up to his camp. He had been able to have a fire that night and had gotten out of his blanket and tossed on all the extra wood he had gathered. Those two had stood 100 feet away, sometimes howling and at other times glaring at him. If one of them took a careful step toward him, he'd pick up a brand of wood from the fire and wave it like a torch at him, and that one would back off again. Finally, with the fire burning lower, he'd had to rush them with a torch, and they'd scooted. As soon as they were out of sight, he had gathered more wood and kept the fire bright until morning. But now he had no fire, and he was tied in place to a tree.

The wolves were still cautious so near a man smell. The

white one edged a bit closer, and the other followed, growling and showing teeth. Wolves can be as cowardly as coyotes, but in groups their fear lessens. They stay clear of Indian villages, although they might attack a child or even a sleeping man. The strength of this pair came from the white one, who was trying to convince the gray to buck up for a charge at Mick.

As the wolves moved closer, smelling the dried blood on his chest perhaps, he stood all the way up, and the blood rushed into his hands with a fierce tingling that burned like shoving them in a fire. He rubbed his hands as vigorously as he could, forcing them back to use, not that it would matter if the wolves started in on him.

The movement of his straightening made the wolves stop. He yelled, then kicked at them. The white one backed a step, the other with it. But after a couple more feints, the white one's grinning snarl grew, and she moved forward, regardless of whatever motion Mick made. They were cunning, too, and it seemed they'd figured out how helpless he was.

Well, Mick, old fellow, he thought to himself, *this looks about like it.* He closed his eyes, stood as straight as he could, and began to sing. He sang the death song, one he'd learned so long ago he didn't know if it would come back. But it did, and he felt somehow comforted by that as he braced himself, waiting for the first leap and tear of flesh. He sang louder.

Thump. There was a whine. Mick's eyes snapped open and there was an arrow deep into the shoulder of the white wolf. She spun, grabbing at the protruding shaft with her teeth, growling and whining at the same time. But as she struggled, she sank to the ground, her heart pumping out a growing red smear of blood. The other wolf circled and howled, not sure what to do.

Bam. A rifle shot. The gray wolf tumbled into a heap and lay still. The movement of the white wolf slowed. Her head fell over to one side, panting. Her tongue lolled out of her mouth. Then her breathing stopped, and the open, fixed eyes seemed to dim as Mick stared.

The brush parted and the first Indian stepped out into the clearing. After him a single file of five others followed. Another, with a rifle, appeared from behind Mick. They checked on the wolves first, and the youngest of them lowered to his knees and started skinning them. He was the only one of them without at least a single eagle feather hanging from his hair. The other Indians moved closer, crowding around Mick.

They were an odd mix. Mick's eyes were drawn first to the tallest of them, a brave well over six feet. He chattered with the others, in a tongue of which Mick could make out only a few words. But he was white. His hair was as red as any Mick had ever seen, and his eyes were pale blue. That stark red hair, though, was long and done in Comanche style, and he, like the others, wore only a breechclout. He was pointing to the wavy line Mytho had made under the word INJUN on Mick's chest, then at the bear claws that still clung on their tight leather cord around Mick's head.

A short but thicker brave, to whom the red-headed one deferred, stepped closer to Mick. He tugged off the bear claws, tossed them to the ground, grabbed Mick's head by the scalp lock, and drew his knife. Mick was close enough to see the stained tassels on his breechclout, the hoops of two fresh scalps hanging from his waist, to smell the beaver oil that made the man's muscled, dark body shiny, to see a pair of hawk's talons hanging from the man's ears. The brave's eyes were like small obsidian fires glaring at Mick from above high dark cheek bones, each painted with two finger swipes of ochre and one of vermilion. A strip of otter fur was woven into each braid of his hair, and the ends of his braids were wrapped in tufts of the same, and, in the rush of seconds he had gathered in all this, Mick even took in the pattern on the man's beaded moccasins, also stylized hawks. Each detail seemed vital, as if it would be his last in the world.

The knife blade started toward him, and Mick said: *"Shi Shi ni Wi he tan iu."*

For a second the knife stopped, and just as it began to move again, an older hand clasped on the wrist. Someone behind the brave muttered something. The brave lowered his knife, shoved it back into its sheath, reluctantly Mick thought, and backed away.

The oldest of them stepped forward, his long white hair hanging loosely, instead of in braids. He had been slow coming into the clearing, hadn't been with the first of them to arrive. His face was wrinkled and his eyes watery, although unflinching, and they seemed to miss little as he looked Mick up and down. This was the peace chief. Mick knew that at once.

White people think, wrongly, that the peace chief is simply old and given his position to calm others in the tribe. This one leaned closely, looked, hard, into Mick's eyes, and Mick could see every particle of the man struggling not to reach and scalp Mick just as the other had begun to do. But his duty, as confusing as the arrival of whites had made it, was to determine what was best for the tribe, to mete out justice. Mick watched the worn face, and it was like waiting for a deliberating jury to come back into the room.

"Snake people," Mick said again in Cheyenne. If his hands had been free, he would have made the same hand sign Mythological Jim had used when he'd talked of the Comanches.

The peace chief turned and looked to the others around him. He turned back to Mick, lifted his chin with a finger, looked even more closely into Mick's eyes. Then he let the finger drift to the scabbed lines on Mick's chest, poking at one spot until the blood started again. He glanced at the others. The tall red-headed one stepped forward, pointed again. He and the chief spoke, and one of the partial scraps Mick caught was "white man".

Well, Mick knew that. He tried to repeat the words and he nodded toward the redhead to say he was a white man, too, wasn't he?

The red-headed brave shouted, denying being white, Mick thought. But the peace chief held up a hand. Whatever it was, he'd decided. Mick braced himself.

The chief bent down, picked up the bear-claw necklace, tugged it back onto Mick's head the way it had been, then backed off a step, his eyes almost laughing now, although the rest of his face changed not at all. The red-headed brave thrust close against Mick, shouted again, making Mick think he was denying again ever being a white man. This wasn't going well.

He tried again in his rusty Cheyenne. The chief's head tilted just a fraction, then he shook it, waved to one of the others, pointed to one of the youngest of them to come.

That brave came up to Mick, opened the end of a water gourd, and held it up. Mick tilted his head up. The brave poured in water, not stopping even when it ran out the sides of Mick's open mouth and poured down his chest. He finally lowered the gourd and, without looking directly at Mick, turned away. The others gathered up the wolf carcasses, and one rolled up the skins. One or two of the men chuckled at something another said. But the joke was among themselves, and none of them looked back. They filed out of the clearing as quietly as they'd entered it.

Mick stood there, staring after the last bushes that had closed on themselves behind the Indians. There went the only tiny ray of hope he'd had. He was no longer thirsty, but that just left him more time in which to die.

Syd awoke to the sound of shots. It was early in the morning. The distant trees were faded clusters of black sticks. She sat up, realized the camp was without anyone watching. Pattie stirred, then Mytho. Laney's blanket didn't move. The rain had let up until it was now a steady mist. Syd shivered in her shirt that was still damp. She scooted closer to the fire. *Poor Mick, he should be dead by now,* was the first thing she thought. She could only hope it had been fairly painless.

From out of the drizzle, Weasel stepped into sight. He was holding two mule-eared rabbits from one hand. He ducked his head and slipped under the tarp.

"Trying out that new pistol?" Pattie asked.

Weasel gave a curt nod and tossed the rabbits by the fire. He took out what had been Syd's ammo belt and began cleaning the small Wells Fargo pistol and reloading it. Then he shoved it into his right boot. By the time he'd done that, Pattie had the two rabbits dressed out and shoved onto sticks that leaned over the fire. He threw on more wood and turned to look at Syd.

"Probably shot them on the move, too." Pattie nodded toward Weasel. "If he bothers you by talking too much, you just have to remember his tongue's hung in the middle like a bell and he just can't go ten minutes without talking up a blue streak. That right, Weasel?"

Weasel just looked away.

All that chatter was probably to keep Syd from lighting out on her own. Here was a man able to shoot moving rabbits with a short-barreled .31-caliber gun Mick had called a belly gun. But, tied up as she was, and out in the middle of who knew where, she didn't have any idea where she would go if she could get a chance to run. She missed Mick then more than ever.

By the time the rabbits were fit to eat, Laney had struggled up and managed to saddle his own horse. But he looked tired before they started.

They all had their bit of the rabbits, and Pattie packed up the last of the camp, and then they were off. All morning they rode steadily, and hard, with Laney on point. It was more of the same as yesterday, up hills, around wide-open patches of grass where Mytho would point out the wallows and where endless backs of buffalos had once crowded. They came across what was once a deep mire, where almost a dozen of the shaggy beasts had gotten stuck in the mud and died. Now just their white, stripped bones stood up amidst the dip in the earth where the tall grass had grown back thickly.

The drizzle kept up, and they were always wet, whether stopping to give the horses a watering or scrambling up another rock-strewn bank. Laney, who had formerly been chatty, now said little. Weasel said less. Pattie and Mytho picked up the slack when they rode close enough to each other to speak. Neither seemed to want to disturb this countryside, where anything might happen and often did.

Shivering was about all that kept Syd awake and upright in the saddle. The ups and downs of hills that had been brown and a little dull before weren't improved by the rain. But they couldn't use a road, even if one went this way. Not with her being bound the way she was. She swayed, tired and half asleep behind Pattie, and Laney looked about as alert in his saddle. He reined in his horse, and the whole line of them stopped. She could hear him cussing. She forced her tired eyes open and leaned around Pattie's rain-soaked red shoulder to look ahead. Someone had put up a fence with posts and a couple of strings of silvery barbed wire.

"Don't just sit there. Do something," Pattie said. Each of the men seemed to have a short temper after a night of sleeping in the rain.

Laney awkwardly slid out of his saddle, using just his right hand on the horn. He dug in one of his saddlebags and came out with a cutter, its metal handles a foot long. He was muttering as he slipped in the mud along the fence line as he went up to it. "Probably some damn' sheep farmer, too, put up a son-bitch fence like this."

"It's not just the sheep farmers. Folks are starting to put up fences all over," Pattie said.

"Don't care if it hare-lips every cow in Texas," Laney muttered as he snipped an opening in the fence and pulled the wire off to the side with a gloved hand. Then he went back, put away the cutters, and struggled back into his saddle after two clumsy tries. He gave his horse a nudge and they were off again.

The grass had been eaten back enough to be starting up greener on this side of the fence.

"You'd better put a loop on that bronco mule," Laney said. "Like as not, if there're sheep in here, someone's put a donkey or mule in with them to keep off coyotes. A donkey'll mother the sheep and kick the bejesus out of any coyote tryin' to make a play for one of 'em."

Sancho was up against Syd's leg, so Pattie tossed the end

of a loop over her neck and snugged it up while they passed through the field. They rode through the far corner of the land, swinging wide to avoid the distant sight of a house, and cut their way through the other side of the fence they came to after a while.

"Never thought I'd live to see this sort of cow flop," Laney muttered. It took him three attempts to get back in the saddle this time. Syd could see beads of sweat on his face, moisture that wasn't from the rain. She could tell he was driving himself along on will alone now, not wanting to be left behind.

Pattie pushed on for a couple more miles, then headed them toward a stream to water the horses and give Laney a chance to rest for a while. The cowhand plopped against a tree, his back upright against it.

"Take a look around, Weasel," Pattie said, and untied the loop that held Syd to his saddle and helped her down. She sat on the ground and watched Laney, his eyes shut and sweat joining the relentless mist to soak his shirt. When she looked up, she saw Mytho squatting and looking at her.

Pattie came back up the bank and handed Laney a canteen before coming over to sit between Syd and Mytho. The buffalo hunter towered above her.

"Know why they call him Mythological Jim?" Pattie asked. Syd didn't nod, but Pattie went on anyway. "It's because of the number of buffalo he could shoot. Why, he's shot as many as two hundred from the same stand, someone pouring water down the barrel of one gun while he heated up another of those big fifties. Kept three skinners pegging out all afternoon fast as they could work."

"Shot ourselves 'bout out of a job's what we did," Mytho said, "don't you know." He turned his head and spit a dark stream. "Had to come south of the Arkansas to hunt Indian territory's what we had to do."

"I thought the Indian territory south of the Arkansas River was protected against hunters," Pattie said.

"It kind of supposed to have, don't you know," Mytho responded. "But a couple of the fellows went to see Major Dodge, over to Fort Dodge there. The great southern herd wasn't migrating north no more, was hardly a buffalo from the Arkansas to the Cimarron to the Canadian. They pitched it to him, and asked what he thought. He didn't tell them they couldn't hunt south of the Arkansas. What he did say was . . . 'Boys, if I were a buffalo hunter, I would hunt where the buffaloes are.' And that's just what we did, though comin' across and shootin' as many buffs as we did has those Injuns stirred up like dammit. If that Quanah's up that way, I'm glad I'm down here."

"This Quanah"—Pattie turned to Syd and leaned closer—"is part white. His mother, I believe, was a Comanche captive when she was only nine. God knows what they did to that woman. She grew up so Comanche that when ol' Captain Sul Ross and his cavalry rescued her after a battle of the Pease River, why she tried to get away again. Now, you want to find one redskin who's really on the warpath, it's this Quanah. Right, Mytho?"

"Just glad I'm way the hell down this way from him." The buffalo hunter shook his head, looked up to where Weasel was retracing the trail from where he'd been scouting ahead.

Weasel reined in, looked from face to face, stopping at Mytho. He nodded, held up a hand with open extended fingers, closed it, opened it, then held up two fingers.

Mythological Jim grinned, reached down to pat the butt of his big fifty Sharps. "Buffalo ahead, just a dozen of them," he said. "Looks like we dine today."

"Someday that man's going to talk himself to death," Pattie said to Syd, nodding toward Weasel.

Mytho rode on ahead and the others sat their horses. Syd leaned forward and whispered to Pattie. He led his horse over to a low agarita bush, slid off, and tied the reins, then he untied the leather thong that held Syd to the saddle.

Laney stayed slumped in his saddle, looking ahead on the trail. It was hard to believe that he was the one about whom Syd had worried most when they'd started. Weasel looked right at her with those perpetually squinting eyes, the kind that said he'd far more enjoy killing her than raping her. She shuddered. If she hadn't heard Weasel speak low a few times to Pattie, she'd have thought he was a mute.

Pattie led the way over a small rise. He undid the leather securing Syd's wrists but left the leather dangling from her left wrist which he looped around his hand a few times. Any thoughts Syd had of making a dash for it passed.

When Pattie had just got her up behind his saddle and was tying her in place again, far off, over the hill, a shot sounded. It was Mytho's .50-caliber Sharps. After a few ticks, there was another shot.

"Hope that doesn't bring in every redskin for fifty miles around," Laney muttered without looking up. He seemed barely able to hold himself in his saddle. But he also seemed to know that the slightest sign of his not being able to ride would get him left behind.

Half an hour later, Mytho came over the hill with a small black buffalo robe wrapped around meat behind his saddle. He reined in and said to Pattie: "Wanted the calf, had to kill the cow, too. Got both tongues, some hump, and the livers. We'll eat well this camp." He grinned at Syd, promising her far more than she ever wanted. Worse, there was blood and smears of dark red flesh on his beard around his grinning mouth.

"Had a little go at the calf liver, did you?" Pattie said. "Heard you runners like it fresh and steaming warm, just out of the body."

The smile slid off Mytho's face. He rubbed a soiled sleeve across his mouth, turned his horse with a jerk of the reins, and started forward again.

Laney and Weasel kept a sharp eye out for Indians after the two shots of the big gun had announced their presence for miles around. It was a long, tense afternoon until Pattie, noticing Laney swaying in his saddle, suggested they camp in a small stand of live oak out in the middle of one of the small seas of grass not far from an old buffalo trail. Pattie reasoned out loud that the brush and trees would give them cover to have a fire, while the open area would let whoever was on watch see a distance around them.

Mytho had regained some of his earlier exuberance as he undid the calf's skin he'd used to carry the meat. Flies buzzed around it, and he waved them away.

Syd couldn't help thinking that two large animals, enough to feed a small tribe for weeks, lay out in a field somewhere for the wolves while they'd kept just enough for a meal or two. But when the slabs of the tongue and liver began steaming and smoking on sticks beside the fire, her stomach kept her quiet about the waste.

Pattie gave the horses and the mule some corn from a bag in the packs Sancho carried. Then he gathered a bit of grass for the horses. As soon as Sancho had eaten, the little mule came to curl up beside Syd, looking up at her with big eyes. Syd reached down to pet the soft nose and scratch behind the twitching long ears.

Laney let his saddle drop, spread his blanket, and grabbed a piece of partially cooked tongue and took it over to his blanket. His face was, if anything, paler than before. His eyes were sunken. He looked gaunt and even a bit haunted to Syd. The others ignored him. As soon as the meat was cooked, they began to eat. By then Laney had already laid down and pulled his blanket over himself.

Mytho bent close to Pattie to whisper. "How much longer, you think?" Pattie shrugged. Then while Mytho was so close, he whispered again: "What say you let me have a go at the girl tonight?"

"No!"

"She'll still be able to talk," Mytho assured Pattie.

"You can be a bit rough," Pattie reminded. "Remember that girl in Dodge."

"Cheap whore tried to bite me," Mytho said.

"You tore her in half. You know that's why they call you Mythological Jim up that way." Pattie had whispered, but his eyes trailed over to Syd. He was registering the look on her face, using it the way he used everything.

Mytho eased away and fiddled with the meat by the fire. He fussed with cooking the last strips of tongue, drying them so they'd have something for the trail tomorrow. Mytho said: "Gonna try to do up some depuyer here."

"*Dépouille,*" Pattie said.

"If you say so. Had a frog runner from down Canada way spoke that sort of flop about as good. Wasn't the best shot of us, though, don't you know." He winked at Syd, appearing to promise her something that didn't make her eager to sleep. "Shame there ain't any kettle of fat a-goin' here," Mytho said then. "All we'd have to do is dip it and hang it till morning." He'd made a frame of sticks and was turning the buffalo hump, leaning it toward the fire, letting each side sear and sizzle as the fat burned. "You cut right along the backbone," he explained, "next to the hide, running down from the shoulder blades to the last ribs. When this stuff gets dipped in hot grease and hung for twelve hours, it's as good as bread. When those ol' Plains Injuns went on a warpath, they'd take some dried meat and this here depuyer and that's all they'd need. You kill one of them carrying this stuff, it's just like getting a free feed. Quite a few of 'em I shot right off their horses while they were on a hill having a look 'round. You can't eat those pretty beaded moccasins, but this stuff'll keep you goin' for days."

Listening to him go on, Syd was beginning to understand why Weasel rarely talked. She had liked sitting around the fire and listening to Mick's stories, but everything this old buffalo hunter said was to intimidate, to gain respect, for which it failed. When she did lay down on her blanket at last, her shirt dry for one of the first times in days, Sancho stood closer to her in the cool evening air.

With Laney asleep and Pattie yawning from having taken first watch last night, Mytho set up to take the first watch without being asked. He knew he was due, and the look he gave Syd kept her eyes open wide for a long time as she lay curled in her blanket. Finally she could fight it no more, and felt her eyes close in spite of all her efforts.

She woke to yelling. The fire had died down to a yellow and red glow. Mytho was the one bellowing, and Pattie was laughing. Weasel had a gun in each hand and was sitting up on his blanket, watching the big buffalo hunter run around the fire, trying to get away from Sancho.

"Make the damn' thing stop!" Mytho yelled, lashing back behind him with his Bowie knife. Sancho kept pace, although moving backward and kicking steadily at Mytho with both hind legs.

"Don't you hurt that pack mule, Mytho," Pattie said, "or you'll have to shoulder its load. She's only protecting the girl, the way that sheep donkey would ward off coyotes."

"I ain't no damn' coyote," Mytho insisted. "Make it stop!"

Pattie stood up, still chuckling, and looped a line over the bronco mule's head. He pulled it back toward Syd, although at first it dug in its legs and tried to get at Mythological Jim. "Just stay away from the girl," Pattie advised, "and you'll be fine." He was still chuckling as he eased back down onto his blanket.

Weasel stood up, indicating he'd take the watch for a while—might as well since he was up. He didn't look happy, so Mytho went to the fire and turned the buffalo hump one more time before going to his blankets.

Syd reached out a hand, and Sancho plopped down beside her. It was the closest Syd had come to smiling to herself since the men had carried her away. She rubbed at the mule's quivering nose until she dozed off to sleep again, this time more sure she would be left alone.

Chapter Eleven

The night stretched long for Mick, like some resistant black taffy being slowly pulled to its limit.

While the shadows were still settling over the clearing from a scrap of moon peeking behind a cloud, five deer came into the far edge of the clearing—a buck, three does, and a fawn far enough along to have lost its spots. Mick could make out their brown shapes against the thick black sticks that were bare trees. Then the buck saw him, or more likely caught Mick's scent. He let out a hard breath, a snort of air, and Mick watched the white tails as they bounded away, pausing once to look back, then bouncing still farther away and out of sight.

At times Mick's legs quivered, and his stomach made low noises. He tried hard not to think of food or eating. But all around him, the night was feeding its own. He heard the slow flap of an owl's soft feathers as it swooped across the clearing to land in a flurry where there'd been a rustle in the dead leaves. It lifted again with its prey, a field mouse, in its talons.

Early in the morning, a huge black hairy sow and five small piglets, all as black as their mother, came into the clearing. The sow was about 500 pounds. Mick knew she'd eat a snake in the beat of an antelope's heart, but didn't know how she'd react to a tied human. He gave a hoarse

172

shout, and her maternal instincts kicked in. She squealed and shooed the piglets out of the clearing. Mick could hear answering squeals from the piglets as she led them out of sight.

He didn't think he'd get to sleep this night, then he woke, and realized he'd slumped down and had been asleep. Light was just filtering through the clutter of dark clouds. At least it was no longer raining, although the air was cool and damp.

A flutter of descending wings preceded two black shapes swooping into sight. He looked up and could see more vultures turning slowly in the air above. The first two may have smelled the spot where the wolves had been dressed out, or perhaps they were here for Mick. He couldn't tell. He watched them flutter to a limb of a tree to watch and wait.

It was hard now to stand straight for long. He felt as filleted as he would if his bones had been removed. He'd bring his head up to find he'd been slumping again, then force himself upright only to have the rage and fire of tingling in his hands. Where his wrists were bound they felt raw, and, now that the rain had stopped, he felt moisture there that could be blood or sweat. He could not tell. But hard as he worked and tugged at the leather, he got nowhere. He'd made a good riata—one of the first things he'd learn to do from Laney in the two years he'd spent as a cowhand—and he still wondered why the Indians hadn't taken it with them when they had had the chance when he and Laney had finally located what was left of McLaren's daughter, Miss Julie, along with the butchered remains of Mick's horse, Pretty Boy. That seemed hundreds of years ago now. He recalled that Laney was his friend back then. But a lot had been different then, and now he could recall only wisps, like a mirage. His vision came and went, sometimes being so keen he could fix on the dim moccasin prints left by the Comanches—although even those had begun to run and fade from the ground, just as sure as that was the way all Indians were headed someday. Another time he would look up and the edge of brush would be a blur, as if it were still raining. He'd blink, it would clear, then it would fade to a blur again. In the times before when he had gone without eating, as a boy in the Cheyenne tests, and when he'd first been on his own out here, his senses had honed, not faded in and out like this. Was he dying? It was a question he put his whole mind to, as if it mattered.

This wasn't so hard, this dying. He could clearly see Yellow Quill, Bear Cub's grandfather, and his own adopted grandfather, wrapping a buffalo robe around his shoulders and walking out of the village one morning. It was the day he'd decided to die.

Mick heard something, realized he was slumping again. He straightened and began to rub his hands together, fighting the needles of sting that shot out to the ends of his fingers. When he looked up, expecting to see the black birds making their move toward him, he saw instead a tall brown horse and its rider push through the low brush on the far side of the clearing.

The horse came all the way over to him. The sun wasn't all the way to the crest of the sky, but when he looked up, the rider's face was in shadow beneath the wide hat rim. The man swung off the horse, lifted his canteen, and came around to stand in front of Mick. He daubed water onto his fingers and rubbed it on Mick's cracked lips. Mick opened his lips, and the canteen came up, and a tiny sip poured across into his mouth. He swirled it around and said: "More."

"Not jus' yet. Let me get you down offa there."

174

Mick forced his eyes wide open, stared. He could see the face more clearly. The skin was as chocolate brown as the horse behind the man.

"Harlan?"

"Sure 'nuff. You better jus' be glad it wasn't some un-weaned calf come 'long findin' you the way like you is."

Mick tried to grin, but his face hurt.

Harlan pulled out his knife, reached up behind the tree while standing ready on the side. Mick wanted to tell him not to cut the riata. But it was too late. He felt the sliced leather let go, and he fell forward into Harlan's arms.

Pattie's horse—well, Syd's horse really, the way she still thought of it, although she rode on it behind Pattie—moved up to where Weasel's horse had stopped and now stood. It stopped, too. She leaned out around Pattie to look down the hill while Mytho and Laney both hove up alongside them.

The sky had been gradually dimming until now the sun was out of sight, hanging on the brink of a horizon they couldn't see, poised to go out as when someone puffs on the wick of an oil lantern. Moisture clung to the dark bark of the leafless trees, making a light aura of mist that gave everything an eerie feel.

Down at the bottom of the hill a small cabin nestled with its back to the sheer hill on the other side, a bend in the river within a short walk of the front door. An outbuilding that had once been a stable or small barn had some while ago been burned to a dark smear on the soil where small starts of trees and grass were taking a greener foothold through the blackened ground. A single horse was tied outside the cabin, and a slender thread of smoke rose from the chimney.

"Sure would be nice to sleep under a roof just once, wouldn't it?" Pattie said.

"There's only the one inside," Mytho responded. "Might could be we could shoot through there from here and take him out." He started to reach down to his long .50-caliber Sharps.

"Hang onto that idea, Mytho. Anyone holed up out here is like as not worried less about Indians than the law. We might know him. And, he might be a crack shot. I think it will be a mite better if we ride up to the door and ask first." Pattie gave the horse a nudge forward.

The others followed, fanning out to spread any possible target. The horses picked their way carefully. Parts of the hill were covered by patches of old scrub berry bushes and low tangles of chaparral; the places where the horses could go were rain-rutted grooves of loose rock that clattered and slipped with each shod hoof that landed.

When they were but halfway down, a voice called out from the cabin: "Stay right there! Off the horses and grab a piece of sky!"

Syd peeked around and could see the cabin door partially open and the barrel of a rifle extended. She heard the lever being worked, a shell being shoved into its chamber. It was a dry, crackling sound, different from the sound of the horses' clicking on stones and the snapping of an occasional dead twig. The ring of it was metal, and more serious.

The horses stopped.

"We're only weary travelers, seeking some comfort along our way!" Pattie called out.

"Bullshit! Off them damn' horses or get knocked off."

Laney, who had been slouching, sat up in his saddle. "Cooley! Is that you, Cooley?" he shouted.

176

Syd watched the man step out farther, peer up the hill at them. "Laney, that you?"

"Yeah."

"Who's that with you?"

"Taking a runaway indentured servant back where he belongs," Laney told him. "That's all. Just passing through. You could stand some company, the Kiowa are stirred up as dammit back there."

The man lowered his rifle, stood outside the door with the rifle's butt resting on the ground and his hand around the barrel. It was the sign to move forward. Hodges Laney clucked and started down, with the rest following.

As they neared the cabin, the man Laney had called Cooley shook his head when he saw Pattie. "I should 'a' knowed."

"How you been keeping, Scott?" Laney asked.

Cooley didn't answer. The line of his mouth got thinner. He was staring at Pattie.

"Do you know Bob Pattie here?" Laney said.

"If that's what he calls himself these days. Yeah, I've met him. I was in Dodge when an empty stagecoach rolled into town and *he* got out."

"Now, Cooley," Pattie said, "those are bygone days."

Syd thought the man looked like he'd bitten into something sour. She recognized the face of a man who had killed before. Mytho had it, and Weasel to a much, much higher degree. But this man, Scott Cooley, he had it, too, maybe not to the extent of Weasel, but it was there, firm as the ground they were standing on.

Pattie slid off the saddle and reached up to untie her hands. Cooley didn't say anything, as if it was natural to ride with someone tied to the back of your saddle. Syd remembered she was back to being the Mex boy, so she kept her head down and let the shadow of her hat brim mask most of her face.

Laney was awkward getting off his horse and almost fell before he righted himself.

"You take a bullet somewheres?" Cooley asked.

"Arrow." Laney winced, tied his horse beside the others.

No one moved to pull the saddles until they saw how things sat here. Cooley was looking them over, glancing up at Mytho's face, but not intimidated by the size of the man. Weasel, though, he gave an extra careful look. When he looked at Pattie again, Syd could swear one end of Cooley's lip curled a tiny bit.

Sensitive to the social necessities of the moment, Pattie dug out a small cloth bag of coffee and a couple of cut plugs of tobacco from the diminished packs on Sancho's back and held them for Cooley to see. It was a smart move, since Cooley nodded at the coffee and reached to take both of the plugs. Syd sensed Cooley didn't own the glorified shack, but was merely squatting in it for a time.

"Kiowa stirred up, you say?" Cooley said, squinting as if in a slightly better mood, but still deciding whether or not to let the group stay.

"Damn' right," Pattie answered. "We lost two horses, and Hodges took an arrow."

"Poisoned, was it?" Cooley asked, watching how Laney moved.

Cooley was of a size with Laney, and wore a shirt that had been white once, a store-bought shirt, above his pants and boots. His hair was somewhere between brown and blond, as was the three or four days of stubble on his cheeks and chin. His eyes were intense and missed nothing.

"Who all's after you?" Laney asked Cooley.

"The Rangers, Sheriff Clark's bunch, and those damn'

Hoodoos." He waved a vague arm at the hills around them, as if his enemies were everywhere.

"Hoodoos?" Pattie echoed, tying Sancho's packs into place and turning back.

"Hell, just those damn' Dutchmen who've blacked their faces. But I know who they all are. Got their names on a list, I have. Same bunch as voted not to secede. Whole damn' Dutch county sided with the Union. You know how everyone 'round here feels about that, Laney . . . you wore gray yourself."

"What say we go inside," Laney suggested, favoring his bad side. "It's getting on dark out here."

Inside, an unlit lantern sat on the table that had one leg repaired—a limb tied to it with rawhide to hold the table nearly level. Cooley went over and shoved the bag of coffee and tobacco plugs into a saddlebag by his bedroll. "If I knew you was comin', Hodges," he said, "I'd have laid in some cards. Could end up rich 'round you. This's the first time I've seen you without your leading along a handful of mossy-horned cattle with brands three deep on them." He straightened.

"Don't know as I'd fuss over a little rustling, Scott," Laney replied, easing into one of the two straight-backed chairs without being asked. "Hain't you sided with the rustling side in all this mess?"

There was no bed in the room. Cooley had stretched his bedroll along one wall, not far from the fireplace where a fire was going under a hanging pot. Extra wood was piled beside the fireplace. Everything was neat by the bedroll, Cooley's saddlebags gathered in one place where he could scoop things up if he had to leave quickly. Syd had noticed he'd left his saddle on his horse with just the cinch loosened.

Cooley lit the lamp on the table, then picked up his tin cup, which was half full. He went over and used a loose glove to lift the pot off the fire. He poured coffee until his cup was full. He hung the pot back and said: "There's a mite more if any of you are of a mind, 'less you have something stronger."

Weasel stood by the wall near the door. Cooley glanced his way, taking in the low-slung gun. Mytho slouched near the fire, but didn't reach for the pot. Pattie went out, came back in with a couple of cups. "Anyone?" he asked.

When neither Mytho nor Weasel spoke, he poured some coffee into the cups and slid one over in front of Laney, and sat down in the other chair, looking at the swollen fingers of Laney's bad arm.

Cooley stood between his bedroll and the fire, drinking coffee with his left hand, although Syd suspected he was right-handed, the side where he wore his pistol. "You still prowling about looking for that lost San Saba Mine?" he asked Pattie.

"Oh, I give the idea a nudge now and again."

"I thought Jim and Rezin Bowie stumbled onto that forty year ago."

"That's what they wanted everyone to think," Pattie answered. "Word I have from the more informed crowds I met at places like Scabtown tell me they never did find it. Way I hear it, they were knocking over Spanish silver wagons and taking the coin and melting it down. Most mines in those days poured the silver into hollow canes. That's the state of any silver they ever turned in."

"I'm surprised you haven't followed in their footsteps," Cooley commented, staring at Pattie.

"Two reasons. One is that there aren't any more Spanish wagons passing through here with silver. The other's that I'm not a common thief."

"Oh, yes, you are. Just maybe a different kind than some."

Pattie didn't respond to that. He looked down into his coffee cup. Mytho's eyes had narrowed, and Weasel, where he stood, looked the opposite of relaxed.

Syd couldn't recall when she'd felt more tension in such a small place. Cooley had barely glanced at her, although her bound hands hung in front of her, as if people go around tied up all the time. The tan of her skin may have dismissed the importance of his asking.

"You said there're Rangers after you," Laney said, taking a sip of his coffee and looking up at Cooley.

It was a pretty heavy-handed shift of subject, but Cooley didn't seem to mind. "Cap'n Roberts and his men were 'bout twenty miles south of Menardville, last I heard. Major Jones was to the north. Ira Long's captaining Jones's bunch. Heard they were fixing to meet up and take care of me and the others. I had a few who've let me know what was going on till Jones stood 'em all up and mustered out anyone who sided my way. I 'spect those left might take a shot or two if they spotted me, but I'm betting they'd miss. They know what's really goin' on 'round here."

Laney spoke to Pattie. "Scott was a Ranger himself once, then had a farm down Menardville way." He turned to Scott Cooley. "What made you leave all that, get into this mess?"

Cooley's being an ex-Ranger explained to Syd why her being tied didn't seem to bother him. Passing through New Mexico, Syd had heard stories that made her think the Texas Rangers weren't friends with anyone of Mexican heritage. She hadn't quite figured out what this mess was about, except a lot of people seemed to be after Cooley.

"Way I hear it," Pattie said, "the Germans . . . Dutch you call them . . . were getting hit hard by rustling, from Indians as well as whites. No one much cared, least those who'd fought for the Rebel cause, since the Germans had all voted to stay with the Union. A lot of cows got taken, so they took matters into their own hands, those Germans did."

Cooley pushed away from the wall, where he'd been leaning, straightened, and threw what was left of his coffee into the fire, almost putting it out.

"So, you go by Bob Pattie, now, do you? *Hmm.* Last I saw you, your hat was a tall silk one, too, a bit worse for wear, but it helped give you a few airs then."

"Hell, man," Pattie exclaimed, "I'm on your side in this! Hasn't that sunk through. I heard what those lynching Germans did up at Hick Springs. Nine men were up for stealing cattle, but about forty of your Hoodoos busted 'em out of Sheriff Clark's jail. Four rustlers got away, but the mob took five of them and strung them up . . . well, shot one, when he tried to get away."

"I wasn't part of it then," Cooley said. "It was nothin' to me at that point."

"How did you get involved?" Laney's voice sounded a lot more patient than he looked.

"That son-bitch Clark's the one. He had his deputy John Worley pick up Tim Williamson. Tim, whose wife nursed me by hand through the typhoid fever. Without them, I wouldn't be here. Twelve of those damned blackened-faced son-bitches came after them. Worley could have let Tim make a run, but, instead, he shot Tim's horse out from under him, let them damn' Hoodoos have their way."

It was still for a second in the cabin. Cooley's voice had been raising as he talked. Syd watched Mytho and Pattie's eyes connect. Cooley was watching Weasel now, ignoring the others, without making any pretense about it.

"Surprised you're out here," Cooley said to Weasel. "There's enough paper on you to make even your friends try to turn you in."

"Maybe try once," Weasel said. His voice was scratchy and unused. It was the first time Syd had heard him speak out loud, and she wished she hadn't.

Standing by the door, Syd watched Cooley step back near his bedroll. She wasn't unfamiliar with feuds, and the only advantage to hearing bits and pieces about this one was that it helped her worry less about Indians.

"Did you do for Worley?" Laney asked. He seemed to be fading, but was obliged to make polite conversation.

Cooley reached into the pocket of his pants, tugged something out, and tossed it onto the table in front of Laney. It was a strip of dried flesh with hair along it.

Syd had seen scalps before, but never one tossed out so handily by someone who'd once been a Texas Ranger.

Laney took a sip of his coffee and poked at the scalp with a finger. "That's Worley, eh?"

"Found him at his farm. He had a guy working down in the well and was cranking him up with the rope. When I shot him, whoever was in the well fell all the way back down. I wished you could 'a' heard him yell. A well like that'll make a man echo real good."

Syd swallowed. All this posturing and swaggering talk led to people shooting each other. If there had been any liquor involved, she was sure this would turn eventually to gun play. Although this sort of banter kept them distracted from her, this was the most uncomfortable she'd ever felt indoors.

"I knocked Daniel Horster right off his horse in front of

the Southern Hotel," Cooley continued, "and got Peter Bardo in Llano. Hell, shot his brother Charles first, couldn't ever tell the two of them apart. Wasn't time to scalp either of *them,* though. Damn' shame. Still a few names on my list. But I've got time."

"Better hope Major Jones or none of those other Rangers gets onto you, then," Pattie said. "Sounds like he's weeded out your supporters. I've heard Sheriff Clark's an able lawman, too. Wouldn't want him dogging my heels."

"That son-bitch Clark went to John Gamel's ranch on Mill Creek looking for him. He wasn't there, so Clark arrested Bill Coke and Gamel's foreman, Ike Beam. He sent them back to Mason, under separate guard, but Coke never showed up, and Clark's men didn't say why. That's why I aim to burn him, as well as those damn' Dutch." Cooley was breathing harder and talking louder. When he stopped, he looked around at each of them, settled on Hodges Laney who was having to strain to keep sitting upright.

This time Pattie didn't make the mistake of explaining Cooley meant Germans. He'd goaded Cooley enough by practically saying kind words about Clark.

Syd was thinking about being out in the woods and on the run. For the first time she had added respect for Mick, who had been out in these wilds without a gun. He hadn't gone nearly mad, whereas it seemed this former Ranger was headed that way. Poor Mick. She wished she could have done more for him. She slowly sank to the dirt floor, her bound hands in front of her and her lowered face covered in the shadow of her hat brim. *These men. These men.* She looked around at them, each swept up in a form of the same madness. Cooley ready to draw and start shooting at any second; Weasel, who was so full of the same bitterness, only knew killing. Pattie, or whoever he was, sly and clever, but

184

just as mad. Mytho and Laney, too. Even poor Mick, probably dead a while by now, was not immune to it. Syd realized the enormity of her foolishness to be out here. Yes, there was opportunity for the courageous and tough, but there was something that sucked away the spirit and soul as well, if you let it. *I've been stupid to come here. Stupid, stupid, stupid.*

Cooley had begun to rant again, something about John Ringgold killing John Cheyney. His eyes glistened red around the white rims, and there was a spatter of spit as he shouted. His hand was close to his pistol, and Weasel, across the room, was so alert he nearly twitched. Then abruptly Cooley stopped and held up a hand. "Listen."

They were all so still Syd could hear Laney sipping his coffee. Then she heard galloping, heading their way. Cooley was to the table and had the lantern blown out before she realized it. He grabbed for his rifle. Weasel had his gun drawn without Syd having seen him reach for it.

The horse pulled up outside. A voice shouted: "Scott! It's George!"

"Oh, it's Gladden," Cooley muttered.

The man who came bursting into the cabin had blood across his chest and down one pant leg.

"Where're the others?" Cooley asked.

"Caught us over to Keller's store, yonder on the Llano River," he panted. "I been ridin' since."

"The others?" Cooley repeated.

"Mose Beard is hurt worse'n me. Didn't think he'd make it. Others scattered. Was Clark and Keller's son did most the shootin'. Bunch o' others . . . a mob really . . . pitched in to help."

"You sure you weren't followed," Cooley said.

" 'Course not."

As he said it, the first shots knocked a hinge off the front door and sent the lantern on the table flying across the room. A flurry of shots followed. Laney and Pattie had rolled off their chairs and were hugging the dirt floor. Mytho kicked the door the rest of the way open and ran out it. Weasel had a gun in each hand and stood along the open doorway, firing a barrage of cover.

"He always impetuous like that?" Cooley asked, easing over to the opening to shoot up the hill at a flash from a rifle. "That buffalo runner, I mean."

"Probably after his Sharps," Laney said from the floor, working to get his gun out of his holster with his good hand.

Sure enough, the shooting picked up and Mytho came rolling through the open doorway clutching his long Sharps Fifty in one hand and the Winchester in the other. He tossed the carbine to Weasel and turned to sight his buffalo gun up the slope. The first shot filled the small cabin like a clap of thunder.

Weasel tucked his pistols away and used the carbine. Syd heard a yell after his first two shots.

"Hell, they're taking cover and settling in for a night of it, boys," Cooley informed them, calmly reloading his revolver.

Syd cowered along the wall. Outside, it was dark, and the low fire was lighting the inside of the cabin. Shots from three directions peppered the walls and knocked a leg out from under the table.

"Make yourself useful," Cooley called to Pattie, "and douse that fire! They can see what they're shooting at, and we can't."

Laney crawled forward to shoot out the doorway. Then the inside of the cabin dimmed to black as the fire went out. But the shooting from both sides continued into the night.

Chapter Twelve

Mick woke and looked up into a worried brown face lit by a full moon and the flames of a fire. Harlan was bent over him. Mick could not remember when it had quit raining and the sky had cleared enough for him to see the moon.

"You sure there aren't a whole buncha other plants you want me to round up?" Harlan asked.

"Damn." Mick went to sit up, found he was still stiff, but, with a boost from Harlan, managed in spite of a sharp stab or two of pain in his chest. He looked around. He was on Harlan's blanket. The shirt he had on was worn, and the pants were those of Union cavalry. They were in a different part of the woods, and the brown horse was tied within sight. "I've got to get moving," he announced.

"Whoa, there," cautioned Harlan. "You sure 'bout that?"

Mick tried to push himself up off the blanket, but his limbs felt like they were filled with lead. His insides ached from the beating. He reached up, felt his face. It was still swollen, and there were rings of scab around his wrists.

"You no beauty to behold, that's sure 'nough," Harlan said.

"Help me onto a horse."

"Only gots one horse, and I think you should ought to rest a touch mo'. Your friends have done right bad by you.

Thought they would. Reason I come back this way."

"Harlan, they've got Syd."

"Don' know no Syd."

"She was the girl, probably looked like a Mexican boy to you. She was with me, and now those men have her."

"Been three days now. Don' 'spect there's much you can do to stop what's already done probably happened."

Mick tried again to lift himself up, but flopped back onto the blanket.

"You ever been beat this bad befo'?"

"I've got to go," Mick insisted even though his body would not respond to his efforts to force it upright.

"You in no shape to travel. Lay back. Got some more o' that tea you wanted mixed up. Tastes like boot polish. No accountin' for tastes. You need to take in some nourishments, too. Got some stock soakin' yonder. Just lay back now and rest."

Mick tried again, couldn't even get partially upright this time.

"You was speakin' some other kind a language there fo' a bit," Harlan informed him.

"Probably Cheyenne," Mick admitted.

"Handy thing to have, I 'spose, out here in Comanche territory."

"It's had a moment or two," he said, thinking: *They would have to keep Syd alive. But would that mean she would have to endure her worst fears? That alone might kill her.*

He looked up. Harlan was back with a cup and was lowering it to Mick's mouth. He used his free hand to lift Mick's head, then tilted the cup. Mick gulped down the bitter tea, although some spilled down his cheeks. Harlan lowered Mick's head and started to rise.

"Why'd you come and help me?" Mick said.

"I owe you a life. I figured you fo' dead, leastwise in bad trouble, soon's I realized Pattie'd sold you bow and arrows as gen-u-ine Cheyenne."

Mick didn't have anything to say to that. He was too exhausted, too beaten. He tried to marshal his will and energy, but there was nothing to draw on. He knew he needed to sleep, to rest, but there wasn't time. *Syd. It was his fault or responsibility . . . they're keeping her alive, but at what price?*

He could hear the sound of water tumbling across the rocks of a stream, and see clouds drift in front of the moon. Then Harlan was back, with a dark blue enamel pan, the kind you'd use for shaving or washing your face. It looked like government issue, the way Harlan's saddle and horse did.

Harlan squatted beside Mick, saw him looking across at the horse. "Horse's name is Blue . . . retired cavalry like my own self."

Mick liked knowing the horse's name, and realized for the first time that he had never known the name of Syd's horse, the gray stallion with its black mane. Each thought of Syd made him gather himself to try and rise. But he wasn't able.

Harlan wet a cloth and wiped at Mick's face and neck. He dipped it in the water, wrung it out again, and wiped some more. Mick could feel thick scabs being softened and wiped clean.

"You been through a lot. You just don' know how lucky you is to be alive."

"That Weasel's pretty fast, Harlan. If it ever comes to it, do you think you could take him?"

"Bein' fast isn't everything. But it don' hurt. Bein' steady's better. That you way of axin' if I plan to ride with you? Answer's yes."

189

"Help me up a minute."

Harlan hesitated.

"Just want to see myself in the pan."

Putting a hand behind Mick's neck, Harlan eased him up until he could twist and look down into the pan. Its dark bottom turned it into a mirror, and Mick's blood gave it a hue.

"You ain't pretty, suh."

Mick's face bobbed and was distorted in the water's surface that was swept by the night breeze. But he could see his face enough to agree with Harlan. One eye was swollen almost shut. The flesh was laid open over a cheek bone. His lips were cracked, split, and still puffy. Two teeth felt loose when he ran his swollen tongue over them. He pulled back and for a moment the image of the moon was caught in the bloody water in the pan. It was a red moon, a red bent moon, as if blood had spattered to reach that far.

"If they've harmed her at all, even scared her the tiniest bit, I'm going to make me the pretty one of them. That's how it's going to be," Mick said, and he fell asleep just like that.

"Wake up." Pattie was shaking Syd. Coming out of a deep sleep, she heard his voice in a whole new way, the unctuous hiss of it. Why didn't others see that from the first moment they met him, she asked herself, then realized it was probably hindsight making her wonder that.

Earlier, sporadic shots had been a reminder that they were surrounded and watched. The shots had peppered the house since they'd been pinned down in it, waking her every few minutes until she was so tired she could fall asleep for short stretches in spite of them. Weasel had slipped through the door some time ago. After a shot or two, there was quiet enough for her to sleep.

Now, awake, she looked around for Sancho, then remembered the little mule had been tied outside. She did hear a low moan from the other side of the dark insides of the cabin.

"Will you shut up?" she heard Mytho hiss. The moaning stopped.

A dark shape slipped in through the front door.

"Weasel?" Pattie said.

"You'd better damn' sure hope so," Mytho said. "Yeah, it's him. The way's clear. Let's go. You comin', Cooley?"

"Damn' straight. George, too."

"Well, help us with Hodges," Mytho said. "He's been hit again . . . been havin' the damnedest luck the last couple o' days."

Pattie grabbed Syd's shoulder and led her to the doorway. Except when helping Laney or leading Syd, they rushed, one by one, from the door into the dark, curled around the side of the house, and started up the hill.

"The horses?" Pattie whispered to Weasel, who pointed ahead as they wove up the hill behind the cabin.

The brush and trees provided some cover. Behind them, they heard the continued sporadic shooting of the men on the one side, who thought they were keeping the men inside pinned down. Weasel had cleared out one area, but that's all they needed. They passed one of the men Weasel had taken care of. Even in the dim light of the moon through the trees, Syd could see the side of the man's bloody head where he was stretched out behind a rock.

The horses were tied to a low limb on the far side of the hill. Two of them had been hit by rifle fire. Weasel had to finish one of them off with his knife, and George Gladden, bleeding less than when he had arrived, found his horse too lame to ride. He got out his knife, and Syd looked away.

In the light of the full moon they led the horses on through the woods before mounting. Laney had been tossed across a saddle, and it was clear from the way he hung there that he was in worse shape. Mytho had taken a shot through the flesh near his neck, the ball passing above the collar bone and out the back above the shoulder blade. His buckskin shirt was soaked as dark as Gladden's now.

When they were far enough away to risk the noise of riding, Cooley put Gladden behind him on his saddle and they were off in a different direction through the dark sticks of the leafless trees in the moon while the others were still mounting.

Laney had to be helped up to ride behind Weasel. Mythological Jim was able to get onto his saddle, but there was nothing cheerful about the way he did it. Pattie was in a rage of an entirely different nature. When the horses had been cut loose, little Sancho had managed to tangle and lose her packs somewhere in the briars. All of the remaining goods and the last of their food was lost somewhere in the woods. They couldn't pause to look for any of it now.

In the distance, Syd could hear shots, still steady and directed at the cabin. Pattie was muttering under his breath. When Sancho came close to nuzzle against Syd's leg, Pattie swung a kick at her with his closest boot, but missed. After that, the mule kept farther back, so she was near Syd, but away from any more kicks. The three horses and mule rode off into the night, with two of the men wounded and with no supplies.

It was a tired, sullen, and beaten group that traveled through the hills and down across the edges of open grass through the night. Syd had not slept much, and the others not at all. She bounced and nodded, the leather tugging at her wrists. Some of the time was spent riding through streams and steering for stretches of flat rock, anything to leave less of a trail, although Cooley's and Gladden's riding off in another direction would be a help, since that's who those men back there were after. But Pattie seemed determined to leave as little and as confusing a trail as possible.

Pattie was in the lead and came up the gravel bank on the other side of a stream when Mytho called out: "Hold up!"

Just past the stream, Laney fell sideways off the back of Weasel's horse and lay in a loose pile in the wet gravel.

The sky was barely becoming a pale gray, and Syd could see up and down the stream a short way. The growth was thicker and greener along the water, although it wasn't light enough to see the green, except as a darker gray.

"Can't stop here," Pattie warned them. "Throw him across in front of Mytho, Weasel, and ride up and find us a place to camp."

By the time a campsite with the least visibility was found, the sun was up enough for Syd to see everything in clear detail. They were leading the horses along a ledge of loose rock that towered in a thirty-foot cliff on one side. To their left was a thick stand of sumac, then cane in huge clumps that stood twelve to fourteen feet high. The thin trail finally opened to a clearing where deer had turned about before settling in to sleep. There was just enough room to picket the horses and to lay their bedrolls in a row along the cliff.

"No fire," Pattie said.

"Nothin' to cook on it any damn' way," Mytho said. He glared at the little mule that was curled beside Syd.

"Take off your shirt, Mytho," Pattie instructed. "Weasel, give me a hand with Hodges. We might as well patch up all who're ailing and hole up here for the day."

Mick woke to the sound of gunshots. He tried to sit up. Sharp knives stabbed him all along his lower abdomen. Before it had been a general pain, a blanket of it. But now it was centered on his lower ribs, those that were cracked or broken. His head felt less swollen, but the ribs barely let him rise to a sitting position by twisting and pushing himself up with his hands. But at least he could do that now. He looked around. A low fire was going. He tried to stay sitting up, but the effort caused his breathing to come in staggering gulps. He lowered himself back onto the blanket. If anyone was going to come after him, he wasn't going to be able to get away. He lay, watching strips of cloud drift across the moon on the other side of a bare tree's limbs.

A rustle and steps easing into the clearing made him turn his head, expecting the worst. But it was Harlan, his white teeth showing in a smile. Over one shoulder he carried the haunch of a deer, and under the other arm he had a rolled up skin.

He hadn't noticed this before, but Harlan had a cavalryman's stride. Mick had known a few cavalry men who had gone on to cowpunching and not left that characteristic behind. Part of it was the upright bearing, the sense of a sailor off his ship and uncertain on dry land, and a composite of alertness and calm that Mick was hard pressed to describe but could sense every time he came across it. He scoured the dark woods around them, then asked Harlan: "You sure it's safe to have a fire out here, and to be shooting?"

"Wasn't the deer I killed. Was the ones carrying it. Got a nice hide, too."

"Were they Comanches?"

"Don' know. Never rightly got onto tellin' 'em apart. We

was told to shoot 'em, and that's what we done."

Mick lay there, watching Harlan start the meat cooking.

"Got meat this way befo'," Harlan said, after setting the sticks, holding strips of dark flesh, the way he wanted them around the fire. "Was 'way up on some plains, where the Injuns we fought started calling us buffalo sodjers. Turns out some o' them thought we was spirits o' the buffalo killed, was why our faces was so dark. That we was there to punish them, somehows. One night we hears crying, loud shouts, not like the war cries, but close. Our watch rushes over and finds piles o' meat on a buffalo robe, eagle feathers, some beaded moccasins. We don' know what to think. One o' the officers . . . all them mens is white . . . says it's a offering. They's trying to make peace with our dark buffalo spirits."

Once the meat was cooking and he'd placed a pan under the biggest piece of it to gather what little fat might drip, Harlan unrolled the deerskin. He hung it to stretch between a limb and two tent pegs he drove into the ground with the butt end of his pistol. Then he took out his side knife and began to scrape the fur off the hide.

"Were you Ninth or Tenth Cavalry?" Mick asked.

"Ninth. Signed on down Greenville, Louisiana way, though I'm a Mississippi boy. Had a disagreement there that consequented in me movin' West." His glance at Mick contained something that could well have been a quick wink.

"Oh?"

"Was a white preacher, name o' Billy Bob Thatcher. He had long white hair and a booming voice we could hear all the way from their church . . . the white church . . . and, oh, them ladies went fo' him. Oh, my, they did. He went fo' them, too, on the sly. Only one was a eleven-year-old girl . . . white girl . . . and she started to swell. Ol' Billy Bob, he rose up, pointed a finger at Jazwell, older brother o' mine who was owned by different folks from me. 'Course the crowd would 'a' waited, they'd 'a' seen that little baby was gonna pop outta there white. But they didn't wanna wait, and there was Preacher Billy Bob a-pointin' that finger. Crowd got ahold o' Jazwell and some big son, white fella name o' Lucas Bradley, pulls me outta where I was hidin' and drags me along, makes me watch.

"He was strong, was Jazwell, and had the neck of a bull. He didn't die right way, just hung there, kickin'. That Lucas hands me his cuttin' knife, wants me to cut off Jazwell's parts, what they thought'd done it. I wrassled with them a bit, but wouldn't do it. So, Lucas, he does it fo' me. He throws those off inter the woods. I can't barely look to where Jazwell's bleedin' down his legs."

Harlan's voice had begun to get scratchy as he talked, but he kept going. "Ol' rope couldn't kill Jazwell. He still weren't dead, even bleedin' like he was. So they threw some lamp oil on him. Lucas gave me a sulphur match and says fo' me to light him up. First, I wouldn't do it. But then Jazwell's screaming at me . . . 'Do it, Harlan. Do it.' So I . . . did. I did it. He screamed and screamed, until he stopped. He were dead then. I wanted to bury him, but they wasn't havin' none o' that, and started lookin' at me, like my neck might need a stretch, so I left outta there. Wasn't no time to be 'round crazy white folks when they all lathered up that way, and Billy Bob there amongst them, leading them on, and him bein' the one that done that awful thing to the girl. I knowed that."

"What . . . what did you do?" Mick asked, watching the knife blade peel loose the stiff hollow deer hairs and softer base hair that fluttered to a growing pile beneath the hide.

"I was young then, and merciful, probably done kilt that preacher quicker'n he deserved. I had to do Lucas Bradley first, needed his gun. Put a kitchen knife clean through his gizzards, twisted some. When he were dead, I took his gun, and I went to see that preacher. Broke in at night, shot him as he sat up in bed. I look enough like Jazwell that I hope that preacher man thought I was a ghost, or some such. I had to light out after that, 'course."

There wasn't much Mick could say to that, so he said: "What are you going to do with that hide?"

"Gonna make you somethin' we can wrap 'round you. Hold your gizzards and them ribs still so's you can ride. You is anxious to ride, isn't you?"

"Very much."

"Ain't much fat in deer meat, but might get enough to soften this hide a bit, maybe work on your boot a lick, too. Found one of them boots yonder, 'most washed down to the stream it was. Something had nibbled on one end, and a whole passel of scorpions had taken up in it. But a bit o' tallow should make it fit to wear once'd it's dried a bit. Be nice to have two of them, but you can't be too wishy. Wished I could 'a' killed a young bear or boar . . . get plenty o' tallow then."

"I've been thinking, Harlan. Much as I could use you along, I've got no right asking you to go with me, to do what it is I think I've got to do."

"Oh, you won' get rid o' Harlan easy as that. No. 'Sides, you don' have no ride. I done found one o' you boots, and you got clothes, though they ain't much. Only one other thing you need." He stood and went over to his saddle, dug in one of the saddlebags, found what he wanted, and came back holding a gun wrapped in its holster and belt. It was a Colt Peacemaker. Someone had taken a knife and cut crosshatches across the smooth rosewood grips. When Mick slid it out of the oiled holster, he could feel three small notches on the grip where his fingers wrapped.

"I can't take this from you, Harlan."

"You goin' to kill those mens by bitin' them with you teeth?"

"I'll have to owe you."

"Don' you worry none. Man owned that ain't gonna need it no mo'. 'Sides, that man had a gun on me, and I knows he's no shy one 'bout usin' bullets. You saved my life. *My life.* How much you think that's worth to me. Powerful lot, I'd say. Least a gun's worth. You might want to practice up a bit, 'course."

"I worry that if I tangle you up in this, you won't be able to settle down, peaceful like, should you choose."

"Won' happen anyways," Harlan said. "Not here." He turned the meat on the sticks, checked his pan for drippings, and went back and took up the knife to finish scraping the hair off the hide. "Ain' no future for no colored mans out here." His voice was wistful, sadder than it had been. "When we was bein' trained down there in San Antonio, we was treated awful . . . bad meat, stale bread, cold water 'stead o' hot . . . kicked and yelled at. Officers was all white. We had no say. Had us a little mut'ny, we did. They put it down, said they might could send us right back to the cotton patches. 'Stead, they brung us out here and turned us loose. Turns out, we're just crazy good at killin' Injuns. But, friend o' mine, Samuel, mustered out befo' me, went to settle down there on some land not far from the fort. But he was burnt out in three weeks. Medal of Honor winner, too. Got one my own self, but hocked it to buy ammo. Ain't no never mind to me. Was a time Menard County was mostly colored folks, like me. But soon's we run them Injuns 'most off it, the white mens figured they could run us off, too. One at a time, they could, and did. Kilt Samuel when he kicked up a fuss. Would 'a' kilt me, too, if I wanted land, or anything they wanted. Just wanted to find me a mine, buy one a those maps, move far 'way as a rich colored man. Maybe then I could get folks to leave be."

"Those maps are no good, Harlan," Mick told him. "Pattie was just shucking folks with those. None of those lead anywhere."

"Guess I should 'a' knowed that."

"But I do know where the mine is," Mick said. "You help me get Syd out of trouble, and you can have it . . . the whole mine, and all the silver in it. I don't care if it goes to the center of the earth."

Harlan lowered the knife and bowed his head.

"What?" Mick said.

"I's gonna he'p you 'cause it's the right thing to do. I owe a life. You don' have to buy my he'p."

"I'm not. I'm rewarding you. This isn't going to be easy, hauling a crippled-up fella like me around and taking on some real hardcases. I want us to be together on this. OK?"

"Sho nuff." Harlan's head lifted, and he smiled. "One thing you should know. I ain't goin' just 'cause I wants to. I goin' 'cause I has to. Just point me the way o' those mens and pass the ammunition. 'K, Mick? Speakin' o' which . . . got a spare box we had oughta spend on gettin' you used to that there new gun. You up to that?"

Mick was sore, but he nodded. "Help me up, Harlan."

"It hurts, you jus' think 'bout those mens done this to you, and they's got your Syd." Harlan helped Mick rise gingerly to his feet and strap on the gun.

When Syd woke, her stomach growled, but not so loud

she couldn't hear Pattie and Mytho talking softly a distance from the mound of Laney's blanket. It was still dark, but the two of them were up, and probably as hungry as she was.

"Not much use to us like this," Pattie said.

"We're rifled up enough. We leave him one?" Mytho said.

"He's got his sidearm. Like as not a rifle'd be a waste."

"And you can always sell a rifle. Right?"

"We get cornered by Indians, Rangers, or those damn' Hoodoos, and you may be glad for an extra gun."

Weasel came into the clearing from the narrow path. Syd realized there were only two horses left. One horse and the mule were gone, had already been led outside the place where once deer had slept. Then Weasel and Mytho got the last two horses, led them quietly out, while Pattie came to her, bent down, and shook her shoulder. She opened her eyes, and he was holding a finger to his lips.

She carried her blanket. Outside the cane stand, Pattie helped her roll it and tie it in place. Then he got her up behind the saddle and tied her in place again. She wanted to ask if they planned just to leave Laney. But the other men were already mounted. Weasel untied Sancho, and she came over to nudge Syd's leg, dodging a kick from Pattie, looking up at Syd with those big eyes, as if wondering why she was no longer petted. She had no way of knowing Syd's hands were tied. Syd felt bad, but she was in worse shape herself than the mule, and hungry on top of that.

With nothing but an empty stomach to keep her awake, Syd bobbed and swayed on the back of the horse, up and down some of the same hills she'd traveled with Mick, although this was quite different.

Several times they stopped, and Pattie would pump her

for information. Were they headed in the right direction? Was she sure? What landmarks made her sure?

Weasel rode off twice, and Mytho another time, looking for game, but finding none.

"Damnedest area for finding a piece of meat," Mytho said when he rode back to them one time. "Usually there's a prairie dog, a turkey, somethin'. It's like this stretch has been hunted dry."

"Not likely," Pattie said. "Though it is possible a big bunch rode through here not long ago and drove everything away or into hiding. If it's the Indians, I just hope they were going the other way. Any sign?"

"Nope. Reckon they all went north with that avenging half-breed son-bitch."

"You?" Pattie asked Weasel, who shook his head no.

It was getting dark, and the horses were as tired as the men, slipping now and then in their steps as they climbed the increasingly steep gravelly slope up to a cliff that ran higher and higher. The little mule, though, made easy work of the climb, especially with no load to carry. Halfway up the steep slope, top-heavy Mytho was the first to dismount and walk his horse, either from concern for the animal, or from a more general, although unexpressed, fear of heights. After one more switchback, Pattie dismounted, too, but he left Syd on the horse's back where she could totter and see down much farther than she would have liked. Twice they had to stop and let the horses wind. Sancho scampered over to look into holes and over the edges of cliffs, but always came back to maintain contact with Syd, who was relieved when they crested the hill onto level ground. The men mounted up again.

"Find some place we can have a fire this time," Pattie said.

Weasel looked back at him, then turned his horse and started up again.

"Man's going to talk himself to death one day," Pattie whispered back to Syd. There was more than mere respect in his tone. There was the tiniest touch of audible fear.

The horizon was a spray of vertical black and blue bars that burst red as they crested the summit of the hill. Below them, the cliff dropped 300 feet to a bed of fallen, large, jagged rocks, some of them as big as horses. Pattie nudged the horse away from the edge and followed Weasel. A short ride down the slope, a flat open spot was nestled in among a stand of trees, enough of them live oak to provide a good shelter.

"Good call, Weasel." Pattie turned to Mytho. "We camp here."

The big buffalo hunter nodded, climbed off his horse, not nearly as hampered by his wounds as Syd might have liked. When he winked at her, she looked away.

"No food," Pattie said, and he was almost gleeful about it.

Weasel had the horses staked while Sancho ran free, munching on a small clump of buffalo grass, then scampering over to Syd when she had spread her blanket and was sitting on it, not far from where Mytho was piling wood for a fire. It made no sense to her for them to risk a fire. They had no coffee and had shot no game.

Mytho got the fire going until it was as big a fire as they'd had so far in the trip. Sheltered high on a cliff side like this, Pattie must have reckoned they weren't all that visible and could see anyone coming. She didn't know how the man thought, or who he really was, for all that. All she wanted to do was lay down and be left alone, free of the sneaking looks Mythological Jim was directing her way again.

Just as the sun was slipping out of sight, Pattie looked around. He was practically grinning. "Weasel?" he said.

Mytho stepped to one side. Weasel came walking right toward Syd. She cringed back onto one elbow. Sancho, who was curled beside her, with her head resting across Syd's knees, looked up, startled, then she clambered awkwardly to her feet, started to run. Weasel drew so fast Syd missed the blur. But she heard the shot, saw Sancho tumble to the ground and lay there, blood pouring from the side of her head.

"Noooo!" Syd screamed, and buried her face in her hands.

"Now," Pattie said, "we eat."

Chapter Thirteen

"You know where they headed. Right?" Harlan drew the cinch tightly on his horse. His glance toward Mick showed one eye narrowed almost into a wink.

"Right." With nothing of his own to pack up, Mick had watched Harlan gather up his few things, realizing, too, for the first time that Harlan had been letting Mick sleep using the only blanket.

"We can cut right to it, use roads iffen we can, maybe gain some time on 'em," Harlan said.

"I don't know if time's going to matter."

Harlan sighed. "Iffen they did fo' her already, it sure 'nuff don'. You wanna do this, o' not?"

"Just get me up there." Mick stood a bit stiffly, wrapped in a corset of leather with ties that held it tightly around his chest and abdomen. He could hardly breathe, but, this way, he could move.

The sun was already an hour up by the time Harlan got Mick strapped in. Mick felt he'd spent enough time in this part of the woods. Who knew when Indians would come roaming through again. Birds were chattering in the limbs of the trees. But there was little other sign of life around them as far as Mick could see.

Harlan boosted him up behind the saddle, then awkwardly climbed on himself. "Never done it with no passenger befo'," he said.

Blue, though cavalry mount he had been, was as stable and sure as the deck of a big riverboat. The first half mile was painful. Even with Blue's methodical gait, Mick's insides jarred and ground with each step. He didn't think he could manage to ride all day. But he gritted his teeth and stood the pain until it gradually eased into a steady aching he thought he could tolerate. Although Mick said nothing, Harlan must have felt him flinch once or twice when Blue jolted down a short, rocky slope.

"You the one's in a hurry 'bout her, couldn' wait to mend first," Harlan reminded.

"I'm fine. We keep going," Mick said between his teeth.

Riding behind Harlan, not having to think over what path to take, was different, as was the feel of the gun belt around him, the weight of the pistol at his side. In too many ways to consider, he felt like he had woke up to find he was another person. It was all too strange, so he focused on the progress they were making.

A couple of times Harlan stopped to examine sign, or wait until a faraway shadow in the trees moved into the light and showed itself. Mick almost welcomed stopping, but wanted to press ahead at the same time. His breathing was more regular now that they'd ridden a while, and the steady ache in his tightly bound chest was just a reminder he owed someone.

They didn't stop at noon, and had ridden at Blue's steady cavalry pace as often as they could, although the frequent ups and downs of hills, even getting to the passes between higher hills, slowed them at times. When they finally did come to a rutted dirt road, Harlan reined in Blue and they sat behind a thick chaparral of mesquite, cactus, and black locust to listen.

Far ahead up the road Mick could hear faint popping sounds. "Guns?"

"Sound like it. Don' wanna go that-a-way."

Harlan twitched the reins and nudged Blue back into the woods. Where they could, he gave the horse his head, and Blue broke into a mile-consuming trot. But there were hills and streams. Mick felt himself covered with sweat from the tight wrap and the constant jarring, but he didn't suggest they slow or stop.

Blue's hoofs were slipping on loose stone going up a hill when Harlan pulled the horse to a stop, even though they were still at an angle.

Mick leaned out, saw the man standing there with a rifle across his knee. Black, like boot polish, was in a ring around the outside of his face, as if it had been darkened once, but wiped partially clear with a handkerchief. In the quiet, the man yelled out: "Lucas, come here and see what I have found! A two-headed horse rider with one head's a nigger. I believe he's ridin' our missin' horse."

The other man stepped from behind a tree, grinning in spite of having far fewer than the normal number of teeth. His teeth weren't white, but, just the same, they stood out against the black painted onto his face. His hand was on the pistol at his waist.

"Got papers fo' this hoss. It's mine. Fo'mer cavalry hoss. You can check its brand. Can't be you hoss." Harlan's voice was calm, but Mick could feel his sitting straighter in the saddle, ready. "You men'd best step out the way. You's imp-eden a rescue."

"Nope," said the one with the rifle. "That's our horse, and I sure ain't gonna argue with no darkie 'bout that."

"Figure you mens was in that ruckus yonder," Harlan

said. "That don' have no never mind to do with us. All we want is past."

"I'm sayin' you have our horse, nig." Mick heard the hammer of the man's cap-and-ball rifle pull back and click at the ready.

Harlan sighed, but, out of the side of his mouth, he whispered to Mick: "That iron on you hip. You got any problem usin' it?"

Mick drew the gun from its holster, held it behind Harlan's back, and drew back the hammer in a series of clicks.

"That there's music to my ears, Mick," Harlan whispered. "Get ready. He's gonna. . . ."

Mick leaned out to his left so Harlan could have his right side free, and saw the man lift the rifle to his shoulder. Mick fired. The recoil of the pistol was more than he'd counted on. All of his practice shooting with Harlan had been on firm ground with Harlan holding him upright. It hadn't been off balance, on the back of a horse. The shot snapped his whole forearm back, and he swung to one side, almost falling from his place behind the saddle. He over-compensated in swinging back and began to slide, then he fell as he heard a shot, then another. Hitting the ground was like getting punched hard by Mythological Jim again. He knew he hadn't been shot, but it hurt as much as if he had. He felt his eyes water. He lay there, like some knight in armor unable to lift himself up. Blue had a big eye turned back to look at him. Harlan dismounted and came around to help Mick up to his feet, slowly, in stages.

Mick swayed for a second and felt his chest throbbing.

"Gun's got some kick to 'er," Harlan commented. "Is why someone's cross-hatched them grips. You OK?"

Mick nodded. He would know about the recoil on

horseback next time. Now that he was upright, he could see the man with few teeth lay back against the slope, with a hole in his forehead. Mick had hit the other man with the rifle in the throat with his shot, and Harlan had finished him off.

"Don' like to shop this way," Harlan said, "but I 'spect we got you a pair o' boots and a new horse, besides." He walked over to the man Mick had shot first. "This 'bout you size?"

"I don't know."

"You wanna keep goin' half barefoots? Otherwise, try these on. Man ain' gonna need 'em no mo'." Harlan tugged off the boots and tossed them to Mick. He went through the pockets of both men while Mick looked away. He was relieved that there seemed to be little on the men worth taking. Their guns were of oldest Civil War vintage.

When Harlan saw Mick frowning, he said: "Figured to bushwhack us, theys did. Only fair we get pickin's."

Mick pulled on the boots, and they did fit, would fit even better should he ever get a pair of socks again.

"You notice somefin funny 'bout the faces o' them mens?" Harlan asked.

"You think they might be a couple of those Hoodoos in that feud over cattle?"

"Heard both sides was hirin' on guns. Gave thought to workin' fo' one side o' t'other. But couldn' cotton much to neither set," Harlan explained, then walked Blue up the hill, Mick following, moving stiffly now that he was back on the ground.

At the top of the hill, they found a sorrel horse, with a white blaze on his face, tied to the base of a young live oak tree. The other horse, a dusty gray mare, lay on her side a few feet away, dead.

"Looks like the mare got lamed in that shootin'. They had to put 'er down."

The two bushwhackers had already pulled the saddle from the dead horse. Harlan bent down and went through the scattered gear, took a blanket and canteen, left everything else. The saddle was better than the one on the sorrel, so they traded it out. As much as Mick felt low about pawing through the dead men's things, he opened the saddlebags and went through them. He found a clean shirt he could use, and Harlan walked back down the hill and came back in a few minutes with a belt. "Might hold them pants up better'n nothin'," he said.

There were caps, powder, and balls in the saddlebags. Like the guns, they weren't worth taking, although leaving them meant they might be found by Comanches. Still, he wanted to lighten the load, so he took them out.

As soon as he had everything he could use, Mick swung himself into the saddle with help from Harlan. They rode off, with Mick's nameless sorrel not only keeping up with Blue, but surging ahead half the time. The horse was competitive. Each time Blue would get into the lead, he would push into a faster pace to regain the lead.

"Believe you oughta name that there horse Blaze. He do like to move," Harlan observed, grinning as he prodded Blue to keep up.

That's how, later in the afternoon, Mick happened to be in the lead when they came across a trail. He knew Biscuit's prints as well as Syd's horse. They were both among the clutter of prints headed in the right direction. The little mule's prints were there, too. Mick gave his horse both heels and they followed along the trail.

As the light grew dimmer, the hoof prints seemed easier to follow. The sun hung off the far horizon like a red orange ball, while from the southeast thick bruised clouds were beginning to spread across the sky.

Mick was first to come to the stand of sumac and cane. The prints went in and came back out along the line of the cliff face next to the thick growth.

"Give me a hand off this horse, if you would, Harlan."

Harlan dismounted and helped Mick do the same. He looped the reins of both horses around a sumac limb in a loose knot. "What you think you gonna find back yonder?"

"Maybe just an old campsite. But might be I can learn something from it . . . about Syd."

Harlan held a finger to his lips. He had his gun drawn, so Mick did the same, and they eased back along the tracks. Mick was stopped when Harlan put the flat of one hand on Mick's chest. Then Harlan stepped to the side, careful not to make a sound. Mick saw the blanket wrapped around the lump of a person against the cliff wall. The first thing he thought was that they'd raped Syd, killed her, and left her here, like this. He forced himself forward and lowered to his knees, which wasn't easy with the constricting leather corset he wore. With his gun in his right hand, he reached with his left and started to pull the blanket back. The person under it rolled to his back and tried to lift his gun. At the same time, they recognized each other.

"Hodges! What the devil are you doing here?" But, as he asked the question, Mick could see the bandages made from torn clothes that stuck through the bloody holes on Hodges's side and arm.

"You're a sore sight for eyes," Laney said, trying to grin, but accomplishing something closer to a rictus. He had tried to lift his gun, but no longer had the strength to do it. He looked down to the half limp hand that could barely hold the gun. "Could get it up, I'd have done for myself a while back, before some wolf did for me." He laughed at himself, let his head plop back onto the blanket, and the hand, too. His fingers fell open from around the pistol.

Mick's eyes were drawn to Laney's left hand, the missing end to the middle finger. Before, it had made the cowhand seem human, vulnerable. Now Laney's wan, thin whiskered face, bloodshot eyes, cracked lips, and limp hands added to that sense. Mick glanced around. They hadn't even left him a rifle. He said: "You still have some of the ingredients for that tea, don't you, Harlan? Maybe you can make up a pot of it while I find some plants to treat these wounds. They've just wrapped them up and left 'em to fester." When he looked up, Harlan's head tilted an inch to the right.

"This 'ere man left you tied up out there in the woods to die," he said. "How can you he'p him?"

"I'm helping him because he needs help."

Harlan shook his head. His half smile said he wondered if Mick had what it took to make it out in these parts.

"I'd like to hear what he has to say about Syd, too," Mick added.

That Harlan could understand. He headed back to where they'd tied the horses to get his pot and the red willow bark and other herbs.

The sky was darker and the tea going well by the time Mick returned with what medicinal plants he was able to gather. But it was the pair of turkeys he carried by the legs that caught Harlan's eye.

"I din' hear no shots," Harlan stated.

"I scared them to death. Just told them you were along and they fell right off the roost." He dropped the birds by the fire and went to Laney.

Harlan started pulling feathers and preparing the birds

211

for cooking, saying: "Good rock throwin'. Might be you don' need no gun."

"Didn't want to risk the noise. Can I use your pan to mix up some medicine?"

Harlan laughed and nodded. The moon was no longer full, had a bite out of one side. Clouds crossed it and obscured it more often than not, but Harlan was able to work by the light of the fire. "Beats me how you found them plants in this dark. You mus' see like a hoot owl."

Mick was squatting awkwardly by Laney, had him sitting upright with his back to the rock while he took off his shirt. Then he began to peel off the torn cloth that had been used to bandage him. "First thing to do is to clean these wounds," he explained. "Then put something on them that'll help. I couldn't find everything I wanted, but I did get enough to make do."

Laney blinked, too weak to do more than watch in a half-disinterested way. He stared at Harlan, and whispered to Mick: "Is that man colored?"

"I heard that, Mister Cow Mans," Harlan said. "You want me to make you any broth, you keep a civil tongue in you head."

The burned flesh from the use of the branding iron was stuck to the cloth of the bandages, and Mick had to soak them with water before peeling them off completely. He applied some of the salve he had made, and tied on the leaves. The bullet hole through Laney's side hadn't torn any organs, but with the blood he'd lost, the shock of the cure for the arrow wound, as well as all of the riding, he was done in. Once Mick had cleaned out the wounds and bound them again, using herbs to help the healing, Laney looked more alert than before. Mick got out the shirt he'd gotten earlier in the day and wrestled Laney into it over the fresh dressings. Then he was given the cup of tea Harlan had made for him. Later he had a cup of broth and even chewed on one of the turkey legs.

While Harlan and Mick were spreading their blankets by the fire that had begun to burn down, Laney cleared his throat and said: "Mick, you've treated me right better than I deserve."

Harlan let out a snap of air, a puff of hard breath that was close to being a snort.

"I'm . . . I'm sorry," Laney continued. "I shouldn't have done what I did . . . stood by and let them do all they did to you. I mean it, and it shouldn't happen again."

Harlan looked away.

"Did you do anything to her?" Mick asked.

"No. Nor anyone else. I was hit by a Kiowa arrow straightaway, and a Hoodoo bullet later. That little mule of Pattie's, he wouldn't let no one near her. Wished you could 'a' seen that bronco mule kickin' up its heels and chasin' that tall drink Mytho 'round the fire. He'd sooner go near a wildcat than mess with that mule. Long as that mule's with them, she'll be OK."

Mick breathed easier for the first time. "You'd better get as much rest as you can. We'll be riding early."

"You're not gonna leave me out here?"

"Of course not," Mick said.

Harlan let out another snap of air, but the fire was so low Mick couldn't see him. That didn't matter. He had hope for the first time in a while, and that's what let him close his eyes at last.

The fire was dying down, but every once in a while fat would drip from one of the ribs held over the fire's edge and flames would shoot up and the smell of cooking meat would sweep over to where Syd lay curled on her blanket. She had refused to eat, could never eat poor little Sancho.

Mytho got up and took another of the ribs. He carried it back to a log where he sat. "You don't know what you're missing. This's one tasty little mule, don't you know." He winked at Syd, letting her know he was glad to be rid of her guardian. He no longer visibly favored the shoulder where he'd been shot, although the spot on his shirt was encrusted with dried blood. Buffalo hunters are made of tough material.

Weasel came into the open area around the fire. He'd been taking a look around. He lowered himself to his blanket, reached for the cooling cup of coffee he'd left there.

Pattie didn't need to ask if he'd seen anything. Instead, he said to Mythological Jim: "Yours is first watch tonight."

"That suits me just fine. Just fine, indeed," he said, staring at Syd over the rib he was gnawing. Grease ran down onto his beard and beads of it sparkled in the light from the fire. The sparkles matched the ones in his eyes.

Syd looked up. The full moon had a bite out of it, then was swallowed by the cloud cover that swept across the sky and darkened everything. *Good.*

Before they settled in for the night, Weasel made one last scout, and brought back more wood for the fire. He'd seen no one. The evening was getting cooler. The men pulled their blankets closer to the fire.

Syd lay there thinking back over every step they'd made to the top of the cliff. The clouds had massed to make the sky as black as it could get. There were no stars to watch as she lay there, her hands still bound. After a while she could hear the steady breathing of Pattie and Weasel beneath the lumps of their blankets. The air wasn't cool enough for her to be able to see her breath, but it approached being nippy. She heard the *thump* and *crackle* of Mytho dropping another log on the fire. There was the *ting* of metal pot lip against the rim of his cup as he poured himself more of the coffee. When she could, she eased back the blanket and looked his way. He was staring at her. He'd sip from his cup, glance at the blanket-covered lumps that were Pattie and Weasel, then go back to staring at her. It was only a matter of time.

The wind had picked up, rustling dead leaves along the ground and adding to the crackle of the fire's noise. That was good, too. Carefully Syd made sure her blanket was only lightly covering her, and flexed her legs and wrists without moving the blanket. When Mytho lifted his cup high to drain the last bit out of it, she jumped to her feet and ran to the fire that burned with intensity as drops of animal fat dripped onto it. He was lowering his cup when he saw her, and she threw the whole coffee pot at him as he dropped his cup and started to get to his feet. The lid flew off and coffee sprayed across his chest and face. She didn't know if any of the coffee got through the thick beard to his neck, but it was hot enough to make him yell. She had already turned and, with her tied hands, grabbed a limb from the fire as big around as her wrist, a fire at one end like a torch. She took off running.

She could hear him yelling, then just the sound of his pounding footsteps increasing as his long legs followed the weaving trail of trees and low brush. Syd put everything she had into the sprint, and was gulping for air by the time she came to the cliff's edge. Clumsily she threw the torch high out into the air and dodged left just as the hammering feet whooshed down the trail and past her.

His scream started as soon as he was in the air and there was no longer ground beneath him. It faded as he fell the

300 feet, before hitting bottom. There was no screaming then.

Syd stood still, breathing hard, trying to catch her breath. She knew she had to move, but make no noise doing so. She eased along the edge of the cliff, moving from tree to tree, hearing the rustle behind her that told her someone was running hard along the same trail. Maybe she would be lucky and they would run off the cliff, too. As the sound got closer, she ducked down behind a fallen log, crouching there, working at getting her wrists free, but having no more luck than before.

"Jim. Where are you? Sing out."

Behind the log, she listened to Pattie thrash around near to where Mytho had gone off the cliff. Then, finally, it was quiet. She waited for what seemed forever until all was quiet in the woods. She heard his steps heading back along the trail toward the campsite. She waited a while longer. The woods settled back into its night sounds, and far away she heard a coyote's howl. Her breathing still came in short, nervous rasps. Slowly she stood, turned, and ran almost straight into the chest of Weasel. He held a knife in one hand and grabbed her by the hair with the other.

Chapter Fourteen

Mick woke and felt like a dry old board that had been secured in place with rusty nails. The sky was still dark, barely beginning to turn gray. The night had been one of the coolest they had had yet. Harlan had gotten up once, that Mick knew of, to gather more firewood. Still he was already up and putting the pot on the fire.

"Harlan."

"What?" He came over and bent down.

"Give me a hand getting up here. I've stiffened up on myself."

"Don' do to brag none, son," he said, and helped Mick sit up.

The leather corset Mick had worn lay beside his blanket, and Harlan helped him into it, although he didn't pull all the ties tight yet. With the binding on, Mick was able to stagger out to the canes, answer the call of nature, and return, where he found Harlan filling their cups.

"Coffee don' taste right," Harlan commented, "all that bark and stuff bein' used in this here pot."

"We ever get near a town I'll buy you a new pot," Mick promised, "if I get some money."

"Iffen we had us some ham, we could have ham and eggs, iffen we had us some eggs," Harlan said, and grinned. He cut a couple strips of meat off one of the cold turkey breasts, and handed one to Mick.

Mick sipped at his coffee. It did taste a bit odd, but was probably good for him

"You sure you wanna do this?" Harlan asked.

"Do what?"

"Take that bag garbage 'long." He nodded toward the lump under Laney's blanket.

"Harlan, everyone deserves a chance."

"Man treats you way theys did you? Don' know, Mick. What's the Injun side of you say? Don' it wanna take the warpath?"

Mick hesitated, looked up at the sky, where the pale gray to the east was taking on some color—white, yellow, even a spray or two of pink. "There must be some middle path," he answered finally. "I get Syd out of this, maybe I can find it. What about you?"

"Don' know what's gonna happen to me. Don' seem to be no place in this here world fo' the likes o' me. I may be past my time, or my time's not come. Man like me's had the fire in his belly this a way has no chance. Ever' man I shoot looks like the ones killed Jazwell to me. I don' knows iffen I can ever shake the mean out."

Laney stirred, and the two of them quit talking. In a minute Laney struggled to sit upright, managing on his own. He ran rough fingers through his hair, then across his grizzled chin, and looked at them. "I believe I could go for a beefsteak, a drink of corn licker, and a loose woman. . . . .hell, a tight one would do." He realized what he'd said, that Mick was right there, so he hurried to add: "As is, a bit of turkey and some of that coffee'd have me obliged to you both."

"You seem a mite better," Harlan observed.

"Don't know what's in that medicine Mick put on me

and in me, but I do feel less rocky than I have." He pushed himself out of his blanket, managed to get to his feet by holding to the rock wall behind him. He took uncertain steps off through the cane, and was back in a few minutes, rubbing his chin. "Could stand some cleaning up."

Mick recalled a distant time he had wanted to be as stubbly and manly as Laney. That, too, seemed ages ago. The cowhand dug around in the saddlebags that had been left, came up with a cup. Mick poured while Hodges held his cup out. Up close, his face was still sallow, and his eyes were rimmed with red.

"They'd taken time to patch you up right, you would've been fit to ride same's them," Harlan said.

"I didn't catch your name before," Laney said, and raised his cup.

"It's Harlan," Mick said before Harlan could. Laney looked at Harlan, and he was unblinking and as near like his former self as Mick could recall.

"I owe you, Harlan," Laney said. "I won't forget that."

When the camp was packed and they were ready to ride, Harlan had to help first Mick and then Hodges up onto Blaze. He swung himself up onto Blue, and the trio was off. Mick and Laney made an odd enough pair, beat up as they both were. But if Blaze minded the extra weight, he sure didn't show it. Instead, his competitive streak came out at once, not wanting Blue to get ahead.

With Blue in full cavalry pace, keeping up, and Blaze galloping, his breath coming out in white puffs, they made good time, exceptional time.

When they came to a stream, Mick and Harlan pulled in the horses and let them drink.

"How're you doing back there?" Mick asked Laney.

"Still puny in spots, but game for the distance. Wouldn't

mind coming across that Pattie myself."

Mick didn't say anything. Harlan's eyes narrowed; for him, the jury was still out on Laney.

"You ever hear of Kiowa arrows being poisoned?" Laney asked.

"I've heard of arrows being poisoned," Mick responded. "Indians who're mad enough do it. Some even roll the arrow tips in dung . . . kind of a slow poison."

"These weren't wearing any paint. Only Kiowa I ever killed before had yellow and red spots on his face, same as on this one's shield."

"Was their hair chopped short?" Mick said.

"Yeah."

"Probably in mourning. That'd explain no war paint. Yeah, I'd say they were grieving."

"Sounds like the same path to me," Laney said. "I'd have steered us onto rock if I'd had the time. Those unshod horses can't take too much of that, especially if hard riding's involved. But there wasn't time before they were on us. They have a tomahawk society or anything?"

"Their warrior society is called *Kaitsenko*. But that wouldn't mean anything if they were stirred up."

"There was a village . . . women and children killed. Didn't you see it back there?"

"We took another way," Mick explained, "tried to cut ahead, but some of this feuding over cattle kept us from heading on that way."

"Wouldn't mind seeing some of those Hoodoos, either," Laney mused.

"You can't begrudge them this. They furnished the horse we're riding . . . thanks to Harlan being handy with a gun."

Mick couldn't see Laney's expression, but he could feel

him turn toward Harlan, saying again: "I said I owe you, and I mean it."

"See 'bout that," Harlan said as he put his canteen back in place and kicked Blue into moving across the stream.

Blaze rushed to follow and take over the lead. Mick watched the trees whiz by. At this rate, they very well might catch up to Pattie and the others. His insides ached as he was jostled, reminding him of one of the reasons for wanting to meet up with Pattie and his men again.

Syd was tied behind Pattie's saddle. Her legs were secured tightly to the horse's sides by a thong running underneath the horse and tied to her boots. They were taking no more chances, and even her trips to the woods had been made more protected and difficult.

When Pattie had stopped by a stream, a mile or two back, and dismounted, he had glared at her the way he'd glared at Sancho after the mule had lost her packs and he'd had her killed. Weasel didn't look at her any more at all, and somehow that was much worse.

She knew this. If she showed them the mine, she would be buried near it. Yet, whenever Pattie asked, she still steered him in the right direction. What would happen if she steered them another way, closer to a town, where she might escape? Then Mick wouldn't be able to find her. But, no, Mick was dead, as dead as any hope she had had.

Pattie asked now: "To the right?"

"No, more to the left," she lied.

"Are you sure?"

"We can go right, if you like."

He turned his horse and started off in the wrong direction. But she knew this couldn't last long.

★ ★ ★ ★ ★

In was just afternoon when the trio came out on the lip
of a hill and looked down at least a mile away on a two-
story, stone house with wooden outbuildings—kitchen on
the back end of the house, barn, shed, and top to a root
cellar. A handful of horses were in the corral along the barn.
It reminded Mick of the McLaren spread. But he'd seen a
Rocking R brand on one or two of the cattle they'd passed,
roaming loose through the woods.

To their left a row of rocks that looked like an abandoned stone fence, but wasn't, ran across the edge of the
higher hill. It wouldn't have surprised him to see a Comanche head poke up over the top. This close to the house,
though, that was less likely.

Harlan gave a nod. "Best take a long ways 'round."

"Man, look at that, Mick!" Laney exclaimed. "Wouldn't
you like a spread like that someday?"

"There's a bit of work to it," Mick responded. "It's not
all rake it in."

"Still and all," Laney said.

"We's coming in," Harlan said. "I see all them trees
chewed up 'bout so high so's you could ride through real
nice, and see a ways, an' I knows we's in the thick o' cattle
country."

"Weren't the cow poking days just about the best,
Mick?" Laney said.

"Maybe he didn't poke so many's you," Harlan suggested.

There was a rustle behind them, and Mick turned his
head with difficulty. Harlan had a gun drawn and pointed
so fast it drew a low whistle from Laney, but it was only a
brindle old steer with long wide white horns with black tips
lumbering through the low brush with cows and a few
calves following.

"Calf wouldn't be missed much," Laney commented.

"We'll go hungry before we poach anyone's cattle," Mick said.

"I wasn't talking about plugging anyone's steer. Just maybe a little unbranded calf."

"That make it less wrong?" Mick asked.

"I thought so." Laney had no guile in his voice.

"Well, I think it's as bad," Mick said.

"Didn't you say once you grew up in a whorehouse, Mick?" Laney said. "You telling me you never once sawed you off a free ride?"

"No. Those gals, whatever brought them to their lives, were like sisters to me."

"You kidding?" Laney said.

"Not even once'd?" Harlan asked.

"No." Mick was adamant.

"None of them, even offered?" Laney persisted.

"Well, sure they did."

"You still said no?"

"That's right."

Something more seemed to be rolling around on Laney's tongue. Maybe it was about the way Mick felt about Syd, what attracted him to her, her being a Mexican and all. Whatever it was, he kept what was gnawing at him to himself.

Harlan gave Blue a nudge, and they rode along, out of sight of the house. Far off, a dog was barking. The wind began to pick up in the high leaves of the live oaks.

As they rode, Blaze pulled farther into the lead. Laney leaned closer as they were going up a hill and said: "You know, Mick, you treat that Harlan 'most as if he was the same as us."

Mick couldn't look back, but he said: "To me, he is."

Laney muttered something, and Mick believed he caught: "Seems like bein' 'round whores too much has addled you a mite."

It was the middle of the afternoon before they came to a stream. Blaze had kept his lead, and Mick pulled up to wait on Blue and Harlan. He heard a rattling whir and looked down to his left. When the horse didn't stir, he looked closer, finally seeing a large grasshopper, settling in at the bottom of a stand of prickly pear cactus loaded with dark purple ends. Harlan pulled up, just as a rattle sounded on the other side of Mick. This time, Blaze danced back, almost knocking into Blue, who was doing a more sedate shuffle away. A rattler, a good four feet long, was coiled up against a flat pile of rocks like a stack of dinner plates. Its pattern was dark, with a darker than usual head, something Mick had seen in a few other rattlers, although there seemed to be no hard rule about which ones were most feisty. This one was ready to strike, though.

"You sure you don' wanna cozy it and take it 'long," Harlan said, his big grin in place.

"You going to shoot it?" Mick asked, having a hard time keeping Blaze from taking off. Behind him, Laney drew and fired. The snake's head disappeared. Blaze settled down right away.

With the snake dead, Harlan led Blue to the water and let him drink. He got down and filled his own canteen, upriver from where the horse was drinking. He kept stealing glances at Mick, and finally said: "Thought you was raised by them Cheyennes."

"I was," Mick answered. "After that by my Aunt Ruth, who just happened to run a house. It wasn't as bad as you might think."

"Bad?" Harlan said.

"When it wasn't a business night, there were social times. Sundays we'd have fried chicken, then sit and talk. Some of the ladies knew some good stories."

"I'll bet," Laney said.

"Racy talk wasn't allowed at table," Mick explained. "Everyone had to be on their manners."

"This Uncle Bill o' yours you huntin'," Harlan continued. "He live in that house?"

"All that came after he'd cut out."

"It would've brought me home," Laney said. "All that opportunity right in your own house."

"I'm telling you, that's not how it worked," Mick insisted.

"You's with all them womens all day long, profess'nal womens, and not once'd?" Harlan said, still not able to believe it.

"Don't know what he's missing, does he?" Laney said.

Mick started to dismount, but when Harlan saw him struggling in the tight harness, he waved him back and came for the canteens.

"Well it sho' 'nuff gonna give you somefin' fine to find out someday," he chuckled.

"This Uncle Bill of yours," Laney said. "He's the one you said you come to Texas hopin' to come across, right?"

"Yeah."

"You know what he looks like?"

"There was a daguerreotype of him hanging in Aunt Ruth's office once. But he took that with him."

"Like to look at hisself, you think?" Harlan said.

Laney asked: "How you gonna know him should you come across him? How you gonna recognize him?"

"I just hope I'll be able to," Mick said.

"And you think you'll find him?" Laney said.

225

That's just it, Mick thought. *If I already have, can I kill him if it comes to that?*

"I've been over and back through this part of Texas so often I have a pretty good handle on it," Pattie was saying, pulling on the horse's reins. "We seem to be getting nearer to town than I would like."

They had just come to a wide-open stretch of buffalo grass that rolled down from a high hill on the right and swept across the hills two miles distant. Out on the far side of the grass were a few black dots, probably small clumps of the buffalo that were no longer migrating north since there were so few of them.

Weasel pulled his horse up short, where the brush was thickest, next to a clump of live oak. His head was cocked just the tiniest bit, Syd observed, but she couldn't see or hear anything.

"What I'm saying, young lady," Pattie went on, "is that you had best not be steering me wrong here. Do you understand?" Although his stiff back was to her, she didn't have to see his face to feel the menace in his tone. "Another reason I bring this up is that all the stories of the old San Saba Mine tell of a break in the soil, where the yellow dirt turns red for a stretch. It's such an important part of the story that I don't put that on none of those maps I sell. The way ahead has none of that. Am I being clear?"

Weasel suddenly stepped high in one stirrup and dismounted. He pulled his horse close to the thicket and waved for Pattie to do the same.

Pattie got down, pulled his knife, and cut the thongs that held Syd's wrists to the back of the saddle and ducked low to cut the leather that bound her legs under the horse. Then he grabbed her sleeve and yanked her off the horse, stepping aside as she smashed to the hard ground. He dragged her with one rough hand while leading the horse over to stand snugged next to Biscuit against the thickest of the brush.

Her shoulder hurt from where she'd fallen, and Pattie's hand pinched her upper arm. Before she could say anything, he let go and she dropped flat to the ground. He put a boot on the middle of her back to hold her down. She looked up at him, caught the finger he held to his lips, then lay painfully still while the two of them peered over the top of the brush. As soon as Pattie's head was turned, she saw the flat, reddish, broken end of a sharp-edged flint spear point laying on the ground inches away from her fingertips. Then she heard the low thunder in her left ear that was nearest the ground. Horses' hoofs. Quite a few of them, and they were riding hard.

Pattie lifted his foot off her and moved closer to Weasel. Syd's bound hands darted for the bit spear point, but Pattie's head snapped back to her. She froze.

"White hats. Did you see them?" Pattie whispered to Weasel while staring at her. "Damned Frontier Battalion we've been hearing about. They're riding fast and hard toward something."

Syd waited. The pounding in her ear peaked, then began to fade. Finally all she could hear was the wind rustling the tops of the bushes. Weasel eased up and looked across the wide open grassy area. Pattie was still glaring at her. He suddenly lunged and crouched over her, grabbed her by her shirt just below the collar. He twisted her until she was sitting upright, and his piercing eyes were boring into her. The spear point lay on the ground.

"You steered us wrong, didn't you? Damn' near took us into that passel of Rangers." He shook her until her head snapped back and forth.

When he stopped, she could see Weasel over Pattie's shoulder, standing there holding the reins of the two horses. She had never seen anything like an expression on his face. But now, she sensed, rather than saw, the glimmer of a smile.

Pattie slapped her, and her head rocked to one side and her left cheek stung. "Now, you're going to tell me everything, and it will be the truth this time."

She said nothing, her tongue feeling the hurt inside of her mouth. She could taste blood.

"Do you know why you're going to tell me everything?" Pattie hissed. "It's because I know the one thing you fear most." His face looked furious, its hue a near purple. He paused, but she said nothing. He clutched her shoulder with his left hand, and his right came slowly down toward her. He reached for the top button of her shirt and undid it. Her eyes opened wide. He undid the next button.

"OK," she said.

He undid the next button.

"I said OK." Her voice went up in pitch.

But he didn't stop. He reached for another button, his eyes locked with hers.

Chapter Fifteen

Hoof prints in the sand and gravel wove up the side of the sharp hill in a narrow path between yucca and cactus, bits of scrub cedar and agarita. Sometimes the trail they followed was faint, at other times clear and unmistakable. Each mark told a story, even those that indicated the scampering, from crevice to edge, of the little bronco mule.

At the point where the men had dismounted, Mick got off Blaze and led him by the reins. Harlan did the same, although Laney, a light sheen of sweat on his face, stayed mounted, gripping the back of the saddle with both hands.

Blaze crested the steep hill and the ground leveled. Mick felt the strain on his tightly bound chest and back after the long, steady climb. Each cracked rib burned, and there was a gnawing ache low in his spine. None of that slowed him. To his left, was a striking view out across the wilderness they'd just crossed. It was the black birds lifting to the trees, though, that caught his attention. Buzzards. His stomach gave a lurch, as if it had fallen all the way back down the cliff. He climbed into the saddle. Ahead were the remains of Pattie's campsite, and he nudged Blaze close, then clumsily swung himself off and went running. He bent over the body the birds had been picking at. It was Sancho, or what was left of the little mule. He could see where she'd been shot in the head, and meat cut from her, even though the birds had been at her a while.

"Thought it was her, din' you?" Harlan said softly. "Syd?"

Mick looked up. Harlan's face was lost in the shadow of his hat, all except for the glitter of white teeth in a smile.

"This means she doesn't have anyone protecting her any more," Mick said.

Harlan's smile faded.

Mick struggled back up into his saddle.

A note of praise in his voice, Laney said: "You mount and ride like an Injun, even stove up like that. I noticed that back when you were cow-pokin'. Bet you'd stay on a horse that was swept up by a tornado."

"Thanks . . . I guess," Mick said, noticing that Laney swayed a bit, and was braving it out, not wanting to show he wasn't up for the ride. His face was washed pale. Mick gave Blaze both heels, even though the horse was moving his front hoofs, already set to pick up the pace.

After their stop at the campsite above the cliff, Mick was puzzled that he no longer saw Mythological Jim's footprints. Mytho's horse was being led along, empty. He wished he had time to go back to that campsite and try to piece together whatever had happened there. But there was no time to stop and read the stories in the dirt. He had to press on now more than ever. The cave wasn't that far ahead.

As they rode, hoofs clicking here and there on bits of stone but otherwise thudding on hard dirt, still moving briskly for having two men on one horse, Mick let Blaze open himself to an even harder gallop while he kept an eye on the trail. Several times he had to pull up on the reins to take a closer look, and he could see places where Pattie had stopped. Although Mytho's were absent, Syd's prints were at the stopping sites, and that kept him pressing forward. Her prints were always next to Pattie's, which suggested she was bound to him, even on the side trips out into the woods to tend to nature.

The spacing of the trees and slightly different pattern of undergrowth told him they were nearing the cave. There, ahead, was a sycamore with a three-foot-wide trunk bent, five feet up, where it had broken years ago and mended itself and started upright again. A large white patch of mottled bark glared at Mick like a signpost pointing toward the cave. His heart beat faster. But he wasn't sure how he felt about taking Laney to the cave and the mine he'd already promised to Harlan. Mick didn't give a whoop about any mine as long as any sense of treasure he had was bound to a bad taste about Pattie. Could he trust Laney, though?

He was studying the trail, bending enough to the side of Blaze to keep the prints in view, even though bending had meant loosening the leather ties of the corset. For a second he thought he was seeing things. He sat upright, loosened the corset further, and bent down to look at the trail again.

"What is it?" Laney asked.

It was there, the trail suddenly veered left. Mick knew the cave was ahead. Yet the horses had taken a decided turn here. That Syd was making her last play was all he could imagine, a desperate move to stall, knowing she'd be dead once Pattie had his mine.

Mick steered Blaze to the left to follow the trail, and he gave him a bit of heel to push him faster. Blaze liked cutting to the chase, and must have run quite a few races for a few dollars in his day. He was off so fast Blue was hard pressed to keep up.

The tree trunks whizzed by. Yet, fast as they were going, Mick stayed bent out over Blaze's neck, reading the trail, looking for the slightest shift or change. He straightened and pulled up on the reins suddenly. Blue came rushing up.

When Harlan was stopped, he looked at Mick. "What you got?" Blue was breathing hard, and light foam ran down his neck across his chest.

Mick pointed at the trail. "Three Kiowa horses from the left, picked up on the trail. See the unshod hoof prints on top of the others?"

"I see 'em. Sho' nuff."

"They're about to be ambushed."

" 'Spect so."

"They're moving fast," Mick said, "maybe a bit too fast. Indians get emotional, like those Kiowas back there who attacked Hodges and the others earlier. They're prone to forget coup and strategy, become reckless, instead of careful."

"Jus' you 'member that you own self, Mick," Harlan said.

Mick gave Blaze a strong nudge, and they were off, even faster than before, Blue falling behind as Blaze surged ahead.

Pattie was reaching for the third button of Syd's shirt when Weasel pushed Pattie flat to the ground, right on top of Syd, knocking the air out of her for a second.

"Dammit, Weasel," Pattie hissed, and went to push himself up when an arrow went right through his straw hat, yanking it off and sticking it into the ground. He collapsed back across Syd as gunshots sounded from Weasel.

Syd lay partially on her back with her legs tucked awkwardly to one side and Pattie's full weight across her. She saw a bare-chested Indian run out of the bushes at them, then snap back as if pulled by a hard rope tug. When the shooting stopped, she tried to get her breath back, but, not until Pattie rose slowly, could her lungs fill all the way. Then she lay there while he reached for his hat, yanked the arrow holding it out of the ground, broke the arrow in half, and dropped the pieces.

Putting his hat back on, Pattie looked over to Weasel, who was bent over the body of one of the Indians. "We don't have time for that," Pattie advised. But Weasel didn't straighten.

As soon as Pattie's head was turned, she saw it—the short round stick, two inches long, the end of the arrow he'd dropped. Tied to the end with sinew was a slender tapered buffalo point knapped of dark gray flint. It lay there. Syd's bound hands darted for the bit of arrow, grabbed it, and she was slipping it up the sleeve of her shirt when Pattie turned back to her.

Mytho's horse whinnied in pain, and that drew Pattie's head away from her again. "Take care of that horse, Weasel!"

Weasel already had his knife out and walked toward the horse that had an arrow sunk to the feathers in its shoulder. Syd turned her head. When she looked up, Pattie grabbed her and yanked her to her feet. He didn't stop her when she reached with her bound hands to start buttoning up, although it was really to let the bit of arrow slide up her sleeve. Then he grabbed her by the ear and took her to the horse, forced her back up into place, tied her to the back of the saddle again.

"Which way?" he snapped.

She nodded back in the right direction. She'd done all she could to delay it. He squinted, but then nodded to himself and mounted. She stared at the sweaty back of his red shirt, and let the arrow slip down into her hand so she could begin sawing at the leather thongs that held her hands.

Weasel closed his saddlebag and mounted, too, rubbing his hands on his pant legs.

Without looking back to her, Pattie said: "You'd better be right this time."

He took the lead, and Weasel drifted behind, Syd keeping her hands still while he could see them. Then they started off, back the way they'd come.

Mick's head was down, studying the trail, moving as fast as he would let Blaze go. They crested a hill and started down the other side. He looked up and pulled on the reins, slowing, then stopping Blaze. There at the bottom of the gradual downward slope was Pattie on Syd's horse, Syd behind him on the saddle, and Weasel on Biscuit just behind them.

The pounding hoofs behind him slowed as Harlan came over the top of the hill and started to pull up, too. As soon as Harlan realized what was going on, he eased Blue around and off to one side, slightly in the front.

Down below, Weasel came around while Pattie sat his horse and stared up at them. The anger rippled across his face like heat lightning, once the stunned amazement at seeing Mick alive had passed. His hand went to the gun at this side, then went back to his reins. He said something to Weasel, who moved forward on the path while Pattie eased his horse to one side, as if getting ready to make a dash for it. He called out: "Think about your share, Laney!"

Harlan's left hand held his reins, and his right hung down beside his gun. Any second the shooting could start. The woods seemed suddenly still, except for the abrupt alarmed cry of a bird and hard flutter of wings high above.

Mick heard the series of *clicks* of a hammer being pulled

back behind him, then felt the end of the barrel poke painfully hard into his right ribs from the back.

"Sorry about this, son," Laney said.

"I'm no son of yours," Mick snapped.

As soon as he saw what had happened, Pattie kicked his horse and they were off, Syd bouncing and looking back at Mick as she was whisked away.

Weasel still stared at Harlan, a glitter in his narrowed eyes.

"Now we'll never know," Harlan said.

"I will." Weasel's voice was, as before, scratchy from lack of use.

"What's the matter with you?" Harlan went on. "Only talks with folk you thinks is mean as youseff?"

"Don't waste words on tomfools."

Then, so fast Mick had no sense of its coming, Harlan drew, spun, and shot Laney out from behind Mick. The body snapped sideways so quickly and so hard it had to be a head shot. Then Weasel's gun was out and he shot at Harlan, who leaped to the side and fell the rest of the way from the saddle.

At the same time, Mick, holding his saddle horn with one hand, dropped down along the far side of Blaze, whose front hoofs were moving in place as he spun sideways. Mick leaned out around Blaze's neck and saw the flame from Weasel's gun, felt Blaze jerk, and begin to fall. Mick rode the fall, shifting in spite of the pain in his ribs. As soon as he could see over the falling Blaze, he lifted his gun and fired. Weasel's right elbow blew off, and his lower arm, holding the gun, drooped and the gun fell. Mick had the hammer back and then fired again. For part of a second he saw the most surprised look on Weasel's face, right before a gaping hole appeared where his nose had been and he fell from Biscuit's back. Mick rolled as Blaze hit the ground, dead from a shot to the head. The horse slid and rolled once, then came to rest against the bole of a tree. Mick's tumble sent him smashing into the trunk of another tree, and, when he hit, it hurt so much he nearly screamed. His head jerked up and came back down on a flat rock with a thud.

As soon as Pattie had taken them over the hill and Syd could no longer see what was clearly the ghost of Mick, she turned, sawing the leather thongs harder and faster against the end the Kiowa arrow. When shots sounded behind them, echoing up over the hill, she felt a hollow punch in her stomach as she realized that, if Mick wasn't dead before, he certainly was now. Then the first leather strand parted as they came to the spot where she had steered them wrong.

"Left here," she said.

Pattie hesitated before turning so they were headed right toward the cave.

Syd cut through another strand. They were almost there. Pattie slowed the horse as they came into the clearing. The mouth of the cave was still obscured by the bushes. She said: "See that tree. The oak." She spoke in part to cover the sawing of the final strand. Then it let go, and she was free. But she kept her hands in front of her, the way they would have been if she were tied.

Pattie rode ahead until the head of a pick was visible where it was stuck in the tree that now grew around it, encasing it tightly.

"Oh, my God!" Pattie cried. "This is it. It's truly the place." He looked around. "Which way?" he asked, although his gaze had fixed in the right direction.

"Over there, behind those bushes."

He nudged the horse into movement again. Just as he did, Syd reached forward and grabbed Pattie's revolver from its holster. She pulled the hammer back while he was reining the horse to a stop. She put the end of the barrel against his back and said: "Get off!" When he didn't move, she shoved hard with her left hand and he tumbled off to the right, landing on his side, his hat falling off. He twisted and looked up at her, his hands flat on the ground. She hopped forward into the saddle, got her feet in the stirrups. She pointed the revolver at him.

"You can't do it. Don't have it in you," Pattie taunted.

She fired. The bullet hit inches from his left knee and ricocheted off a stone in an angry whine.

Pattie froze. His eyes said he wasn't so sure.

Here it was. Everything she'd told herself she wanted. He'd never admitted to being Bill Hinton, but for the way he'd treated her and Mick, she should do it anyway. She felt her fist clenching and her finger tightening on the trigger. *Pull it.* Then she stopped.

"You're probably right," she said. "I doubt it'd be a clean kill. Probably just hurt you, and then leave you, bleeding, to die after a few days."

She had seen his face when he was being smooth and convincing, and she'd seen it in a rage enough to kill. What was there now, in the twisting features beneath the tousled thinning hair, was first fear, but that quickly eroded enough to show stark greed.

It was just a matter of seconds before he jumped to his feet and rushed her. Syd had him figured for that. She had read the struggle in his face. With her left hand, she undid the coil of rope that hung from the saddle horn and tossed it down in front of him. "You'll be needing this," she said.

He jumped up at the same time she kicked the horse's sides and took off at a gallop. Pattie ran only a few steps, then turned and was reaching for the rope when she glanced back as she and her horse went around a stand of trees and out of sight.

Blinking, Mick came to. It took a second for his eyes to focus, then he remembered everything. The pain in his ribs was as bad as it had ever been. He thought of Syd and Harlan and shoved his palms against the hard slope of the ground, sitting up first, and then forcing himself up to his feet. There stood Biscuit, eating at a clump of grass. Weasel lay on the ground beside her in a tangle of limbs. He was never going to kill again.

Mick hobbled over past Blaze, and then past Blue, who stood with his reins hanging down. On the other side, Harlan lay, face down, his cheek and shoulder pressed to the earth, the rest of him slightly bent at the waist. Mick grabbed a shoulder and rolled Harlan over onto his back. A groove was sliced across the top of the outside of his left shoulder, and blood oozed from that, but he seemed otherwise unhurt.

His eyes fluttered open. "Oh, Lawdy. Them angels is uglier'n I thought."

"You're not dead, Harlan."

"I knows that." He grinned, then winced.

Mick tore off a piece of his own shirt sleeve. He wadded it and put it on the flesh wound. "Hold this in place," he instructed Harlan. "I'll fix you better when I get back. Gotta go for Syd."

"You ain' leavin' me behind." Then something dawned on Harlan. He struggled to rise, and Mick helped him sit up, bent at the waist with his legs straight out. He looked around, finally located the pile that was Weasel. He looked up at Mick. "You did that?"

"I'll explain later. I've got to get to Syd."

They both heard the horse galloping at the same time. Mick moved to one side of Harlan, keeping an arm around his back so he wouldn't fall over. Harlan let go of the cloth over his wound and drew his gun.

The horse came up over the hill and was reined in as soon as Syd saw them.

"Well, you two have sure gotten close," she said.

Mick snapped his arm from behind Harlan, who instantly fell on his back.

Mick helped him upright again, mumbling: "Sorry."

"And you. Aren't they wearing corsets a bit lower in Paris this time of year," Syd said, grinning.

Mick didn't know what to say or do as Syd hopped from the side of her horse and came running. Mick stood, his supporting hand slipping from behind Harlan's back again. He heard Harlan hit the ground as Syd's arms wrapped around him. Past their pressed lips, Mick repeated: "Sorry."

Aside from the texture of her lips and tongue—that sent a tingle to the tips of his sockless toes in his borrowed boots—was her hand on his arm, pulling him closer, the glitter of those half-closed eyes as she kissed him back. They stepped apart awkwardly after a minute. Mick turned to help Harlan, who was pushing himself upright this time.

"No, thanks," he said, and held out the flat of one hand to Mick. "Do it my own self."

When Mick turned to Syd, he said: "Pattie?"

She shook her head.

"You couldn't do it, could you, when it came right down to it?"

"I'm not as unhappy about that as I thought. It came out OK. I wouldn't worry about him just now."

"Did you . . . is he . . . ?"

She grinned and stepped around to pick up the cloth for Harlan's wound. "Let's get this tended to first," she said.

They cleaned and bandaged Harlan's wound. Mick sighed when he went past the corpse of Blaze, but he was glad to have Biscuit back, even if she couldn't run as fast and she had a weakness for eating. He took the Winchester from Weasel's gear and put it in his own scabbard.

"I hope you're not attached to those saddlebags," Syd said. "I'd get rid of them."

Mick lifted a flap and looked in. He took a step back.

"What's in there?" Harlan asked.

"Ears. The whole things full of ears. Some are on a string, but several are in there loose yet, I suppose waiting to be strung later."

"Man was sho' somefin," Harlan commented.

By the time all three were mounted on their horses, buzzards had begun to circle, although that might have been for the Kiowa, dead, back on the trail.

"They had bare chests and backs, no paint," Syd told Mick.

"My guess is they tailed Pattie all the way from where Laney had been shot by them. Cut across somewhere or they'd have come onto us. Nice of them to supply you with means of getting free, though." He winked at Syd, feeling a warm rush each time he looked at her and knew she was safe. But he was also anxious to get to the cave and Pattie.

The day was becoming increasingly gray. Clouds bunched dark on the horizon and the air was cooling enough that they might need jackets or a fire soon. They started down the hill beside the cave. The scuttle of a lizard in the leaves to one side made Harlan draw his gun so fast the three of them laughed.

"I didn't expect him to be out here, waiting," Syd said.

When they stopped, Mick said: "I suppose you want a look at your mine, Harlan."

"You think you got treasure 'nuff right now I don' need to share witch you?"

"I said earlier . . . ," Mick began.

"Mine's half yours, Mick," Harlan said. "But you gotta he'p work it."

Mick dismounted and went to help Harlan down.

"I can get my own self down," he said. "But thanks."

The two men drew their guns and eased toward and into the entrance of the cave. There was just enough light, a beam of pale yellow filtering from the hole high in the cave's roof, for Mick to see one end of the rope tied to stalagmite by the shaft.

Then they heard the screams: "Oh, sweet Jesus!" They could also hear the echoing sound of rattles between screams.

Mick and Harlan holstered their guns and went back outside to find Syd, grinning from the back of her horse.

"Can't never tell no ones we's found this here mine? Can we's?" Harlan commented.

"No, Harlan," Mick answered, "and it may take someone handy with a gun to de-snake it first. I only want enough for a start somewhere else, like yourself. I'll help you get what you need, then I may just settle down somewhere and raise nothing wilder than kids."

Syd blushed a dark copper, but she didn't look away.

Even this far out, although they could no longer hear the rattles, they could hear the echoing cries: "Lordy. Lordy. Oh, sweet Jesus!"

"Don't you want to go back and help that man, Harlan?" Syd said.

"He'p him? Why would I? Man like that's on fust name basis with far greater powers'n me."

About the Author

Born in Colorado, Russ Hall lives in Texas hill country on the waterfront of Lake Marble Falls on the path of an old stagecoach line where a coach has not come along in quite a spell. He first moved to Texas in 1983 from New York City, but has lived variously in Connecticut, Florida, Pennsylvania, North Carolina, and Ohio. Beginning with Harper & Row, he worked as an editor for over twenty-five years with major publishing firms. Among his eight previously published books, primarily mysteries, are *Island* (2001) and *No Murder Before Its Time* (2004). He has also published numerous short stories and was winner of the Nancy Pickard Fiction Award. Part Indian himself, his collection of short stories, *The Blue-Eyed Indian* (1997), showcases that background. When not researching and writing Westerns, he fishes in order to keep his truth-stretching skills honed. His next Five Star Western will be *Wind Won't Quit*, a sequel to *Bent Red Moon*.